Month-to-Maybe

HARLOW SCOTT

Author's Note

For the most part, this is a fun, lighthearted story. However, a few elements may be sensitive for some readers, including:

- Body dysmorphia (discussed on page)

- Death of a parent (occurs in the past but mentioned briefly)

This story also touches on body image struggles and internalized fatphobia. Please know these moments are not meant to promote negative views of weight or appearance. Blaine's experiences reflect some of my own challenges with body image and the lasting impact of society's attitudes toward weight. My hope is that readers who have faced similar struggles will feel seen and reminded that beauty and worth are never defined by a number on the scale.

A quick note of appreciation: at one point, Hattie receives a card from her friend Jayne featuring a specific image. This was inspired by something I came across online. Despite my best efforts, I couldn't locate the original artist or creator, as there seem to be many versions circulating. If you are that original creator, please know I tried to credit you — and also, you have a wicked sense of humor, and we should be friends.

And finally, yes — I'm aware that, in reality, you can't book a therapy appointment quite that easily or quickly. But that's one of the perks of fiction, isn't it?

Chapter 1

Hattie

Hattie tossed from one side to the other and back again. Her gaze drifted to Galen, who slept peacefully beside her, oblivious to her restlessness. She sighed in frustration, then replayed the day's events in her mind for what felt like the hundredth time. Not for the first time, she had been blindsided by Galen and one of his "relationship talks." Everything had seemed fine until it wasn't. Once again, she felt like no matter what she did or said, it would never be good enough for him.

That's when it hit her—whenever they had one of these little chats, it was because of something she did or said, or something he believed she said or did. He was always the one to instigate these little chats. He was always the one asking her to change. To change the things she said or did to suit him.

Hattie had never noticed before—he was always asking her to change.

Madison called Hattie the next afternoon to ask her if she could borrow a fancy dress from her closet. Almost immediately after Hattie said hello, Madison sensed something was wrong. Within minutes, she had organized an emergency girls' night, which Sophia volunteered to host.

When Hattie walked through the door of the apartment that evening, Sophia took one look at her and asked, "What did that asshole do to you?"

Hattie counted herself lucky—she really did have the best of friends. They were always there for her when she needed them.

Madison came in from the kitchen with a bottle and three glasses in hand and said, "At least give the girl a glass of wine first."

"Fine, fine," Sophia said as she placed a platter of cheese, crackers, and various cured meats on the oversized tufted ottoman that served as her footrest and coffee table. Madison followed, setting the now open bottle on the wooden tray in the center after pouring each of them a glass. Handing a glass to Hattie, she sat on the opposite end of the couch after helping herself to a plate.

Sophia settled in, sinking back into the plush peacock-colored velvet couch, then repeated her earlier question, "So what did that asshole do to you?"

"It's complicated," she started.

"Isn't it always?" Madison asked. Hattie filled them in on her late-night revelation, along with a few things she hadn't told them before.

"It almost sounds like emotional neglect. You might want to talk to someone about his behavior and get a professional opinion,"

Sophia said. "My aunt had a partner, and some of what Galen has done or said reminds me just a little bit of the kinds of things this guy did. He never treated her like an equal, but she was so afraid of being alone that she stayed with him and was miserable."

Hattie paused, Sophia's words ringing true in her soul. "I never thought about it like that. He pays attention to me, but it's almost always when he wants something. It feels... I don't know, like he sees me as an accessory instead of a partner." Hattie stared into her wine glass, watching the light shift on the dark red liquid.

"So what are you going to do?" Sophia asked.

"I don't know," Hattie replied, looking up at her friend, and sighing. "I guess start by talking to someone, and then go from there."

"Well, whatever happens, you know we're here for you, whatever you need," Madison said, refilling her almost empty glass of wine.

"Thank you," Hattie said with a sad smile, "both for the wine and the sentiment. I wish I didn't need anything, but I appreciate it nonetheless."

Sophia, Madison, and Hattie met in graduate school and stayed close ever since. They understood Hattie in a way that Galen never did. They shared her love of museums and knew how incredible it was to see the spark in someone's eye after learning or discovering something in an exhibit or at a program. They also understood how little money she made. Passion for the work didn't necessarily equate to a great salary in the nonprofit museum world—something that was occasionally a point of contention between her and Galen. While he was generous with his money, often paying for things outright rather than demanding they split the cost, it wasn't like they shared an account and contributed equally, so she was always conscious of the difference in their situations. Honestly, it was probably part of what led her to be in this situation to begin with—because he paid for so much, she felt like she needed to be more accommodating to his wants and needs.

"Have you guys ever thought about going to couples therapy?" Sophia asked, interrupting Hattie's thoughts about the ups and downs of her relationship with Galen.

"I tried to suggest it once, and he just laughed it off," Hattie responded. In fact, Galen had nearly mocked the practice, so she wasn't keen to bring it up again.

"My therapist is a godsend," Madison said. "As long as I talk to him every two weeks, I'm good. If not, I start to lose my shit a little."

"I think everyone needs a therapist," Sophia said matter-of-factly.

"I agree with that, although people like our friend, Galen, will never go. Even though they may be the ones who need to most. Ironically, his insecurities make him too, well, insecure to go," Madison said.

Sophia jumped in, "It's funny because he doesn't come off as insecure until you get to know him. I mean, from the outside, what does he have to be insecure about? He's good-looking, not my type, but still attractive. He's a pretty generic, handsome, blonde dude with great cheekbones. He has a job that isn't too evil and pays well. He knows how to dress like a grown-ass man, not like someone stuck in his early twenties. Hell, he's got a car and a mortgage."

"And a great girlfriend!" Madison proclaimed.

"Well, that goes without saying," Sophia continued, tucking her long blonde hair behind her ear. "Clearly, there's more to him than that, though, or else our friend here wouldn't have fallen in love with him. I obviously don't know him as well as you do. What is it you love about him, Hattie?"

"There were a lot of things that made me love him at first, but honestly, I don't know if I care anymore. I... I'm just tired," Hattie said, shaking her head.

Both Sophia and Madison looked shocked. Hattie wasn't surprised. She hadn't been as open with them about everything that happened as she wished she had been. If she had, maybe she wouldn't feel so lost. If she was being honest, she hadn't wanted to admit it out loud because that would make everything feel that much more real.

"Are you going to leave him?" Madison asked tentatively, her dark brows knitting together.

Hattie took a sip of her wine, considering Madison's question. "I don't know, I really don't. I mean, we've been together for four years. Maybe this is something we just need to push through?"

"Do you want us to be honest? Or be there to support whatever decision you make?" Sophia asked, taking Hattie's mostly empty wine glass from her and refilling it. She would normally stop at two, but she felt like an emotional crisis was at least a three-glass situation.

"I'm such an emotional mess right now, I don't know."

"Then we'll just be here for now," Madison said. Sophia nodded in agreement.

"Thanks," Hattie said. "I don't know what I would do without the two of you!"

Madison and Sophia moved at the same time to embrace Hattie, resulting in a squishy group hug, which quickly devolved into fits of giggles.

They spent the rest of the night drinking wine and talking about the misadventures of Sophia's brother James, who was currently traveling Europe with his best friend, whom he secretly had a crush on for years. Sophia was betting they'd be more than friends before they got back, assuming they survived camping on park benches and running down hills to catch trains and otherwise being twenty-two in Europe.

Hattie climbed out of her ride share and dragged her tipsy self home. As she quietly entered the apartment, she thought about her friend's earlier question. *Are you going to leave him?*

She walked into the bedroom to get ready for bed and paused for a moment at the foot of the bed, watching Galen sleep. The sheet was low around his waist, and his left arm was bent near his head. She took a moment to appreciate his toned body in the moonlight.

The sight made her core warm. Maybe she should forget everything that was discussed tonight and wake Galen with kisses across his bare torso. He would probably be up for her riding his cock, then again, there was no guarantee that she'd get to come, which would just leave her angry and frustrated—much like she was now. That was one of the other things that had changed in their relationship, somewhere along the line. Anymore, when they had sex, which had become less and less frequent (thank god for whoever had invented the vibrator), Galen put his pleasure first and foremost. Then, if she was lucky, he might worry about Hattie and hers. Not to mention, it had become so vanilla.

Hattie wasn't the kinkiest by any means, but still, she liked to spice things up every so often. Their sex life had become so predictable and boring that she could almost tell when he was going to climax based on mattress squeaks alone. Was it too much to ask to have him boss her around a little, pull on her hair some, or tie her wrists together every so often? Hattie sighed and decided to just go to bed instead.

After putting on her pajamas, she slid into bed. Normally, she would crawl into bed and snuggle into the crook of his arm—she loved that crook! But without thinking about it, Hattie put as much distance as possible between her and Galen's gleaming body.

When she woke up in the morning, it was obvious from the silence that Galen had already left for the day. Realizing she was alone in the apartment, she let a sigh of relief escape her lips. Just like that, she knew she had her answer.

Hattie got up and started some more coffee—because, of course, the asshole hadn't made more after finishing off the pot—and texted her boss that she was taking a sick day, something she rarely did. While she wasn't physically sick, she admittedly felt a little worse for wear from all the wine, and she was sick of this situation.

Today, she was going to do something about it.

Chapter 2

Blaine

Blaine groaned as the alarm blared, pulling him from sleep. He reached over and slapped it off. The bedside clock read five o'clock. He really didn't want to get out of bed or go for a run, but it wasn't much of a choice. He knew he had to stay disciplined with his exercise if he wanted to keep his body in the shape he'd worked so hard to achieve. Going from a size XXL to a Large hadn't happened overnight. Plus, he'd indulged in an extra beer last night. Perhaps he should just give up. He was never going to be able to easily maintain the body he wanted.

Man, negative self-image was hard to shake. *Give yourself some credit, you bastard.*

Blaine had come a long way from being a pudgy little kid and an overweight teen. Still, he didn't know many men who tracked calories like he did. After much hard work, he managed to lose a lot of weight over the past four years, reaching his goal weight around the time he moved to Oceanside two years ago. He was no

Chris Hemsworth, but he'd even managed to put on some muscle. However, if he stopped paying attention or broke his routine, it was easy to slip back into old habits—especially stress eating. So, instead of cream cheese frosting, it was crunches. He didn't enjoy it nearly as much (what he wouldn't do for a cupcake), but he refused to go back to being "Blubber Blaine," as his middle school classmates had called him. With that thought, Blaine forced himself to get out of bed.

Throwing on a pair of sweats and an old 5K race t-shirt, Blaine headed the short distance to the beach to start his run. He wasn't really a fan of running, but it was great exercise, and the view was tough to beat, no matter the weather.

Blaine was one of those people who actually liked the grey, foggy mornings. He enjoyed how peaceful the beach was with its roaring waves. The only people who tended to be down there early in the morning were folks like him out to exercise and, of course, the surfers.

Blaine enjoyed surfing but wasn't very good at it and definitely wasn't hardcore enough to do it at five a.m. He was more of an 11:30-on-a-sunny-morning kind of surfer. Blaine paused for a few moments, watching the surfers weave hypnotically in and out of the waves. A small shiver ran down his spine. Deciding he'd better get moving to warm up before his balls fell off from the cold, he took off down the beach.

As Blaine ran, he let the sight and sound of the surf calm him. The ocean always had that effect on him. Growing up in Oregon, his family went camping on the coast during the summer. He remembered how much he loved sitting and watching the waves crash upon the sand as a kid. He often wondered if he had grown up somewhere like Oceanside, where the beach was warm enough to play on and the water warm enough to swim in, if he would have the same love for just watching and listening to the sea. The Oregon Coast was a very different place from the beaches of Southern California in both temperature and culture. No matter where he was, though, the ocean gave him some peace. Some people meditated; Blaine stared contemplatively at the waves.

After about a mile, he decided to turn back. It wasn't as far as he had planned to go, but Blaine wasn't feeling it this morning. At least he'd get in two miles. Maybe he'd go out again after work. His thoughts weighed heavily on him this morning. Last night's dinner date had been a disaster. Again. He had no idea why he agreed to a second date with Laurel, whom he met through a friend of a friend. The first one had been awkward and uncomfortable. They'd gone to the Padres game and didn't talk much during the game, but it was an interesting match, so he didn't dwell on it. Afterward, they went to dinner, and the conversation was stilted and sometimes cringeworthy. At one point, he recalled saying, "So...." When they got back to her house, where they'd met earlier to carpool, she hugged him, leaving him extremely confused about what had just happened. She called a few days later, asking him out again, and he didn't know what to say, so he said yes.

Date number two was just dinner this time. At least the food was exceptional (unlike the mediocre sports bar food they'd had on their first date). They went to a new pub in town that opened about a month ago. The conversation was still pretty awkward, and at the end of the night, when he mentioned helping her install a window air conditioner she needed help with, she told him, "Listen, Blaine, you're really nice, but..." He didn't remember what he said in reply, but he had been reeling all night about what had happened. It's not like he liked this girl, but she was the one throwing around mixed signals! Then to be given a "You're nice, but..."! What the hell was he supposed to do with that? This is why you never let friends set you up with other friends. Then he started to wonder if the problem really was him. He was a nice guy. Was he too nice? Was that the problem? Moments like this always caused his already sizable self-doubt to flare up and negative thoughts to intrude: *Maybe it's because you aren't attractive. Maybe you're not good enough. Why would she want to date you? There are so many other, better-looking, funnier men out there.* Fuck you, inner voice, fuck you.

After a few rounds with the punching bag and a hot shower, he was starting to feel better. Blaine stood in front of the mirror, a towel wrapped around his waist, and quickly ran a comb through his dark brown, fairly close-cropped hair. He ran his hand through his short beard. It was going to need trimming soon, but not today, or he was going to run out of time. Blaine threw on some jeans, a white button-down shirt, and a vest. While he didn't have to dress up for his job, he never felt quite right showing up in just a T-shirt, so he usually chose a mix of casual and business casual. He glanced at the clock as he finished buttoning his vest. Luckily, he still had time for breakfast and a cup of coffee. He strolled into the kitchen, tossing a few slices of whole wheat bread into the toaster. He grabbed ricotta from the fridge and honey from the cupboard. As he spread ricotta on the warm bread, Marmalade, his orange tabby, came over and rubbed herself in and around his legs.

"Is this your way of reminding me that I haven't fed you?" he asked as he bent down to scratch her chin. She closed her eyes in ecstasy and rubbed her face against his hand. At fifteen, her fur was starting to lose some of its color, and her teeth were starting to go bad. Blaine pulled out a can of her special diet wet food and dished some up as she continued to wind in and out of his legs.

Whenever he had a bad day, Marmalade could always make it better. He knew his time with her was running out, and it broke his heart to think about it. At this point, he had had Marmalade for more than half his life. She had been the stray kitten who wandered into his life and heart when he was a geeky, gawky, unpopular 13-year-old boy. They had been together through high school heartbreaks, college late nights, the death of his dad, and several moves. He was convinced he would never find a woman who loved him as unconditionally as his cat did. Maybe it was better that he just stayed single?

Chapter 3

Hattie

Hattie's suitcase lay open on the floral jungle-printed comforter, surrounded by piles of semi-open packing cubes, clear plastic bags filled with toiletries, and various charging cables. From somewhere beneath a pile of clothes, Hattie's phone started to ring. After digging around, she finally found it under a green cashmere sweater. Her best friend's name and picture lit up the screen. Hattie wasted no time hitting accept on the video call.

"Jayne! Hi!" Hattie exclaimed.

"Hey, you. What's going on? I saw your text earlier and knew this was a phone call kind of situation. Plus, you know I've been out of the country and unreachable for several weeks, and I've missed hearing from and seeing you dearly. Everything okay?"

While Jayne had been talking, Hattie moved from the bedroom portion of her rented hotel room into the kitchenette. Leaning her phone against the backsplash, she grabbed a mug from the cupboard and poured herself a cup of the coffee that had just finished brewing.

Adding a dollop of cream from the fridge, she picked up her phone and then carried it and her mug to the couch and sat down.

"Sorry to text you so early in the morning," Hattie apologized.

"Please! I'm your best friend. You can call me at four in the morning, and I won't get mad. I'll just ask what you need from me to make whatever situation is causing you to call me at four a.m. better. So, what's going on, hun?"

"I... I think..." Hattie started. She stopped, took a deep breath, and began again. After all, if she couldn't tell Jayne, she couldn't tell anyone. "I'm done. With Galen."

"Wow. Okay." Jayne looked about as shocked as she seemed to feel.

"A few weeks ago, we had one of those little chats I'm so fond of..." Jayne gave a massive eye roll in understanding. It wasn't the first time Jayne had heard Hattie complain about Galen and his approach to relationship communication. "The next night, I met up with Sophia and Madison, drank too much, and came to the realization that I really wasn't happy. The morning after, I called in sick and spent the morning applying for jobs all over the country. Anywhere but upstate New York."

"For a minute, I thought you might be calling to tell me he had proposed," Jayne said, shaking her head.

"Oh, lord, no. I thought he might for a while, but he didn't. Then I started to worry that he actually would, which probably should have been a sign. At first, I wanted to stay and try to work it out, but actually, it was something you said that finally made me realize I was done."

"What? What did I say?" Jayne asked, looking perplexed.

"It was a while ago, but you said you should only do things that make you happy—after all, you only live once! That came to mind the morning I sat down to look for jobs."

"It is very sage advice," Jayne said with a smile. Without missing a beat, Jayne asked, "So what was the straw that finally broke the camel's back?"

"I don't know, exactly. It was more of a slow-burn realization, if you know what I mean, but not the good kind. We've had our ups and downs, as you know, and I could never say anything to him without him turning it against me, so eventually, I just stopped saying anything. If he approached me with something, I would say, 'Sorry, how can I make it better?' and then try to change. Again.

"I just realized that I was the one making all the changes. That I was the one giving things up. That it felt like I was living in a house of cards with eggshell floors." Hattie paused and took a sip of her coffee.

"Wow, that sucks. I had no idea it was that bad, Hattie."

"How could you? It's not like I shared. I think I was afraid that if I said anything, it would make it real. And if it was real, then I'd have to deal with it, and I just didn't want to. I was losing myself, but I was so immersed in him and his life that I didn't notice it right away."

"How do you mean? I think I can guess because I know you pretty well, but what do you mean?" Jayne asked.

"Well, to avoid conflict, I would just try to go along. So, when there was something I wanted or wanted to do, I found it was better not to do it or not bring it up. Like that three-month fellowship in L.A. that I wanted to apply for. Do you remember that? I never even bothered to submit the application because Galen was all 'But what would I do without you, babe?' In the end, we were really living his life, and I was just part of it. Does that make sense?"

Jayne was quiet for a moment, then said, "As your friend, I wanted to say something, Hattie, but also, as your friend, it didn't feel like it was my place. There were a few times I saw you give up on opportunities because of Galen's work or other things, and I hated to see you lose out. I sometimes wondered if you were becoming less and less of your old self, but like you said, it was so gradual that I somehow always managed to talk myself out of saying something, convincing myself that we were just mellowing with age, or something like that. I'm sorry I didn't say anything sooner."

"No, you were right not to. I probably wouldn't have seen it anyway and would have just been mad at you. What I really needed was for you to be there to pick up the pieces, so thanks for that."

"I hate that there are pieces, but I'm glad I get to be the one to help put you back together. I love you, bestie."

"I love you too!" For a moment, they just looked at each other, sending love through the phone screen.

"So, what are you going to do?" Jayne asked, breaking up their love-fest.

"Well, I texted you this morning because I just accepted a job in Oceanside. Remember when we went there on vacation?"

"You bitch! You're moving to Oceanside without me?" Jayne asked in mock protest.

"You're welcome to come with me, but I know with your professorship, you can't exactly just pick up and move easily," Hattie said.

"Le sigh. Yes, that's true. So when are you leaving? Does Galen know yet?" Jayne asked.

"Actually…"

"No! You are not already there, are you? I was going to ask about that atrocious wallpaper behind you!"

"I am!" Hattie confirmed. "One of the jobs I applied for that one morning was at the art museum in Oceanside. They were looking to fill the position quickly, and I was looking to leave even faster, so it worked out for everyone involved."

"What does your family think?"

"My mom is supportive, but worried. She didn't see anything wrong with Galen but trusts me to know my own heart. Up until a few weeks ago, I hadn't talked to anyone openly about what was going on or how I was feeling, so her reaction makes sense to me. I also texted Andy, and her response was along the lines of 'Good for kicking that loser to the curb.' That was it."

"I've never understood why you two aren't closer," Jayne stated.

"We used to be when we were kids. We've just drifted apart. Maybe this break with Galen will help with that, too. At least it will be easier to travel to see her since she's up in Seattle, so it's a relatively quick flight, versus having to fly for five plus hours to get there. Who knows, maybe we can even convince Mom and Jeremy to fly out from Denver and spend Christmas with us in Seattle."

"Or in Oceanside! You are going to be so happy there, Hattie. I just know it!" Jayne said excitedly. "What did Galen say? How did you break the news to him?"

"After accepting the job in Oceanside, I started packing my belongings into a few boxes and kept them in the closet. He never even noticed. I put my notice in at work right away and booked a plane ticket for last night, my last day in the office. So, yesterday, before he got home, I threw the rest of my stuff into a suitcase and sat waiting for Galen to come home." Hattie pulled her legs up onto the small hotel couch, pulling her knees almost to her chin, reflecting on last night.

Hattie sat surrounded by white tile and marble at their kitchen island, drinking a glass of red wine. Galen walked in the door and set his things down. He hung up his keys and took his shoes off. While he did all of this, Hattie admired his muscular body, his handsome face, and his immaculately trimmed blonde beard. He was handsome, there was no denying that, but a handsome face and a good paycheck weren't enough anymore.

"Hey, babe," Galen said without really looking at her. He walked into the kitchen and poured himself a Scotch, two fingers, neat. She had always hated the smell of that stupid Scotch. It smelled like he was drinking a peat bog that had been set on fire. Galen knew she couldn't stand the smell of it, but he insisted on drinking it anyway.

Galen leaned back against the counter and seemed to look at her for the first time. He took in the keys in her hand, her purse strapped across her body, and her suitcase sitting next to a stack of boxes against the back of the white leather sofa. Starting to look a little confused, he finally said, "Babe, what's going on? You going somewhere for work?" Galen clearly had no idea how little Hattie made or what the budget of her museum was if he thought they were sending her somewhere for work.

"No," she said, standing. "I'm leaving, Galen. I'm tired of being asked to change. I'm tired of being treated like your assistant instead of your partner." She picked up the boxes, grabbed her suitcase, and opened the door, waiting to see if he would stop her or protest in some way.

"But who's going to pick up my dry cleaning tomorrow?" he asked with a confused look on his face. And with that, she pulled the door shut and walked down the hall toward her new life.

"I told Galen last night when he got home. Then I stopped by Madison's to leave a few boxes for her to ship to me later, and then headed to the airport. I still have to find an apartment. I priced them before I accepted the job, but given my need to get out of there, I didn't try to secure one before I hopped on a plane out here."

Jayne shook her head in disbelief. "I still can't believe you just left him standing there and that you live in Oceanside now!"

"I know, it's not very like me. I'm always the one with a plan, who likes to color-code and make spreadsheets. I don't know how to explain it, Jayne, but I woke up that morning and my only thought was I had to get out of there. I didn't want to try to talk to him. I didn't want to ease out of the situation. I didn't feel like I could breathe. I just wanted out and to get far away. It made me wonder who I even was to be having thoughts like that. I barely recognized myself. It's time to find myself again. But first, an apartment. I'm staying in one of those extended-stay places for the time being. This way, I don't have to eat every meal out and do things like that. It's nice, but it's still a hotel in the end. After we finish chatting, I'll hop online and start looking in earnest."

"Well, what are you doing talking to me? Get searching! And while you're doing that, I will start pricing airline tickets, so the second you have a place, I can come help you celebrate and move in."

"Jayne, you don't have to do that!"

"I know I don't, but I love you, and I want to. Plus, there are worse things than a trip to the ocean!"

"What would I do without you?" Hattie asked.

"You'd fall to pieces," Jayne retorted.

"Love you too, Jayne," Hattie said with a warm laugh.

"Talk to you soon! Let me know what you find!"

"I will!"

After hanging up with Jayne, Hattie finished her coffee and organized her belongings, clearing off the bed in the process so she would have a place to sleep that night. Grabbing her laptop, she sat down at the small dining table with one goal in mind—to find a place to start her new life.

Chapter 4

Hattie

"Any luck with the apartment search?" Jayne asked. It had been almost a week since Hattie arrived in Oceanside, and in that week, before she started her new job, she had been doing nothing but trying to find an apartment and despairing about the lack of available units in her price range.

"Yes, actually! I found a great place today. The only problem is that I can't move in for a month. I went ahead and took it because it really is perfect, but I'm not thrilled about living in this hotel for another month. I even debated passing it up and trying to find something I could move into sooner, but I absolutely loved this place, and there aren't many options for someone on my salary! And this place has these cute little built-in shelves, a great closet, and the cutest little patio. Plus, it's set back from the road, so it's fairly quiet. Most importantly, it was in my price range. Now that I'm on a single-nonprofit income, I'll have to get used to being a bit more frugal again, like I used to be before Galen and I moved in together. It will be fine. I did it once before, I can do it again."

"It does sound perfect for you. I wish you could make the money you deserve while being in public service," Jayne said, folding laundry while she and Hattie chatted.

"Sadly, we public servants are supposed to live off warm fuzzies instead of real money. I know my parents wish I had become a doctor or something, but you know me, Jayne. I never would have been happy doing anything other than what I'm doing now. I love museum work. Don't get me wrong, I wish I got paid more, but at least I love my job, which a lot of people I know who make more can't say."

"Well, I'm sure it will be great," Jayne commented.

"I'll send you some pics once we're done. It's not big, but it will be just right for me." Hattie paused, looking at the hotel room wall. "No!" she groaned.

"What is it?" Jayne inquired.

Hattie sighed audibly. "They're at it again!"

"Who is? What are they doing?"

"I didn't tell you about my new neighbors, did I?" Jayne shook her head. Hattie continued, "They arrived a few days ago. I met them on their way in. They seem super nice, but I swear it is nonstop sex over there!"

"Maybe you could join them?" Jayne laughed.

"Har, har. So not my scene," Hattie said.

"Well, they probably won't be there too long, right?"

"Wrong. They mentioned they were here for work. For a month. I don't know how they're getting any work done because I swear all they do is screw each other's brains out!" Hattie sighed again, picking her laptop up from the micro-kitchen counter and moving it over to the coffee table.

"Maybe they work in the porn industry?" Jayne teased, loading her folded clothes back into the now-empty laundry basket.

"Doubtful, that's the San Fernando Valley, not San Diego. What am I going to do, Jayne?" Hattie whined as she sat back in the one armchair in the room.

"Wait, how do you know that?"

Hattie ignored her question and said, "It's like they're going for some sort of Guinness world record or something."

The volume from next door increased. "Oh, wow. I can hear that from here! Could you look for someplace else temporarily?"

"Easier said than done. With Camp Pendleton so close, temporary housing is hard to come by. I got lucky with the place I'm in now." Hattie popped the top open on the pop she'd grabbed from the fridge.

"I'm sure it will get better. Maybe. Besides, don't you start work soon? At least you won't be there much during the day anymore, other than on weekends. And hey, there's a beach right there!" Jayne reminded her.

"Right, beach. I need to keep reminding myself of that. I suppose I can spend all my waking hours on the beach."

"Tell me more about this amazing job of yours. I know you haven't started yet, but what are you going to be doing?"

"I'm actually really excited about it, Jayne, and not just because it got me out here. The Californios Museum is an art museum that focuses on the art of Hispanic Californians. They've been open for about a decade now, and are still fairly small, but they are growing. While the collection focuses on art, the programming they offer blends art, culture, and history. So, I'll be overseeing the educators who run the programs, while taking a lead in designing the programs, liaising with the curatorial staff, and doing things like that. So, part programs, part management, and part whatever else they need because, again, it's a small staff."

"You are going to love that! You've always been really good at juggling a lot of different things at once, and you're really good with people. Your staff will be lucky to have you for their manager."

"That's sweet of you to say, Jayne." The noises from next door were increasingly getting louder. Hattie didn't want to subject her friend to the torture as well, so she said, "Ok, I should go. Sorry. I've been so busy apartment hunting that I haven't done much in the way of grocery shopping, and I ran out of all the food I had except for this," she said, raising her pop can. "I need to grab some dinner and some lunch to take with me. After that, I'll start stressing about what I'll wear to my first day of work tomorrow!"

"You're going to knock 'em dead! Good luck. I know you're going to be amazing. Call or text me tomorrow when you're off and tell me all about your first day!" Jayne said enthusiastically.

"I will. I miss your face!" Hattie said in closing.

"Not as much as I miss yours. You got this, Hattie!" Jayne blew a kiss at the screen and then disconnected the call.

After a quick run to the grocery store, Hattie looked at the clothes she had hung up as potential first-day outfits. Her role at the museum was different from her previous jobs, blending elements of several into one. It was a smaller museum, and she gathered from what they told her during the interview process that she would need to get used to wearing multiple hats, beyond simply education and programs. She was looking forward to the challenge and hoped that a smaller environment might encourage better collaboration. She had loved all of the museums she had worked at so far, but noticed that the larger they became, the more siloed people seemed. She enjoyed the camaraderie and teamwork that came with smaller museums.

Hattie searched through her clothes and finally chose charcoal pencil pants, a loose floral top, and a casual blazer. It was a bit more relaxed than what she might wear if she were starting a new job at an East Coast museum, but she figured it might be a little bit more laid back than upstate New York. After all, this was a beach town in California! Still, she knew she needed to dress to impress. After picking out what she hoped was the perfect outfit, she made a quick run to the store for some basic supplies. When she got back, she prepared a quick meal and ate it while enjoying a temporary lull in the noises from the next room. Even though she was nervous about the next day, she was determined to get a good night's sleep. Somewhere between dinner and bedtime, the neighbors started again. Hattie set her alarm, put on headphones to block out the romp next door, slipped into bed, and drifted off to sleep.

Two days after her last conversation with Jayne, Hattie received an email from her best friend titled, "Solution to Your Problem." She clicked it open and read:

Hiya!

So I did a little looking around after our call the other night (remind me once again that espresso after six p.m. is a bad idea!), and I found this ad on Craigslist. I know, I know, but hear me out. This sounds like it's the real deal, and the guy doesn't sound like a total psycho creep. Just take a look at the posting and consider reaching out, okay? Here's the link*.*

Hugs and loves and all that!

Jayne

With a great amount of trepidation, Hattie clicked the link in Jayne's email, which took her to a Craigslist post titled, "Long-term Cat-Loving Housesitter Needed."

Live rent-free for a month! Due to an unexpected business trip, I need someone who is willing to come to stay at my place and take care of my slightly neurotic senior cat for a month. Looking for someone who is responsible, doesn't smoke/do drugs, and won't kill all my plants (or my cat). I do have a home monitoring system set up so I can check on the place, and I don't own anything that exciting, so if you're hoping to rob me blind, you may want to reconsider applying.

Hattie read through the application requirements and noted that the email address he provided was for a legit, locally-based company. That, at least, was a good sign. She picked up her phone and texted Jayne.

Hattie: *Craigslist? Seriously, are you trying to get me killed before you can even come to visit?*
Jayne: *I know, I know, but like I said, this feels real. Just check it out. The dates line up perfectly with yours!*

Hattie still wasn't sure about reaching out to this guy, but when she got home, it sounded like there was an orgy happening next door. She immediately sat down, flipped open her laptop, and started composing an email to Mr. Craigslist.

"Please don't be a psycho..." she thought as she hit send.

Blaine

Blaine cursed himself for posting that ad. His inbox was full of responses from some seriously questionable people. He just couldn't leave Marmalade alone anymore, and her usual cat sitter was already working another job and then on vacation. The vet wasn't an option either, since they could only take her for part of the time he needed.

Being anti-social had its ups and downs, and this was one of those moments when he wished he had a few more friends locally. He kept scrolling, deleting, and blocking the various replies. There were a few he flagged to respond to. Hopefully, one of them would work out. He needed to leave town on Monday and only had a few days left to find a solution. He wished he could just postpone this trip, but when the government came calling and told him to be in D.C. on Monday, he had to be in D.C. on Monday.

Just as he was about to head home for the day, another message popped up in response to his ad. He decided to go ahead and take a quick look before he shut things down for the night.

Hi,

I'm really hoping you're not some sort of serial killer or otherwise unbalanced person. My name is Hattie, and I'm moving to Oceanside from out of state. I'm already in the area and have a job, but I can't move into my new apartment for a month. The dates line up nicely with when you need someone. If you're interested, I'd be happy to meet in a public place to discuss further and see if this arrangement might work out for both of us.

Per his request, she had included a few references, including for her current boss. So far, she seemed like she was the most normal one who had reached out. He responded and suggested a meeting place around lunchtime, near where she worked. Fingers crossed, she, too, wasn't a serial killer or otherwise unbalanced.

Chapter 5

Hattie

Hattie anxiously waited for Mr. Craigslist to show up for their meeting. She figured she should stop thinking of him that way and rather think of him as Blaine. It was a few minutes past 1:00 p.m., their agreed-upon meeting time, and he still hadn't shown up. She decided to give him five more minutes before heading back to work. As she was about to give up and go back to the museum, a man fitting Blaine's description walked into the café where she was waiting. Six foot? Check. Close-shaven beard? Check. Dark brown hair and eyes that almost matched? Check. He failed to mention that he was sexy in an understated way. He had definitely downplayed his looks. He described himself as medium build, which was mostly true. His broad shoulders were hard to miss, especially in the crowded café. The man clearly lifted weights. He looked around and stopped when he saw her. He approached and said, "Hattie?"

"Hi, you must be Blaine," she replied. He extended his hand for a shake. Hattie had to resist the urge to stare at the well-developed forearms poking out of his rolled-back shirt sleeves.

"Sorry, I'm late. Usually, parking down here is really easy, but I forgot that today was the Farmer's Market. I hope you were able to get here ok." He sat down across from her, leaning back comfortably in the chair.

"Yes, super easy for me," she said. "I was able to walk over. Thanks for choosing a spot so close to where I work."

"Well, I wanted to make sure you felt comfortable. Thanks for suggesting a public place. I was going to insist on it, but I'm glad you were similarly concerned. You wouldn't believe some of the responses I got to that ad!"

"Do I want to know?" she asked.

"No," Blaine said adamantly.

Hattie chuckled. "That good, huh?"

"Let's just say, some of them made me question my sanity by putting the ad out there, others... you know what, never mind. Let's just go with no," Blaine said, smiling.

"I'll admit, I was really hesitant to respond. In fact, my best friend saw it and sent it to me. I'm not the kind of person who would normally look at Craigslist for a situation like the one I find myself in." *I'm not normally the kind of person who would be in this situation, to begin with*, she thought.

"You said you recently arrived from Syracuse. Where are you staying now? Wait, never mind. Please don't tell me—that sounds creepy." Blaine held his hands up in an almost protective gesture.

Hattie smiled. She liked him so far. He seemed nice. He had a rich timbre to his voice that was weirdly soothing. While she didn't necessarily trust him, she was pretty sure he was who he said he was and not some creeper on the internet. "I'm staying at a place temporarily, but let's say it's not ideal, hence my looking for an alternate situation."

Blaine nodded as if he understood what she meant. "Sounds perfectly reasonable. So, tell me a little about yourself. Only what you're comfortable sharing, of course. What made you move all the way out to California without a place to stay? It must have been a quick move."

Hattie appreciated that he was trying to ensure she was comfortable and not pressing her for details she wasn't ready to share. She took a sip of her latte and told him a very watered-down version of what had happened. "The short version is that I was in a long-term relationship and decided it was time to end it. We were living in a fairly small area in upstate New York, and I didn't want to risk running into him, so I decided to start applying for jobs elsewhere. The museum here needed someone to start quickly, and I was eager to get out of there, so I broke the news and hopped on a plane as soon as I could. I probably should have thought a little more about housing than I did. Normally, I'm much more of a planner than that!"

"Wow, it must have been rough if you just up and left like that," he commented, eyebrows slightly raised.

"He wasn't abusive or anything; I just realized that I was living his life instead of my own, and once I had that realization, I couldn't stand to be there anymore. I felt like I was suffocating living in the same space as him."

"That's really awful, Hattie. I'm sorry you were in that situation."

They talked a little longer, sharing what felt safe and appropriate given the situation they both found themselves in. Blaine glanced at his phone on the table and said, "I know you've got to get back since your lunch hour is almost over. I just wanted to thank you for meeting with me." Blaine looked unsure of what to say next. This was such a strange situation for them both. "If you're interested, I'd like to go ahead and offer you the position, or whatever you want to call it. If you'd rather come over and check the place out and meet the little lady, you're welcome to do that as well," he said. "Feel free to bring someone along if you'd like," he added quickly.

Hattie thought about it for a moment and then said, "I accept." She hoped she would make it through the experience, but with how little sleep she'd been getting because of her energetic neighbors, she was willing to try. Blaine seemed like a decent guy (she might have done a bit of light internet stalking). She just hoped she was right.

"Great! Would you like to come over tonight so I can show you around, introduce you to the cat, and do all those sorts of things? Assuming you're free, that is."

"I'll have to check my schedule... hmm, looks like I have a pretty busy evening. I need to take a walk on the beach, wash my hair, and make some mac and cheese. I just don't know how I'll ever fit it all in!" Hattie said with a smile.

Blaine grinned at Hattie. "How about this then? Let me handle dinner in exchange for you meeting Marmalade. How does that sound?"

"I suppose I can make that work," Hattie said with affected indifference. Blaine laughed, the sound warm and inviting, like cuddling up next to a cozy fire on a cold day.

"I think you and Marmalade are going to get along just fine," he said with a smile.

Later that evening, Hattie cautiously approached the door of the address Blaine had given her. It was a 1940s Mission-style home, small and utterly charming from the outside. It certainly didn't look like a place where a serial killer would live, though she had no real idea of where they would. The house was on a well-lit, but not too busy, street within easy walking distance to the beach. Hattie couldn't believe her luck. It even had a palm tree in the front yard!

She'd come this far, she might as well go all the way in. Hattie raised her hand to the door, paused, took a breath, and then knocked firmly. A moment later, the door opened, and Blaine stood there. He'd changed out of his work clothes into jeans and a faded college t-shirt. She couldn't help but notice how the fabric strained slightly against his biceps.

"Hi," she said nervously.

"Hi! Did you find the place okay?" he asked.

"Yeah, it wasn't too hard. I mean, I have no idea where anything is yet. When we visited a few years ago, we mostly just stuck to the beach, but thank goodness for GPS."

"Luckily, this town isn't that big. You'll learn it in no time," Blaine said with a smile. He stepped to the side and said, "Come on in."

Hattie stepped into the house and glanced around. It was small, but cozy. The living room was to the right. Hattie was delighted to see that Blaine believed in cushy furniture, none of that modern, sleek stuff that some people (ahem, Galen) preferred. The space looked lived-in but tidy.

"Are you ok with pizza?" Blaine asked. "There's a gourmet pizza place that just opened, and I've been meaning to try it."

"It's one of my top three favorite foods," she replied, setting her bag down by the door.

"Hmm, let me see if I can guess the other two..." Blaine said. He closed one eye and put his hand on his chin, stroking his beard, looking deep in thought. "I've got it. Mac and cheese is one, and chocolate cake is another. Hopefully not together, of course!" he said.

Hattie laughed heartily. "Well, you're not wrong about the mac and cheese. Anything carb-based with cheese is at the top of my list."

"But no chocolate cake?" he asked, leaning against the back of the couch.

"It's okay. I know, I know," she said when he gave her a look of disbelief. "It's good, and it's not like I don't like it, I just prefer white cake if I have a choice. Lemon cake above all other cakes, though."

"I do love a good lemon cake," he said, nodding his head in agreement. "Although I don't tend to eat a lot of sweets myself. So, mac and cheese, pizza, or really anything cheese-covered are two of the three. So what are your other top three? Do you want me to guess?"

Hattie smiled. "I doubt you'd ever figure it out, so I'll just tell you. You have to promise not to laugh when I tell you, though."

"How about this? How about I try not to laugh too hard when you tell me?" he asked with a grin.

"Deal. It's Brussels sprouts, actually." Blaine didn't laugh but did look a little surprised.

"Yeah, you're right, I was never going to guess that," he said. "Brussels sprouts? Really? Huh."

"I know it sounds strange, but I always liked them as a kid, despite the fact that the only way my mom ever prepared them was by boiling them and tossing them in some salt. I loved them anyway. Then, as an adult, I discovered you can do the most amazing things to them. Pan-fry them, broil them, serve them with a red wine butter sauce, mix them with cranberries—there are so many options! And each one is just as delicious. Now, any chance I get to eat them, I will."

"Well, Hattie, I'm about to blow your mind because the place I was going to order from just happens to have a Brussels sprout pizza." Hattie's mouth dropped open, but she quickly shut it.

"You mean I could have my pizza, and eat it, too?" she asked incredulously.

Blaine chuckled. "I guess that settles it then. Let me place the order real quick, and then I'll show you around. Marmalade will make an appearance soon. She's usually a bit shy around new people at first. Why don't you have a seat, and I'll call the pizza place?"

Hattie wandered over to the overstuffed chair facing the window and sat down. She was glad that Blaine didn't seem creepy or psychotic. The fact that she found him attractive was the most upsetting thing so far. *Get it together, Hattie! That's not what you're here for. You didn't move out here to jump into another relationship,* she thought to herself.

A few minutes later, Blaine approached and sat on the couch next to the chair Hattie was in. He smiled shyly and said, "I don't really know what to say now."

Hattie laughed nervously. "Yeah, I know what you mean. This is an odd situation. What is taking you out of town? I think you said in the ad that it had something to do with your work?"

"I have to go on an unexpected trip to Washington, D.C. The aerospace logistics company I work for contracts with the Marine Corps here at Camp Pendleton, and we were summoned to a meeting in D.C. I have a great cat sitter who normally comes and stays with Marmalade, but because it was such short notice, she can't do it since she has another gig already."

"Lucky for me, I guess," Hattie said with a smile. "I can't wait to get out of the place I'm staying in," she said, rolling her eyes.

"Why's that, if you don't mind me asking? Noisy neighbors?"

"Ha! You have no idea. They go at it like rabbits day and night, and since it's a long-stay hotel kind of place, the walls aren't that thick, and unfortunately for me, they aren't going anywhere for the next month."

"Oh man, that's terrible. I lived in a cheap apartment when I first started grad school, and one of the guys who lived on the other side of us would listen to Metallica loudly day and night. The other guy who lived there had a girlfriend who I'm pretty sure was faking her very loud orgasms. Either that, or I've been doing something wrong all these years. I was never so glad to move as I was from that place!"

"That's pretty much how I feel. I mean, I could have dealt with it for the next month until I move into my new place, but I have a feeling I'd be a lot happier hanging out with Marmalade." And now, maybe they should stop talking about sex. *You're the one who brought it up!* she thought.

"Speaking of, here she comes now," Blaine said as an orange and white cat sauntered down the hall. She stopped and looked at Hattie before jumping onto the couch next to Blaine. She butted his hand with her head until he lifted it and started to pet her. "I hope you don't think I'm a total weirdo, but I'm one of those people who talk to their pets," he said.

Hattie smiled and said, "I promise I won't think any less of you." Then, addressing her comment to the cat, "It's nice to meet you, Miss Marmalade. My name is Hattie, and I'll be hanging out with you for a while, while your daddy is out of town." She looked up at Blaine, "Hey, I'm just as much of a weirdo as you are."

Blaine laughed warmly. "Can I get you something to drink?" he asked with an amused smirk.

Chapter 6

Hattie

When Hattie came back from Blaine's, she picked up the phone and called Jayne. "Oh, thank the gods you're still alive!" Jayne exclaimed when she answered.

"Yes, I'm still very much alive, thank you." She set her bag down and took off her shoes. It felt good to be 'home,' but she would be glad to leave this place in a few days.

"So, not a total psycho then?" Jayne inquired.

"No, he actually seems sweet. I mean, he talks to his cat like she's a person, but other than that, he seems pretty normal. I think I told you when I was doing my internet sleuthing that he works for a local company that makes logistics software, or something like that. It turns out they contract with the Marines, and he unexpectedly has to take someone's place at a training session and some meetings in Washington, D.C., which is why he needs someone to care for his cat."

"Is he cute?"

"Jayne!"

"I'm going to take it from that reaction that he is." Hattie could hear Jayne's smile on the other end of the line. Normally, they opted for video calls, but Hattie didn't have the energy for a long call tonight, so she went for a simple phone call instead.

"Yes, he's attractive; however, I'm not interested. Remember that whole 'I just got out of a long-term relationship thing where I couldn't be myself' thing? I'm not dating anyone until I can remember who the real me is, whoever she is. Plus, I'm about seventy percent sure he's gay. I mean, he did name his cat after a Moulin Rouge song." Hattie cracked up at the memory of how much Blaine had blushed when he admitted that to her.

"No!" Jayne gasped. "You're joking!"

"Not in the slightest. He told me that her full name is Lady Marmalade, but he usually just calls her Marmalade or Miss Marmalade."

Jayne started laughing. "That is the absolute best thing I have heard all week! Please tell me he has an elephant somewhere in his house!"

"Not that I saw, however, it's not like I saw everything. Actually, his smile does remind me a bit of Ewan McGregor..." Hattie paused, thinking of the handsome Scot. Simultaneously, she and Jayne let out dreamy little sighs. Hattie had always been drawn to men in kilts, and Jayne shared her love for them.

"Are you sure you don't want to date him?" Jayne asked.

"Yes. Plus, I barely met the guy. Oh my god, Jayne, we had the best pizza! When you come out here, I'm so taking you there—it had

Brussels sprouts on it!" Hattie grabbed a bottle of sparkling water from the small refrigerator and twisted off the cap.

"You must have been in heaven. I know how much you love your pizza, but topping it with Brussels sprouts? I can hardly imagine. Did you leave any for him?"

"Hush, you. I'll have you know I only had three pieces. Like a lady."

"Uh-huh."

"It's true!" she paused, taking a drink, "But he did let me bring the leftovers home," she said with a big grin.

"You totally ate it already, didn't you?" Jayne accused.

"I did no such thing!"

"Uh-huh..." Jayne said with a knowing pause.

"Fine! I plan on eating another slice after I'm done talking to you. The rest is going to be lunch tomorrow."

"You and Brussels sprouts." Hattie could easily picture Jayne shaking her head, rolling her eyes, and smiling. "You're such a weirdo."

"Love you too!" Hattie teased.

"So, are you going to do it? Move in, that is?" Jayne asked after she was done playfully harassing Hattie.

"Yeah, I think so. It's a nice neighborhood. You'd love the house, and he seems legit. Don't get me wrong, I'm still nervous and cautious, but I've checked him out online, and he didn't do anything tonight when he could have. He leaves super early on Monday, so I'm planning to swing by on my way to work and drop off my stuff. Then I'll stay there until I can move into my new place."

"I'm so glad you found something that will work out. Just remember who found it for you," Jayne finished in a singsong voice.

"Like you'd ever let me forget."

"Not a chance."

The next day was Saturday. Hattie woke up to silence. She climbed out of bed and headed to the kitchen. She filled the coffee pot with cold water and inserted one of the paper filters provided by the extended stay hotel. Hattie looked forward to having a place she could call her own, where she could make choices, like using a reusable filter in her coffee pot. It was silly, she thought, to care about coffee filters, but it wasn't just about the filter; it symbolized her choices and what she wanted. For so long, her life had been wrapped up in Galen's. Her choices had been his choices.

Now, the only person she needed to worry about was herself, and that felt incredible. It was also a little scary. She'd been with Galen so long that she'd forgotten how to be herself. Hattie was excited to begin this new chapter and find out what made her happy. No matter what, she knew she could never go back to being that person again. When she decided to dip her toes back into the dating pool, she wasn't going to tolerate the kind of crap Galen had pulled. Having experienced that before, and now understanding it, she hoped she'd be able to spot someone like him right away. She wasn't in any rush, though, despite Jayne's urging.

Hattie was happy for the first time in a long time, and she planned to enjoy life on her own for a while.

Chapter 7

Blaine

Blaine had been hesitant about the whole strange-person-living-in-his-house situation, but he was glad that Hattie had agreed to watch over Marmalade for him. He couldn't believe how she devoured that pizza last night! He wondered how long she had waited before finishing the rest of it. That woman hadn't been kidding when she said she loved Brussels sprouts.

Blaine found himself thinking about how beautiful Hattie's eyes were. He'd never seen anything like them before. They were a deep green with golden flecks. He reminded himself that she was simply taking care of his cat and that she had just gotten out of an emotionally-complicated, long-term relationship. There was no way she was ready to date. Especially, a guy like him. He needed to get his mind off her and onto the task at hand. She'd be moving into his house on Monday. That gave him two days to clean, pack for D.C., and make sure he had enough supplies for Marmalade while he was gone. Plus, dinner with his best friend, Eli, later tonight.

Blaine walked into the restaurant and looked around for Eli. Spotting the man who looked like a young and slightly more chiseled version of Taye Diggs in one of the booths, he made his way over.

"Hey man, how's it going?" Eli asked as Blaine slid into the booth opposite him.

Blaine picked up the drink menu and started to look over the beers on tap. Since he was conscious of how many calories were in a beer, he didn't drink them that often, but tonight was definitely one of those times. "It's been a really long week," he replied. "I see you got started without me," he added, nodding toward the plate of half-eaten fries in front of Eli.

Eli had a weird look on his face that vanished almost as quickly as it appeared. Blaine wondered what that was about, but decided not to ask him about it. He knew Eli well enough by now to know that if he wasn't ready to share something, he wouldn't. When he was ready to tell him, Eli would let Blaine know if something was going on. "Yeah, well, I was in the area and didn't have enough time to go home, so I came here and grabbed an appetizer while I waited for your slow ass to get here." He pushed the plate toward the middle of the table. "Feel free to help yourself if you want any."

Blaine picked up a few of the crispy fries and bit into them. Eli knew Blaine would never get a whole order himself, so he always shared a few of them with him. This place really did have the best fries. They were always perfectly crunchy and salty. "Thanks, man."

"So, you found someone to hang with my favorite furry lady for the next month? I still can't believe you posted a Craigslist ad."

"I know! I was desperate. And yes, I did find someone, and she actually seems, dare I say it, normal."

"You sure about that?" Eli asked suspiciously, eyebrow raised.

"As strange as it sounds, yeah. Her name is Hattie, and she just moved here from New York. She's started a new job and came out here without having an apartment lined up yet. She's been staying at that extended-stay place on the edge of town while she found a place to live, and before you ask, yes, she has a place now. Her dates almost exactly match when I'm supposed to be gone, so it works out perfectly for both of us."

"Just looking out for you, man. I need to make sure my boy isn't coming home to a torched house or some sort of madness like that."

"I'm not a total idiot. I did some internet stalking, checked her references, made sure she actually works where she claims to, that sort of thing."

The server came over and took their order. Blaine couldn't help but notice Eli's eyes following the guy as he went to put in their order. *Interesting*, he thought. Eli had never expressed any interest in men, but there was a first time for everything. Curious, he asked, "You met anyone lately?" he asked his friend.

"Like, romantically?" Blaine nodded in affirmation. "Man, I wish. My dick's been so dry, I'm worried it might snap off one of these days."

"That's what lotion is for, you cretin." Both men chuckled. Maybe he was wrong, and there was something else that had caught his interest about that guy.

Before he could inquire, Eli asked, "What about you? What about this Hattie chick? She cute?"

Blaine envisioned Hattie laughing and snuggling with Marmalade, and that stray lock of hair he'd been dying to push back.

"Ooh boy, if that look is anything to go by, I'll take that as a yes," Eli said with a knowing grin.

"Shut up. She's not interested, I'm sure. Apparently, she broke up with her long-term, live-in boyfriend and came out here in a rush to get away from him. Not that she would want to date me anyway," Blaine said dismissively.

"Man, give yourself some credit. Have you looked at yourself in the mirror lately? You look great. You've even got the start of a pretty sexy V-cut. The ladies love that shit. You gotta get rid of that image in your head of you as a pudgy kid, because you definitely are not that anymore."

Blaine appreciated his friend standing up for him, even if it went against what Blaine just said. Eli wasn't usually quite so vehement, though. Something seemed a bit off tonight, but Blaine couldn't quite pinpoint what it was. "Thanks, man. Sorry, I still have a hard time feeling worthy, especially when it comes to relationships. Looking like this takes a lot of work and discipline, and unfortunately, the mental stuff takes more work and time. You have to remember that it's only been a few years since I lost all that weight. I'm still dealing with the emotional weight, even if the literal weight is gone."

"I know, but you're an amazing guy, and I'll keep reminding you of that whenever you need it. I would hang out with you regardless of what you look like because you're a great guy to be around."

"Thanks, man."

"Anytime. I can, on occasion, be more than a good-time friend. Just don't make it a habit," Eli said with a wink.

Blaine laughed warmly. "I promise I won't. What about you? You good?"

"Yeah, why?"

"You just seem a bit off tonight, is all. I just wanted to make sure you're doing okay, is all."

"I'm fine. I'm just annoyed about something that happened at work today. I need to let it go, especially since in the grand scheme of things, it's really not important." Eli visibly tried to shake off whatever was bothering him. Returning this attention to Blaine, he said, "So, you take off early Monday morning? When are you back? Do you want me to drive by and check on the place for you?"

"I fly out of San Diego at the asscrack of dawn on Monday, and I'll be gone until the end of the month. If you're okay with it, do you mind if I give Hattie your contact info? Since she's new to town, it would be helpful for her to have someone local to call if anything goes wrong."

"That's fine, man. I'm sorry I can't help you out, so having me as a support person makes me feel a little less guilty."

"I'm not going to hold it against you that you can't come hang with my cat when you're helping take care of Nana. She's like a grandmother to me."

"I swear she likes you better than any of us," Eli said, taking a drink of his beer. Blaine chuckled because he wasn't wrong. Nana treated him like family and never made him feel like anything other than that.

The server brought their food and another round of drinks, depositing them on the table with efficiency. The restaurant had gotten significantly busier since Blaine arrived. Despite that, their server, Marcus, stayed and chatted with them longer than was strictly necessary. Although he included Blaine in the conversation, his attention was definitely focused on his friend. Was he flirting with Eli?

Marcus eventually left them to their meal. Eli dove into his food while Blaine sipped his beer, continuing to observe his friend. "So, Marcus seems nice. Do you know him?" Despite the dim lighting in the restaurant and his friend's higher melanin count, Blaine could have sworn Eli was blushing.

Eli cleared his throat. "Not really. I mean, he's helped me out a few times when I've been in here. Turns out he also goes to the same yoga studio that I do, but in a different class. I ran into him on my way out the other night. We got to chatting and were talking about maybe hitting that salsa club up since I can never find anyone to go with me." Eli avoided looking at Blaine, picked up his beer, and took a drink.

Interesting, indeed, Blaine thought. He could tell that Eli didn't want to talk about whatever it was that was going on, so he changed topics. "Who knows, maybe you and Hattie will hit it off, and you can go with her."

"You never know!" Eli laughed.

They spent the rest of the time talking about other things before Blaine said his goodbyes. If he didn't hurry, the pet store where he got Marmalade's special diet food from would close, and he'd be out of luck since they weren't open on Sundays. He gave Eli a thumping man hug and said his goodbyes.

"See you in a month, man. Don't get into too much trouble without me," Blaine said with a wink as he walked back to his car.

Chapter 8

Hattie

Thoughtless. Selfish. Inconsiderate. Those words kept echoing in Hattie's mind. She remembered Galen's accusations when she was unpacking a few things that first evening at Blaine's. Tucked inside the pages of one of her books was a photo from a long-forgotten girls' trip with Madison and Sophia. Months after the trip, Galen had been acting moody for a couple of days until he finally approached her and essentially told her that she was thoughtless, selfish, and inconsiderate for going on that trip, even though he had said it was okay at the time. That conversation had blindsided her. No one other than Galen had ever described her that way. She had been dumbfounded and didn't know what to say or how to express her feelings without upsetting him even more. That was when she'd decided it was better to say nothing besides, "I'm sorry. I'll try to be more..." and then insert whatever the problem was.

Marmalade chose that moment to jump into her lap and lay down. Once again, she was reminded that, although her decision had been impulsive, it had been the right choice. She gave Marmalade a scratch and said, "I sure hope you never had to deal with an asshole for an owner, Miss M." Marmalade let out a little meow, which Hattie interpreted as a *no*.

Hattie's phone buzzed in her back pocket. Carefully avoiding disturbing Marmalade, she slid it out and checked who was calling. It was Blaine, probably wanting to check on how things were going. "Hello," she answered.

"Hi! I just wanted to call and check in. Did you find everything you needed so far?" he asked.

"So far, so good. Marmalade is sitting on my lap right now. I really hope she gets hungry soon, because I know I am. I wouldn't dare disturb her, though."

"Smart move, especially since it's your first night there. Okay, well, I won't keep you. I just wanted to check in and see if you're settling in okay. Feel free to call or text if you're having trouble finding something or if you have any questions."

"I will. And Blaine, I just wanted to say thank you again. I know that we're both helping each other out here, but I want you to know that I really do appreciate it. This is already so much nicer than the place I was staying."

"I'm glad that it's working out. And I meant to leave you my friend Eli's number, but I think I may have forgotten. He's a great guy and can help you if anything comes up. I'll text it to you after we hang up."

"I'd love that! I doubt I'll need it, but better safe than sorry, right?"

It was a good thing that Blaine had given her Eli's number, because two days later, the dishwasher stopped working. Hattie felt bad texting Blaine, but he reassured her that it had been on the fritz anyway, so it probably wasn't anything having to do with her. He suggested she contact Eli to see if he could take a look at it. Luckily, Eli said he could stop by on his way home from work.

When Hattie arrived at Blaine's after work, she spotted a tall, gorgeous man sitting on the front steps. As she approached the sidewalk, he looked up from his phone and said, "Hattie? I'm Eli. Nice to meet you."

Damn, his voice was like velvet. Jayne would be absolutely dying if she were here. Blaine sure knew how to pick his friends.

"Hi! Nice to meet you. Thank you so much for coming over."

"Not a problem. I'm practically Marmalade's step-daddy, so I gotta take care of my little lady," he said with a smile.

"Oh! I didn't realize you and Blaine were..."

Surprise colored Eli's face.

"Oh! No, no, no. Nothing like that. Straight man here," Eli said, gesturing to himself. "Blaine and I are just friends." Both of them blushed with embarrassment.

"I'm so sorry," Hattie said. "The way you said it..."

Eli laughed awkwardly, running a hand down his face. "Yeah, I can see that. What I should have said is step-uncle or something like that. You know, something totally unrelated to being married to, or in any other way, being romantically connected to Blaine. Oh man, he will die if he ever finds out about this. Please tell me there is some way to buy your silence," Eli pleaded.

Now, it was Hattie's turn to laugh. "I'm sure we can come to some sort of arrangement. Let's start by seeing if I need to buy Blaine a new dishwasher."

Together, they headed into the house, and Eli got to work investigating the problem. While Eli futzed around with the dishwasher, Hattie changed out of her work clothes and into something more casual. Marmalade followed her back from the bedroom into the kitchen. Eli reached over and scratched her. When he returned to what he was doing, she butted her head into his side, rubbing up against him.

"Hey, little lady, I've missed you too, but in case you haven't noticed, I'm kind of in the middle of something." Marmalade completely ignored him, continuing to rub up against him.

"Let me help you out," Hattie said, picking up Marmalade's food dish. The cat took off like a shot when she heard the sound of the can opening, meowing as if she hadn't been fed in weeks. Hattie just laughed warmly. "I swear I fed her this morning!"

Eli stood up, wiping his hands on a towel. "I'm sure you did. She can be a bit dramatic sometimes. I've helped out here and there when Blaine's been out of town for a night or two if Cassie, his usual sitter, can't do it. I think that's what comes of naming your cat after a *Moulin Rouge* song," he said wryly.

"I appreciate that she takes her role seriously," Hattie said, doing a terrible job of smothering a grin.

Eli looked at Hattie for a moment and said, "I like you. You're good people." Hattie felt a slight blush creep up her cheeks at the compliment. Eli continued, "So, I've got good news and bad news."

"Give me the bad news first, please." She cringed.

"Bad news is that I can't fix it. The good news is that it looks fixable. You'll need to get someone to come do the work. It looks electrical to me, and I like to leave all things electrical to the pros. I've got a guy I can recommend, so you don't have to try to find someone." Hattie let out a sigh of relief. "Now, as far as buying your silence for my stepdad mishap, can I buy you dinner?"

"Hmm..." Hattie pretended to think. "That sounds fair," she said.

"Do you like Mexican? There's a great place down on the water that makes killer margaritas."

"You just said two of my favorite words: Mexican and margaritas. Let's go."

"You weren't kidding about these margs, Eli!" Hattie exclaimed, taking another sip. "Wow."

"Yeah, I've been accidentally shitfaced a few more times than I'd like to admit as a result of one too many of these. Depending on how much of a lightweight you are, you might want to stop at two," he said.

After they had placed their order, Eli asked, "So, what do you think about Oceanside?"

"I love it so much. My best friend and I took a short trip out here a few years ago on vacation. We spent most of our time on the beach or at the museums, so I'm still getting to know the town, but we said at that time that we would move here in a heartbeat if given the chance.

Unfortunately, I was in a committed relationship, and she was starting a tenure-track position, so it had to remain a dream—until now, that is. What about you? Are you from Oceanside originally?"

"Not Oceanside, but San Diego. I've been blessed to live in the area my whole life. I did the typical college thing, though, and fled as far away as possible without hitting another ocean. I decided to try land-locked living for a change and spent four years in the middle of cornfields at Notre Dame."

"Ooh la la! So you're Mr. Fancy-pants, huh? What did you study?"

"Sports medicine. I work at the university. UC San Diego, that is."

"So you work with the student athletes?"

"Yes, and I occasionally teach, too."

"How long have you and Blaine been friends?" Hattie asked.

"He and I actually met almost on his first day in Oceanside. We hit it off immediately, and he's quickly become my best friend. The guy's a rock."

"I'm hoping to get to know him a bit better once he gets back. It feels really weird living in his house and not knowing him. But from what little I did get to know him before he left, he seems like a nice guy. You do, too. Thanks for taking me to dinner. Maybe the three of us can do this when he gets back? I don't really have other friends yet since I moved out here on a whim."

"You seem friendly enough. I'm sure you won't have trouble making friends."

"I'm friendly with a few people at my new job, and I have hopes that those will turn into full friendships, but you know how it goes, though. It's always hard being in a new place, and it only seems to get harder as we get older."

"Ain't that the truth?"

"I don't want you to take this the wrong way, so just to be clear, I'm just making conversation."

"Ah, I think I see where this is going. I'm currently single, but don't worry, you're not really my type, so you'd have been safe from heartbreak either way." Eli gave her a wink.

Hattie laughed. "I'm glad you could see where I was heading. It's such a strange thing between single men and women. I'm just curious about your life, and yet I don't feel like I can ask without it seeming like I'm hitting on you, ya know? It's one thing if you're not straight, but fully another if you are."

Eli smiled. "I like you. I know I already said that, but you're typically a straight shooter, aren't you?"

"It's funny, actually, because I think if you had met me before I moved out here, you would have had a different impression of me. I'm not sure how much Blaine told you, but I broke up with my long-time, live-in boyfriend and moved out here after waking up one morning and realizing I was living his life. I was acting the way he wanted me to. Doing the things he wanted to. Being who he wanted me to be. We were together for over four years, and in that time, I forgot who I am, so I'm now rediscovering that. If I've learned anything from the breakup, it's that you have to be true to yourself in order to be truly happy."

Eli was quiet for a moment, then slowly nodded in agreement. "Wow, yeah. I guess I've never really thought about it like that, but if you're living a life that's a lie, what's the point of living it?" He chuckled. "That sounded way darker than I meant it to. I just mean that I think your point is, if you aren't living a life that is genuine to who you are, then you need to choose a different life, one that is true to who you are."

"Exactly. I just wish I had realized it sooner because I feel like I've lost years of my life to someone else."

They talked some more, and Hattie decided she really liked Eli. He was easy to get along with, easy on the eyes, and seemed fun to hang out with. She hoped they could do it again. It was nice knowing that neither of them was interested in the other beyond friendship. Hattie was determined to be man-free for a while, but despite that, while she clicked with Eli on a friend level, that spark of interest just wasn't there. If anything, she felt more attracted to Blaine, a thought she shoved to the side as their entrees arrived. They ate their fill of enchiladas, tacos, and carne asada.

Hattie wasn't sure she could eat another bite when Eli said, "Wait until you try the fried ice cream."

"Fried ice cream? I think I've died and gone to heaven," she said, rolling her eyes and leaning back in the booth.

"I'm not sure I can manage one on my own. Want to split one? Or is that too weird, considering we just met?" Eli asked.

"Many people would probably say yes, but I feel like I've known you for a long time. Plus, fried ice cream," as if that explained everything. Eli just laughed.

"The true test then... chocolate or strawberry topping?"

"What kind of monster do you take me for?" she asked in disbelief. "Both. The answer is both."

Eli laughed heartily. "You and I are going to get along just fine, Hattie."

Chapter 9

Blaine

Blaine shrugged his suit coat back on once again. The air conditioner was turned up high enough to be too cold without a jacket, but slightly uncomfortable with one on. He'd been taking his jacket off and on all morning, and it was starting to drive him a little mad. Mike, his coworker, reentered the small conference room that had become their makeshift office for the day.

"Wilson, I have news," Mike said as he entered. Sitting in a black swivel chair across from Blaine, Mike pulled out his laptop. "They're sending us home early."

Relief washed over Blaine. While the hotel they were staying in was nice, it was still a hotel, and he longed for his own bed, not to mention snuggles from Marmalade. Shit, Marmalade. Hattie. Crap, what was he going to do about Hattie? He'd have to call her later and explain what was up.

Mike started to chuckle. "A lot just happened on your face, and I can't tell if it was good or not."

Blaine reminded Mike that Hattie was staying at his place and wouldn't move into her new place for another week and a half.

"Oh, yeah. I forgot you didn't know her before you let her move into your place—bold move on your part, by the way."

"I know. I'm still unsure if it was brave or stupid, but she seems solid. She and Eli became friends after he came over to fix the dishwasher, which, of course, broke only a few days after we came to D.C. Plus, Marmalade seems to like her, too, at least based on the pictures I've seen." Blaine pulled up one of the selfies that Hattie had sent him of the two of them snuggling together, handing his phone over to Mike to show him.

"She's cute. Is she single?" Blaine balked a little at Mike's question, but then again, Mike didn't know the whole story. He was newly single himself and should probably take a page out of Hattie's playbook, Blaine mused.

"She is, but she's not interested," he replied.

"That's too bad. Oh well, plenty of fish in the sea and all that. Wanna grab dinner after we are done today?"

"Actually, I was planning on hitting one of the Smithsonian museums. We've been here for several weeks now, and I've barely left the hotel except to come here. I'm not in D.C. very often, so I wanted to take advantage of the opportunity. Fancy spending the evening at the National Gallery of Art?"

"Blaine, you know I love you and enjoy hanging out with you, but art bores me to tears. I'll stick to my original plan, which was to find some chick at the bar and hopefully go home with her. Enjoy your art, though."

After they wrapped up for the day, Blaine wandered through the immense halls of the NGA until it was nearly closing time. The size of the collection impressed Blaine. He had visited many art museums in his life, but never seen Van Gogh's paintings in person. He marveled at the visible brush strokes and the thickness of the paint. This was far better than spending the evening in a noisy, crowded restaurant while Mike chased tail.

Before leaving, he stopped by the gift shop. Honestly, it was one of his favorite parts about visiting museums. They always had the best stuff in their stores. Even though Christmas was still a few months away, he picked up a few presents for his mom and sister. As he headed to the checkout, something bright orange and yellow caught his eye. It turned out to be a cat figurine that looked almost like Marmalade. Without thinking about it too much, he grabbed it to give to Hattie as a thank-you gift. After paying, he made his way back to the hotel, picking up some street food for dinner on the way.

It was late enough now on the West Coast that he could call Hattie without bothering her at work. He tapped her saved number, popping his earbuds in while he waited for the call to connect. After a few rings, she answered.

"Hi, Blaine!" she answered enthusiastically.

"Hi, Hattie."

"Marmalade says 'hi' too, by the way. She would come to tell you personally, but, true to her name, she's too busy practicing lounging like a courtesan to come to the phone." Blaine smiled and shook his head. He had lucked into finding Hattie to take care of Marmalade for sure.

"Well, I wouldn't want to disturb that, so I'll talk to her later. Actually, and please don't tell her this," he said, lowering his voice almost to a whisper, "but I was calling specifically to talk to you."

Hattie laughed. "Oh, is that so?"

"I wanted to share some news with you. I found out this afternoon that our trip is being cut short, so I'll be coming home earlier than expected."

"Oh." He could hear the surprise in her voice.

"Yeah, the news caught me off guard, too. I wanted to let you know as soon as I could. I realize you can't move into your new place yet, and I don't want to put you in a bind by asking you to stay in a hotel for that long. So I wanted to run a few options by you and see what you think."

"Okay... when will you be back?" she asked hesitantly.

"We're scheduled to be here through Monday and then head back on Tuesday. The way I see it, I can get a hotel..."

Hattie interrupted, "Don't be silly! This is your house, Blaine. If anyone should be getting a hotel, it's me."

"Yes, but you weren't expecting to have to do this, and I don't want to ask that of you. Another option—and it's okay to say no to this—is that you could stay with me for the few days I'll unexpectedly be home. If that's too weird or uncomfortable, just say so, and I won't be offended. After all, you don't really know me, and it's one thing to be there taking care of my cat; it's entirely another to see me stumble out of bed in my pajamas, desperately searching for coffee like a bear coming out of hibernation."

Hattie barked out a laugh at his description. Blaine was doing his best to put her at ease; hopefully, it worked. He felt really bad about putting her in this situation. Staying put and sharing the space for a few days, while it sounded a bit insane on the one hand, likely made the most sense. Plus, she'd been hanging out occasionally with Eli, so between that and a few phone calls and text messages with Blaine to check on Marmalade, he felt like she knew him well enough to be comfortable staying there for a few days together. In reality, it would only be for a few hours each day when they were awake and together in the house, so it couldn't be all that bad.

After a pause, Hattie replied, "It's fine, Blaine. I really appreciate you thinking of me, and if you're truly okay with it, I'd be grateful if I could stay here. Packing up and moving to a hotel only to pack again and move to my new place sounds like a whole lot of not fun. Thanks for offering."

Blaine felt relieved. He had been feeling bad—he didn't want her to feel like she was being kicked out. "Great, well then that's sorted. I should be back before you get home on Tuesday, but I'll let you know if something unexpected happens or we're delayed for some reason. Otherwise, expect me to be there by the time you get home from work. I know it doesn't make it less weird, but let me buy you dinner on Tuesday for the inconvenience."

"If Brussels sprouts are involved, I'm absolutely on board." It was Blaine's turn to chuckle. If she hadn't already been, he was going to take her to that place that had pan-fried sprouts with a spicy BBQ sauce on them.

"Done. I'll let you get back to things. I just wanted to call and let you know."

"See you Tuesday, Daddy." Blood shot straight to his dick, causing Blaine to jerk back on the bed.

"Um…" was the only reply he could muster.

"Oh shit, I forgot we weren't on video!" Hattie started cackling, clearly amused. Taking a breath, she said, "Sorry, that probably sounded really weird. What you would have seen, if you could, was Marmalade waving her paw at you."

"Oh, heh heh," he laughed hesitatingly. "Well, yeah, see you Tuesday," he said, trying not to sound off.

After hanging up the phone, he stared, confusedly, at his lap. The evidence of the beginnings of a hard-on was obvious in his grey sweats. While Blaine hadn't had a lot of sexual partners, he had been pretty adventurous with the ones he'd had. Never in his time had anyone called him "Daddy," but maybe they should have, based on his body's reaction. *Well*, he thought, *new kink unlocked, I suppose. Note to self: to explore that later with a partner.* In the meantime, he was going to rid himself of this hard-on in the shower.

Chapter 10

Hattie

Hattie was just sitting down for lunch in the breakroom when Carly, who worked in collections, came up to the table.

"Mind if I sit with you?"

"Not at all! Please," Hattie said, gesturing across from her to the open seats.

"How are you settling in?" Carly asked as she unpacked her salad and chips from her lunchbox.

"Pretty good. I mean, it's only been a month, but I've learned a ton and I think I'm starting to get the hang of all the different things the job requires."

"The Manager of Audience Engagement is an interesting mix of duties, for sure."

"I think my title should be changed to Managing Octopus, honestly. I've got so many different types of things I'm doing and overseeing, it seems appropriate."

Carly giggled. "That would be an amazing job title! I definitely think you should advocate for that when your review comes up." Carly pulled the tab on her sparkling water and asked, "So, when you aren't at work, what do you do for fun?"

"I'm still trying to get my bearings some, but if I'm not hanging out in a museum, I'm usually baking, reading, or hanging out with friends, although I'm still working on making those."

"You came from New York City, right? I think that's what I remember reading in the staff announcement email."

"Not NYC, but from upstate New York. I was living around Syracuse."

"Nice. I haven't been to upstate New York, just the city. I was there in December a few years ago, and it was wicked cold."

"The weather here is so much nicer," Hattie said with a laugh.

"Definitely. It rarely gets below sixty for daytime highs, although the nights can sometimes drop below freezing, but that's pretty rare."

"We won't talk about the lows in upstate New York," Hattie said with a playful laugh.

"I don't even want to know," Carly said, smiling. "So, what kind of things do you like to read?" Carly asked, taking a drink.

"I read a lot of different things, mostly biographies, historical fiction, and lots of romance." Hattie had no shame when it came to her book consumption. A woman's pleasure and sexual health were just as important as a man's. While Galen had become a less-than-generous lover, Hattie still got in plenty of O's thanks to her trusty vibrator.

"Nice! I'm a big romance reader as well. What are your favorite tropes?" She already liked Carly a lot, but if they could talk about books together, they were definitely going to get along. Hattie loved it when she found a fellow romance junkie.

"I love me a good enemies-to-lovers or one-bed. What about you?"

"Mmm, same," Carly said, swallowing her water. "I also love a good dark romance, but I really prefer them with a little bit of humor in them. Marco, who works in the early childhood programs, he's my boyfriend, and he thinks that it is strange that something can be both dark and funny." She shook her head in disbelief.

"Did you two know each other before you worked here, or did you meet on the job?" Hattie asked.

"We met here. We both started around the same time and would occasionally cross paths at lunch or out in the exhibits, but you know, collections and youth programs don't have too much crossover, generally speaking. I thought he was cute, but didn't really know much about him. He's pretty quiet unless he's in front of a room full of toddlers—then he just lights up!

"Well, one day, I was getting something out of the exhibit storage space that is off the smaller education classroom. I was in a little bit of a hurry. The cart that was supposed to be back there was missing, so I decided to carry the piece I had gone in there to get. It wasn't heavy, just a little awkward. Marco didn't realize I was back there because he had been out saying goodbye to his students for the week when I came in. When he returned, he started to clean his program up and had leaned the broom he'd been using near the doorway to the exhibits room."

"Oh no," Hattie said, sensing where the story was going.

"Oh, yes," Carly said. "So, I come out, hands full, and only sort of being able to see. Needless to say, I tripped. The component I was carrying flew across the room, and in trying to catch myself on the edge of the table, I ended up hitting the edge of a tray of tempera paints that was sticking off the edge just a bit. The tray went flying, I continued falling, and ended up covered head to toe in primary colors and with a sore ass. Marco felt so bad. He tried to help me get cleaned up, and well, let's just say, in the end, I wasn't the only one with paint on my hands."

Hattie gasped, "At work?"

"I know! It's remarkable that we didn't get caught, given the amount of noise the whole incident made. It was just a few kisses. Still, if it hadn't been for that misplaced broom, who knows if we would have ever gotten up the nerve to approach each other," Carly said with a shrug.

"I'm sure you two would have found your way to each other somehow or another," Hattie said. She loved a good meet-cute. She could just picture Carly, looking a bit like a deranged clown, covered in dripping paint.

"What about you? Are you seeing anyone?" Carly asked.

"No, I'm sort of off men right now," Hattie said adamantly.

"Oh, that has the sounds of a bad breakup written all over it," Carly said. "Is that why you moved?"

"Actually, it is. Galen and I were together for four years. For the first couple of years, we were happy. Then it felt like more and more he was upset about something or another. I started giving things up and only doing what he wanted, in an effort to keep him happy. I finally woke up one morning and realized my life was no longer my own, and I was done with that. Long story short, I moved out here and started anew."

"Four years, wow! That's a long time to be with someone. How did you two meet?" she asked, starting to repack her lunch containers into her lunch box.

"It was through a mutual friend in grad school. I was getting my Master's in Museum Studies, and he was getting his in Urban Planning. We were at a BBQ, and she introduced us. He was smart, funny, charming, and very handsome. I loved that he wanted to help create more livable cities, especially for low-income families. He seemed like the total package. We hit it off, and like I said, for the first part of our relationship, it was great. After a while, though, something shifted—I didn't notice it at the time—and I started to feel like an accessory rather than a partner."

"That's no way to be in a relationship. I'm sorry that he was such an ass to you, but I'm glad you made the leap and joined us out here on the Best Coast," Carly said with a wink. "We're lucky to have you, Hattie!"

Hattie smiled, "Thanks, Carly. That's really nice of you to say."

"Well, it's the truth. Hey, if you're looking to make some more friends, there is a group of gals who get together once a month or so for dinner or drinks. We try to mix it up a bit. Sometimes we head to someone's house. Sometimes we meet at a bar or something like that. Other times we pack a picnic and eat on the beach. Based on what I know about you, I think you would fit in really well with our little group. If you're interested, I can let you know when the next one is."

"That would be amazing! I'm definitely looking to make more friends. Thank you for the invitation, Carly." Hattie was grateful for the opportunity. While she had only been in Oceanside just over a month, making friends was harder than she had thought it might be. It made sense, though, given the lack of built-in networks she had, other than work. It had been much easier to form new relationships with people when she was younger, or even in grad school. The fact that Carly had offered her this opportunity warmed her heart.

"Here," Carly said, pulling out her phone. "Give me your number and I'll send you the info when I get back to my desk." Hattie took the phone, put in her number, and thanked Carly again. "Speaking of, I should get back to it. See you around!" Carly said as she tossed her water can into the recycling and headed back to her office.

After lunch, Hattie was settling back into work when her cell phone chimed with a new email. Before she could check to see who it was from, her phone rang with a local number. She assumed it was the apartment manager calling to check in on her upcoming move on Sunday.

"Hello," she answered.

"Hattie? This is Cecilia over at Shoreside Apartments. How are you this afternoon?"

"I'm great, thanks. I'm excited to move in on Sunday."

Cecilia sighed. "That's actually why I'm calling. We've run into a bit of an issue in the unit you are going to be renting."

Panic immediately started to rise in Hattie's chest. "What kind of issue?"

Cecilia explained that when the cleaning crew went in to give the unit a standard once-over, they discovered that part of the kitchen floor was sagging. Somewhere between the last tenants moving out and the cleaning crew coming in, there had been a leak that worsened the already old flooring. The tenants in the unit below were on vacation, so they hadn't noticed the water dripping through from the floor above. The flooring throughout the entire unit would need to be replaced, and since they were doing that, they decided to go ahead and do some upgrades to the kitchen and bathroom while they were in there, especially as they were going to be working to repair the downstairs unit at the same time.

"What does that mean for my being able to move in? How long will all of that take?" Hattie asked, trying to keep her voice steady and her panic hidden.

"Unfortunately, you won't be able to move in on Sunday as planned. The unit will be ready in about a month. If we had another unit available, or coming up soon, I would offer that to you instead. As it is, we just don't. We wanted to give you the option to wait, in which case you'll end up with a nearly new apartment, or, if you find somewhere else you can move in sooner, we'd be happy to refund your deposit since this is clearly on us."

"How long do I have to decide?" she asked.

"We'll be happy to give you two weeks. Does that work for you?"

Hattie closed her eyes, doing her best not to break down into tears while Cecilia was still on the phone. She took a deep breath and responded, "Yes, and thank you for being so generous. I'll let you know what I decide as soon as I know what I'm doing."

They said their goodbyes and hung up. Hattie closed her office door, sank down to the floor, and wept as silently as she could manage. This was a disaster. It had been difficult enough to find this place as it was. Hattie dried her eyes and stood up. Pulling herself together, she reminded herself that there was nothing she could do right now. She had a job to do, after all. After she finished work, she would figure out her options and come up with a plan.

On her way back to Blaine's house, she stopped at the Post Office to check her mail. She had set up a P.O. box right after she arrived, not knowing where she might end up living. It was fortunate she did, considering she had moved from the long-stay hotel to Blaine's and eventually to her new apartment. There wasn't much exciting—her museum association membership magazine, a few ads, assorted junk mail, and a card from Jayne. Just what she needed after this morning's crappy news.

She and Jayne tried their best to out-card each other, so she knew whatever was in this seemingly innocent envelope would be good. Hattie relocked her box and headed back to her car. Not wanting to wait until she got home, she slid her finger under the flap of Jayne's envelope and tore it open. Pulling out the card, Hattie looked at it and burst into loud laughter. She was laughing so hard that tears streamed down her face. Jayne had really outdone herself this time. The front of the card featured a cross-stitch style design with a pink rabbit vibrator on the left and a similarly sized and shaped saguaro cactus on the right. Underneath the images was written, "Dil-do Dil-don't." Deciding there was no way she would be able to read what Jayne had written without losing it again, she tossed the card and envelope onto the passenger seat and headed home.

After she got settled and fed Marmalade, Hattie sat down and read the rest of Jayne's card. As predicted, it made her laugh, lightening her mood.

Picking up her phone, Hattie texted Jayne to see if she could chat. She hoped her friend might help her work through her housing problem. Speaking of which, she opened her laptop and immediately started looking for available apartments. Hattie wasn't surprised when she couldn't find anything within her price range. Well, that was one option out. Her phone pinged with an incoming message.

Jayne: *I've got 15 minutes now. Is that enough?*
Hattie: *No idea. I'll call you.*

"What's up, buttercup?" Jayne asked when she answered.

"I'll keep it brief since I know your time is limited." Hattie quickly updated Jayne on the phone call this morning and her apartment search just now. "So I think the only option I really have is to wait. I guess I could always go back to that extended-stay place." Jayne groaned on Hattie's behalf.

"Have you asked Blaine or anyone else about leads? Maybe they know someone with a room to rent or something like that."

"I haven't, but that's a really good idea. Honestly, things were so busy at work today that I just put dealing with it on hold until I got home. I haven't done anything besides doing a quick search just now. Other than panic, that is."

"Please tell me you at least know where your towel is," Jayne said.

"Got it right here," Hattie responded, immediately understanding Jayne's *Hitchhiker's Guide to the Galaxy* reference.

"Look, babe, I gotta go, but seriously, start with Eli and Blaine. I'm sure they'll be able to help. I'll call you tomorrow, okay? I should have time after work. Today's just madness," Jayne apologized.

"No need to apologize. Wish me luck. Love you."

"Love you too! Good luck!"

Chapter 11

Hattie

Hattie fired off a text to Eli, bribing him with pizza if he could come over. She didn't want to explain the whole situation via text, and honestly, she just needed a friend. She would take any time she could get with Jayne, but she also wished it could have been more. Luckily, Eli said yes and even offered to pick the pizza up on his way over. Hattie happily accepted, giving her a chance to tidy up a little. Not that the house was messy, but Blaine was coming home tomorrow, so she wanted it to look nice—especially since they would be staying there together for the next week.

Eli showed up about thirty minutes later, pizza in hand. "When you said you were getting Brussels sprouts on pizza, I thought you were kidding," he said, placing the pizza boxes on the counter.

"Blame Blaine," she said. "He's the one who introduced me to this place."

"Of course, that man would be the one to find the only place in town that puts mini-cabbages on pizza. He's always finding the weirdest food to eat. I'll stick to my meat-laden pizza, thank you very much."

Hattie grabbed a couple of beers from the fridge, handing one to Eli. They plated the pizza and headed to the table.

"So, half-pint, what's up? I'm assuming you didn't call me over on a Monday night just to shoot the shit," Eli said.

"Am I that obvious?" she smiled, slightly embarrassed.

"Hey, I'm not one to turn down free pizza when I thought I would have to eat leftover spaghetti. Again." It was Eli's turn to smile.

"Well, regardless, I'm glad you could come over. I needed some company tonight, and I have a problem I'm hoping you can help me with, or at least help me figure out."

"Hit me. What's going on?" he asked, taking a bite of pizza.

Hattie sighed and leaned back in her chair. "So this afternoon, I got a call from my new landlord, and long story short, I can't move into my place on Sunday as planned. In fact, I can't move in for at least another month."

"Oh shit, that sucks!" Eli empathized.

"Thanks, and yeah, it does suck. I looked already, and there isn't anything else available right now in my price range."

"That isn't surprising. This is an expensive city to live in—totally worth it, but expensive—so anything remotely reasonable goes quickly, if you even hear about it."

"After living here for the past few weeks," she said, gesturing around the house, "the thought of moving back into the extended-stay place has zero appeal. So, I'm trying to figure out what to do. I'll ask around at work tomorrow, but I was hoping maybe you knew of someone who had a room to rent for the next few weeks, especially with Blaine getting back tomorrow."

"I can ask my buddy, Mick. He might still have a place to rent, especially if it's only for a few weeks. Have you asked Blaine? You know he'd probably let you stay here."

"I didn't want to impose on him. He seems like the kind of guy who likes his peace and quiet."

"Be that as it may, he also needs to get out more and live a little. Having someone else here could help with that. Just talk to him about it tomorrow and tell him what you told me. See what he says."

"Speaking of getting out," she said, "what about you? You always avoid any questions about relationships. Don't think I haven't noticed." Eli suddenly became very interested in the pizza on his plate.

"It's been a long time since I was in a relationship," he started. "I mostly just date, if you can even call it that. Nothing serious." He looked like he wanted to say more, so Hattie encouraged him to continue.

"And, is that changing?"

Eli started to blush.

"That look tells me there is someone!" she said excitedly.

"Fine," he said, turning an even darker shade of red, which was impressive considering his already dark skin tone. "There is someone I really like. It's new, though. They're very different from anyone else I've ever dated, and I don't know if that's a good thing or bad. We're just exploring things, so I don't really want to talk about it."

"I get it. Thank you for sharing what you did." Hattie stood and grabbed two more slices of pizza from the box.

Eli twisted in his chair to face her at the counter. "Thanks for understanding, Hattie. I haven't really told anyone else about it since all of my other friends are nosy and wouldn't let up until they knew every detail, so thanks."

"Anytime you want or need to talk about it, I'm here. I promise I won't push you to say more than you're comfortable with."

Eli looked a little embarrassed again. "Would you mind keeping this between us? I mean, do you mind not saying anything to Blaine? He's the only one who's an exception to my asshole friends, but I'd still prefer to keep this one close to the chest for now, even with him."

"Your secret is safe with me."

Chapter 12

Blaine

Blaine opened the front door, unsure of what he'd find. He was honestly a little surprised that it looked like nothing had moved from when he left. Marmalade poked her head out at the end of the hallway. When she saw it was him, she meowed and hurried over to him, rubbing her head against his legs. Blaine let out a sigh of relief, letting go of the stress he didn't realize he'd been holding onto. He tossed his jacket over the handle of his roller bag and bent down to pick her up.

"Hello, darling," he said while she butted her head into his chin. "Did you miss me, sweet girl? I missed you. But it seems like Hattie's been taking good care of you while I was gone." Marmalade meowed in response, butting Blaine's chin again. With a scratch to the ear, Blaine set her down and rolled his bag into his room to begin the process of unpacking.

After changing out of his suit into a pair of jeans and a black T-shirt, Blaine carried his hamper to the laundry to start a load.

Usually, on a long trip like this, he would take advantage of the hotel laundry service before heading home, but because they were so busy trying to finish everything early, he wasn't organized enough to make that happen, so instead, here he was.

While he sorted through his darks and lights, Blaine ticked through his mental to-do list. Deciding that nothing was so urgent it couldn't wait until tomorrow, Blaine decided he was officially taking the rest of the day off to settle in. It had been a long trip, and aside from the night he spent at the museum, he hadn't truly relaxed.

As he was adding the soap, his stomach growled, reminding him that although he had eaten a little on the plane, he still needed to eat more. After he started this load, he would see what was in the kitchen. He didn't want to eat anything Hattie might have bought, but there had to be some protein bars or something like that left in his pantry.

Walking over to the kitchen, he noticed a note tented on the counter:

Dear Blaine,

Welcome back! Marmalade has, I'm sure, already given you lots of rubs by now. Given the timing of your flight, I thought you might want something to eat when you got back. In the fridge, there is a container of rice and stir-fry that I made last night. I saved it for you, so feel free to eat it. If you've already eaten, no worries. I can always take it for lunch tomorrow.

See you this evening!
Hattie

Wow. That was really thoughtful of Hattie. Blaine was honestly taken aback by the gesture. He opened the fridge, finding the container in question. He removed the lid and took a sniff—it smelled delicious! Popping the dish into the microwave, Blaine grabbed the soy sauce and some utensils. When the beep sounded, he grabbed the hot plate and settled at the table. He scrolled through his personal email while he ate, woefully behind on responding to much of anything other than work-related messages. There was an email from his mom, which he'd need to respond to sooner rather than later, forms to fill out for his upcoming doctor's appointment, and a vet reminder for Marmalade's annual appointment. Everything else could wait or be deleted. If he got through those and finished his laundry by the time Hattie returned, he'd feel like he'd accomplished enough for today. He was looking forward to taking her to dinner tonight, probably more than he should be. Instead of dwelling on that thought, Blaine threw himself into filling out insurance forms while he sat on hold to make an appointment for Marmalade.

A little after 5:30, Hattie arrived home.

"Blaine! Welcome back," she said, seeming a little unsure of how to act. He understood. While talking about living together for a week was one thing, it was another to know what to do in the situation.

"Thanks. It's good to be home. The place looks great, by the way," he finally said. "It barely looks like you've lived here for the past three weeks."

"Thanks. I did try to keep things the way you had them. I know if it were my house, I would hate to come back and reach for the spatula only to find it not there, for example." Blaine smiled, glad she was as type-A as he was.

"Yeah, that's the worst. I hate it when I can't reach my spatula," he teased. Hattie smiled, lighting up the room. "So, are we still on for dinner?"

"Absolutely. When did you want to go?"

"No rush, whenever you want. I had that stir-fry you left me—thanks for that, by the way. So, I'm not starving, but I could definitely eat. Whatever works for you. I'm just catching up on some personal things, so I can go pretty much whenever."

"I'm actually really hungry right now. Would you mind if we go in, say, fifteen minutes? I just want to change into something more casual and feed Marmalade. Oh, wait, did you already do that?"

"Actually, no, I haven't. Why don't I do that while you get changed? Settle for a few minutes; it's fine."

The door to Hattie's room snicked shut. Blaine leaned against the kitchen island and closed his eyes. She was so much prettier in person than he remembered. *Hey, asshole, you can't hit on the girl who's going to be living with you for the next week.* Not to mention that whole she-just-got-out-of-a-relationship thing. Blaine groaned inwardly. It was going to be fine. He would get over it, and she would be gone soon enough anyway.

Hattie was acting nervous as they were seated and the server took their drink orders. Her eyes lit up when Blaine pointed out the Brussels sprouts. They sat there in relative silence, examining the menu. Blaine decided on the house burger (he would push himself to go the extra mile tomorrow to make up for it).

"What are you thinking about?"

Hattie looked startled at his question. "What do you mean?"

"To eat?" he asked, eyebrows raised.

"Oh," she almost seemed relieved, "to eat. Yeah, um, I was thinking about the Italian salad. That or the chicken piccata."

"Both are great options. I like them both a lot, so I'm afraid I can't help you make a decision one way or the other. Do you want pasta or salad?"

"When you put it that way, pasta."

"See, that wasn't so hard," Blaine said with a smile.

After they placed their orders, Blaine said, "I hope you don't take offense to this, but you seem jumpy tonight. I know I don't know you well, but something feels off this evening. Is everything okay?"

Hattie sighed and paused for a moment before responding. She looked like she was taking a moment to gather her thoughts, but who knew what was really going on in her head. "I got a call yesterday that's kind of thrown me for a loop. I actually wanted to talk to you about it, but for some reason, I'm really nervous to."

"What's going on, Hattie? Is there something you need help with?" he asked, concerned.

"I can't move into my new place on Sunday." Hattie proceeded to tell him everything that had happened in the last thirty-six hours. "Anyway, I was hoping you might have some leads on a room to rent or another temporary house-sitting gig or something. I asked a few people at work if they had any leads, and Eli is asking his friend Mick, I think he said, but he suggested I ask you, too."

Blaine racked his brain for possible solutions to Hattie's problem, but nothing came to mind. Then it hit him: why didn't she just stay with him? It would be torture for him, sure, but he couldn't see any good reason why not.

"Well, I can't think of anyone I know, but assuming this week goes well, and assuming you'd want to, that is, why don't you just stay with me? There's a chance, after all, that I'll need to make another impromptu trip to D.C., and this way, I wouldn't have to worry about a last-minute person for Marmalade if Katie can't do it again for some reason. What do you think? Do you want to live with me temporarily?"

"Really? That would be absolutely amazing, Blaine! I'm happy to pay you rent and take care of Marmalade whenever you need me to. I promise you'll barely notice I'm there."

"Hattie, if you stay, I want you to feel like it's your home, too, even if it's only temporary. You don't need to hide in your room when I'm home or anything like that. Feel free to use the living room and kitchen just like you have been. And I don't need your rent money."

"Please let me contribute somehow, Blaine; otherwise, I'll feel bad."

"Fine, how about this: you buy any communal groceries."

"I'll do you one better than that; not only will I buy the groceries, but how about I plan on cooking for both of us, say three times a week?"

"Deal."

Blaine reached across the table, offering her a hand, and said, "Welcome home, roomie."

Hattie

Hattie did her best not to squeal with delight when Blaine offered to let her stay with him. He truly was such a kind man. It was a huge relief to have a place secured for the next month and not have to pack everything up for yet another temporary move.

"Blaine, I can't begin to thank you!"

"It's really okay, Hattie. So, roomie, why don't you tell me some more about you? We didn't really have a chance to get into it too much before I left. Tell me about yourself."

"Where should I start? You already know about my breakup and how I ended up out here."

"Start with the basics. Where did you grow up? Who else is in your family? That sort of thing," Blaine said, taking a drink of his water.

"Sure, okay. Well, I grew up outside of Denver. I lived there until I moved away for college, and then I moved to Syracuse for grad school, which is where I met Galen."

"Is it just you, or do you have any siblings?"

"I have one sister, she's two years younger. We used to be really close, but we drifted apart some, basically since I moved to New York. Her name is Andy, it's short for Andrea. She lives in Seattle, so I'm hoping that maybe now that I'm closer, we'll be able to reconnect some. I actually wonder if part of the reason was Galen. She never seemed overly fond of him, not that she was going to say anything to me about it."

"I hope that happens for you, Hattie. I have a younger sister, too. Her name is Brooke. She lives in Central Oregon. She works as an occupational therapist during the school year, and in the summer, she works at a camp for kids with special needs."

"That's awesome! We need more people out there doing that kind of work. Andy is in her last year of law school at UW. She's going to be an environmental lawyer, or at least that's the plan."

"Law school is tough. I flirted with the idea of becoming a lawyer, but I like what I do better than I think I would have liked law."

"I'll stick to the social sciences, thank you. Where do your parents live?" Hattie asked.

"My mom moved a few years ago to a small town on the Oregon Coast, which was always a dream of hers. It's been a good change for her... I don't know if it came up in conversations with Eli or not, but my dad passed away a little over four years ago."

"Oh, Blaine! I'm so sorry to hear that."

"It's okay. I mean, don't get me wrong, it sucks, but it is what it is. Each day gets a little easier, you know? Anyway, being at the house where I grew up held too many memories for my mom, so she decided to sell it and move over to the Coast. She absolutely loves it and I'm happy for her."

"So, you both live by the ocean?" she asked with a smile.

"Haha, yeah. I guess the apple doesn't fall far from the tree," Blaine replied. "What about you? Are there any parental figures in your life?"

Hattie understood Blaine's pain from personal experience. It wasn't often that she found someone else who was as young as she was who had lost a parent, too. "My dad died in a car accident when I was still pretty young. I was four when it happened. He slipped on some ice and crashed. Luckily, no one else was hurt. My mom still lives in Denver. She remarried after Andy started college, although they had been dating for years. Jeremy is a nice guy and he seems to make my mom happy, so that's all that really matters. Blaine, can I ask, how did you lose your dad? And it's totally fine if you don't want to share, so don't feel like you have to. I know it's not always an easy thing to talk about."

"He had a massive heart attack. It killed him instantly, so at least he didn't suffer. It's why I am so strict about what I eat and staying on top of my exercise routine." Blaine looked warmly at Hattie from across the table. "We make quite the pair, don't we?"

"We do," she agreed with a little smile. Thankfully, the server arrived with their food, and their conversation turned to more pleasant things.

Chapter 13

Hattie

Hattie felt stuffed to the gills upon their return from dinner. "I'm so full I'm sleepy. I might just get ready for bed and then read a little. Give you time to settle a bit more and get some Marmalade snuggles in."

"Oh!" Blaine exclaimed. "Speaking of Marmalade, I have a little something for you. Hang on, I'll be right back." Blaine disappeared into his room, where Hattie heard him rustling around. The feline in question wound her way around Hattie's legs while she was waiting. A moment later, Blaine returned with a small tissue-wrapped package.

"For me?" she asked, accepting the gift he was offering her.

"Yeah, it's just a little something I picked up for you—at a museum, I'll have you know. It's just a small thank you for taking care of Marmalade. It was a relief to know she was being loved and cared for. Anyway, I hope you like it."

Hattie carefully unwrapped the package, pulling back the last layer of tissue paper to reveal a small, enameled, orange tabby figurine. "Oh my gosh!" she exclaimed. "It looks just like her!"

"That's what I thought, too. It even has the same big white patch that she has on her belly."

"Blaine, this is perfect. Thank you." Without thinking, Hattie leaned forward and kissed Blaine on the cheek. The realization of what she had done slammed into her, and heat rushed to her cheeks. "Okay, well then, thank you so much for this. I'm just going to head to bed now. Goodnight, Blaine!" she said quickly, heading down the hall and into her room.

Shutting the door behind her, Hattie leaned against it. "You idiot!" she whisper-yelled to herself. "You can't just go around kissing men you barely know." *Even if you are living with them*, the voice in her head said. "Especially not then!" *But you're attracted to him.* An even better reason not to kiss him, she reasoned with her inner voice.

Hattie decided to ignore what had just happened. It was just a simple thank-you kiss, and chances were he barely noticed it anyway. The figurine was still clenched in her hand, so she made a space on the bedside table for it. It was a really thoughtful gift, and she would treasure it once she moved into her own place.

Hattie started to undress so she could change into her pajamas. "Shit!" she called out when her arm, hair, and earring somehow managed to all get caught in each other, and in a spot that she couldn't easily reach. "Ow!" she cried out as she tried to untangle herself. Hattie stood there for a moment trying to decide how best to get out of this situation.

Blaine knocked lightly on Hattie's door. "Hang on!" she cried out, trying not to panic.

"You okay in there?" he called through the door.

"Um..."

"Hattie?"

"This is really embarrassing, but, um, I'm sort of stuck. My sweater... it's all caught, and... uh, I can't get out," she finally said.

There was a pause before Blaine responded again. "Do you want me to come in and help you?"

"Um... ow! Shit!" she exclaimed, having little luck trying to free herself and hurting herself in the process.

"Hattie?" Blaine said, sounding increasingly concerned.

"This is so embarrassing," she groaned.

"I'm going to come in now... unless you tell me you don't want me to."

"Okay, um, I should warn you, I was getting changed, so, um, I'm mostly not clothed." Hattie couldn't hear anything from the other side of the door for a moment.

"Okay, I'm coming in." Hattie stepped away from the door so Blaine could enter. "Let me just take a look here," he said, stepping closer.

Hattie's breathing increased, causing her bra-clad breasts to rise and fall more quickly. At least she had her pretty bra on today, she mused. Scents of pine and leather wafted towards her as he made his way closer. She'd smelled a little bit of it when they'd been in the car before, but the scent of it was so much stronger now with his nearness.

Blaine was quiet while he slowly moved around her, examining the situation. "I think I can see the problem. Are you okay if I touch you?" Blaine asked.

"Mmhmm," was all that she could manage to get out. What the hell sort of soap or deodorant or whatever did Blaine use? He smelled amazing. It reminded Hattie of her favorite "Lumberjack's Cabin" scented candle. She closed her eyes and inhaled as deeply as she could without being conspicuous.

Blaine reached up and started to help untangle her, his chest lightly brushed her breast while he worked to free her trapped right arm. Hattie had to repress the shudder that wanted to run through her body at the touch. Twisting around her side, he continued working. Suddenly, she was free. Blaine quickly took a step back, turning towards the door. Over his shoulder, he asked, "You good now?"

"Yes," she replied huskily. Trying to lighten up what felt like a tense room, she said, "Didn't think we'd cross that bridge on day one, but, oh well! I appreciate your help."

"Of course," he said, clearing his throat. "I'm going to hop in the shower unless you need in there," he said.

"No, that's fine. I don't need in the bathroom just yet. Go ahead," she said. Blaine closed the door behind him. She heard the bathroom door snick shut and the shower start.

Hattie threw herself down on the bed in relief, holding the trouble-making sweater against her belly. Did that really just happen?

What the hell? If Blaine had run his hand down any part of her body, she would have either turned into a puddle on the floor or jumped on him like a monkey. Warmth pooled at her sex when she thought about him brushing against her breast. Another inch closer, and he would have brushed her nipple. Her imagination loved the idea of that.

One thing she hadn't considered with this whole roommate situation was how she was going to take care of her sexual health with her sexy roommate just across the hall. No matter how much Hattie wanted to deny that Blaine was sexy, she had to admit it was true.

Now's your chance, the little voice in her head told her. *He's in the shower. There's no way he'll hear your vibrator over the noise of the water and the fan.* She was taking all of her clothes off anyway. Jumping up and grabbing her toiletries bag from the desk, she stripped in record time, threw herself back on the bed, lined up her vibrator, and turned it on. Normally, the lowest setting was enough to get her off; tonight, though, she kicked it up a few notches in order to get the job done quickly. With one hand on the vibrator and the other pinching and playing with her nipple, it didn't take long to get her close to the edge. She grabbed the pillow and cried out into it as she came. Turning the toy off and tossing it to the side, Hattie lay against the comforter, panting. Wow, she had needed that.

Thankfully, by the time she heard Blaine turn off the water, her breathing had gone back to normal. She put on her sleep pants and tank top, grabbed her toiletries bag (with the vibe safely tucked back inside for cleaning), and headed to the bathroom after she heard Blaine's door close.

Chapter 14

Blaine

"I hate you," Blaine said to Eli as he slid into the booth at London's.

"Why, man? What did I do?" Eli asked, brows arched in surprise.

"You suggested Hattie talk to me about needing a place to stay. You knew I wouldn't be able to say no to her."

Eli chuckled. "I just said she should ask if you had any ideas for her, man. Why? Is she awful to live with? Your place always looked great whenever I was over there while you were gone."

"No, she's actually the model roommate. It's Hattie. She's the problem. Hey, hand me the specials menu, will you?"

Eli handed the menu over and started to chuckle. "Ah, I see. You've got the hots for her."

"Yes, which is awkward as hell." Blaine proceeded to tell Eli about what he was referring to as the sweater incident. "Thank god I have a loud shower, not one of those quiet, low-flow things. Otherwise, I might have died from pent-up misery waiting for her to go to sleep so I could relieve myself." Blaine set his menu aside, ready to order whenever the server arrived.

"It really is a noisy shower," Eli confirmed. "So what if you like her? I mean, maybe wait until you're not living together to start something, just in case it goes badly. Otherwise, what's holding you back?"

"A woman like that will never go for a guy like me."

"We've been over this, Blaine," Eli growled. "You are objectively sexy."

Blaine cringed. "You know it weirds me out when you say stuff like that."

"Then don't make me fucking say it. You're kind, funny, have a good job, live in a great place, and have a nice body."

"Again..."

Annoyance flickered across Eli's face. "Yeah, yeah. I don't like this any better than you do. But I'll do what I gotta do to make you understand who you are in this moment. Don't take this the wrong way, because I'm asking out of a place of love, but have you ever thought about going to therapy to help you get over your body issues and childhood trauma and shit like that? It might do you a world of good."

Blaine hadn't considered therapy, but now that Eli mentioned it, it made some sense. After all, people went to therapy for eating disorders. Not that this was the same, but if it could help them, maybe it could help him.

"I haven't, but there might be some truth to what you're saying. I know I've mentioned this before, but whenever I look in the mirror,

I only see my flaws. I know I've come a long way in the past few years, but I tend to focus on the areas that need improvement instead of all the work I've accomplished."

"Well, think about it. My cousin went to see someone. Therapy helped him immensely."

Their server approached the table, so they paused their conversation for a moment.

"Hey, ya'll. My name is Leslie, and I'll be your server for a bit. I'm about to head off shift, but I didn't want you to have to wait too much longer, so I thought I'd get you guys started. What can I get for you?"

After placing their orders, Eli asked, "So what are you going to do about Hattie?"

"For now, nothing. You're right that I need to sort my own shit out first," Blaine said, "And remember, she isn't looking for any sort of relationship right now, anyway. I guess I'll just be sexually frustrated while I try to get my head sorted out. That, and research the best thing to use in the shower since I think my hands will be getting a workout in there for the next month."

Eli looked across the restaurant at something, seeming not to want to meet Blaine's eyes, and said, "You didn't hear it from me, but if you want something you can leave out without raising suspicion, give coconut oil a try. Bonus: it smells good. If she asks, it's for your hair."

"Do I even want to know how you know that?" Blaine asked, equally uncomfortable, keeping his gaze on the tabletop.

"Nope," Eli said, with a pop on his 'p', avoiding eye contact with Blaine.

"Noted."

Leslie, the server, dropped off their drinks, and their conversation turned to other things. Blaine was telling Eli about seeing the Van Goghs in D.C. when a server came over to bring them their entrees. It was the same guy who had helped them the last time they had been here.

"Hi, I'm Marcus. I'll be taking over for Leslie. Who had the salad?" Blaine raised his hand to indicate it was his. "Which means this big ol' sausage must be for you," he said, inclining his head towards Eli. Blaine could have sworn that Eli was blushing, but with the lighting in there and his naturally dark skin, it was hard to tell.

After Marcus left, Blaine asked, "You okay? You seem a little flustered."

Eli took a breath, seeming to recenter himself. "No, man, I'm good. That guy is just a lot. He's super flirty every time I've been in here."

"Yeah, he sure seems to have a thing for you," Blaine said.

Eli huffed out a laugh. "Yeah, obviously, I'm not interested."

They ate and chatted a while longer. After a bit, Marcus made his way back over to their table to check on them. "How's everything? Is there anything else I can get you?" Marcus asked, smiling.

Eli looked over to Blaine. "You up for dessert?" Every fiber of Blaine's body wanted to say yes, but he didn't want to stress about the calories.

"Nah, I think I'm good."

"I'd like to take a look at the menu if you don't mind. Maybe I'll get something to go," Eli mused.

Marcus pulled the menu from his apron pocket and placed it in front of Eli. Eli picked it up and began to look over the list. "What would you recommend? Or, what's your favorite thing on here?"

"A lot of people get the cheesecake, which is really good, but personally, my favorite is the panna cotta. It's good with the salted caramel or the berries on top."

"Sounds amazing. I'll take one of each of the panna cotta. Thanks," Eli said, handing the small menu back to Marcus.

"Great, I'll get those right out. To go, correct?"

"Yes, please."

"Hungry?" Blaine asked with a smirk.

"Haha, yeah, they aren't both for me. They both sounded amazing, so I thought I'd take them home and share with my sister."

"I forgot she was in town visiting this week."

Eli glanced around. "I'll be right back. I'm gonna go take a piss before we head out."

Blaine picked up his phone from the table, checking his messages while Eli was gone. As he was responding to an email from his mom, a message alert from Hattie popped up. Tapping on it, the message showed a picture of Marmalade lying peacefully on Hattie's lap, clearly fast asleep. The message read:

Hattie: *I've been catnapped for at least 30 minutes. I'm starting to need to pee. Either I have to move her or pay to get your chair cleaned. What should I do?*

Blaine: *Screw the chair, I'll get a new one.*
Hattie: *Oh, thank god. I'd hate to think of what might happen if I did try to move her.*

Blaine smiled at Hattie's reply. This woman! Blaine looked Eli over as he slid back into the booth. Something was definitely off. He looked almost disheveled. "What happened between the bathroom and here?" he asked. "You look a little worse for wear."

Eli laughed warily. "I feel that way, too. There was a drunk woman by the bar who tried to throw herself at me. Apparently, she's nursing a bad breakup and will regret much more than just her dating choices come morning. She's going to have one hell of a hangover from the looks of her. I did my best to get out of there in one piece."

Marcus arrived at their table with a to-go container and their check. "Here's this as well; no rush, though. Whenever you're ready, I can take your payment."

Eli pulled out his wallet and handed his card to Marcus as Blaine started to pull his wallet out of his pocket. "I got this. You can pick up the tab next time. Deal?"

"Thanks, man. Sounds good."

Together, they headed out to the parking lot. "Oh shit!" Eli exclaimed. "I don't have my sweater. I must have left it inside. I bet it fell off the bench and onto the floor, so I didn't notice it. I'm just gonna run back in and grab it. I'll catch you later, man," he said, giving Blaine a quick hug before turning and heading back inside the restaurant.

"Yeah, see ya." Blaine climbed into his car and leaned his head back against the headrest. He both wanted and didn't want to go home to where he knew Hattie would be. "Suck it up, buttercup," he said to himself. "You can't avoid her for the next month." And with that, he started for home.

Chapter 15

Hattie

H attie shuffled bottles of nail polish around, looking for the one she wanted. When she couldn't find it, she held up two bottles and asked Jayne via video call which one she should pick. It was their monthly girls' night, a tradition they'd kept since her college days, despite the distance that often separated them. Blaine was out for the evening, so Hattie had the house to herself.

"Ooh, I like that tealish-colored one! It looks almost Tiffany blue," Jayne said.

"It is really pretty. Oh! I know what I'll do. I'll use this one, and then I've got a pearly, semi-sheer color that I can use as a top coat."

"That will look amazing! So now that we've got that all sorted out, what the heck is going on with your living situation?" Jayne hadn't been able to check in last night, so Hattie hadn't had the chance to fill her in on Blaine's offer or what had happened after they got home. She started to tell Jayne about the very eventful few hours of that evening.

"Shut up! That did not happen!" Jayne gasped after Hattie finished telling her about the earring debacle.

Hattie twisted the lid back on her polish and held her hand up to examine her work. "Yeah, unfortunately, it did. And Jayne…" Hattie began. Should she admit this part to her friend? Yeah, she should. "So, um, this probably won't come as a surprise, but I'm attracted to him."

Jayne shrieked in delight. "I totally called it! Ha! So, what's the big deal?"

"Well, to start with, I'm living with him. Also, I want to be single. I knew I should have kept this to myself!" Hattie began applying polish to her other hand.

"Love, just because you find someone attractive doesn't mean you're going to jump their bones or anything like that. And even if you do, it doesn't mean it's a relationship. It could just be—gasp—sex."

"Sorry, I'm overthinking things again. This is what I mean, though! This is why it's so important that I figure out who I am on my own."

"So let the man supply you with some fantasy material."

"Jayne!"

"What? You've already admitted that you have the hots for him. Use him for his body if you want, and then move on. Or don't, and keep things simple since you're living with him for at least the next month."

"Yeah, that's probably the safer route. I think I just need some really good sex or orgasms, and then I'll be better. It's been a while since I've had a toe-curling level of release. Galen was usually more focused on his needs than mine, and eventually, sex just became the same, almost mechanical." Hattie finished her nails, setting the polish bottle to the side, and made herself comfortable on her bed, careful not to smudge her nails.

"So your vibrator was working overtime?"

Hattie barked out a laugh at the look on Jayne's face. She was probably going for lascivious but ended up looking slightly deranged instead. "Yes, but it's only so good, too, ya know? My battery-operated boyfriend gets me to where I need, but not beyond that."

"That won't do! Sounds like you need to go shopping for some new toys. Especially, if you're committed to being single for a bit. Have you used one of those air pulse vibrators? I tried one, and oh my god. I nearly broke my damn leg off in the shower."

"Ooh, maybe that's what I need! Minus the near-leg break," she said, chuckling.

"I'll send you the link to the article I read about it, and you can check out the other options, too. Highly recommend it. Great orgasms, quick, and low effort. It's a win-win-win if you ask me."

"Well, if I'm going to keep living with a sexy man sleeping across the hall, I'm going to need something quick and quiet."

"So other than the housing snafu that is resolved, everything else is going well?" Jayne asked.

Hattie smiled. "Yeah. I'm starting to get the hang of things at the museum, and I'm beginning to make friends. Carly, who works in collections, has invited me to join her and a group of friends that get together once a month, so I'm doing that next week, and Eli has been a blessing. I can see why he and Blaine get along. They're both such good guys. I can't wait for you to meet them someday."

"I'm excited to meet both of them, especially Blaine. I want to see if he's as sexy in person as that one photo you sent me. But enough about them. Please tell me you've been to the beach!"

Jayne picked up her glass of white wine and took a sip.

"Yes, although not as often as I'd like. I think once I get moved in and fully settled, I'll be able to go more often, but I'm still trying to establish roots here and figure things out. But yes, I've been there several times. Blaine gets up at 5:30 every morning and goes down there to run, apparently."

"You should go with him sometime," Jayne suggested. There was a brief pause, and then they both started laughing. This was why she loved Jayne so much. It was great to still be friends with someone who knew her so well.

"Yeah, hard pass on that one. I'll take my sleeping until seven a.m., thank you very much." Hattie's smile faded as she saw the email that had just popped up in her desktop notifications. It was from Galen.

"What's wrong, babe? Your face just did this thing, and now you look constipated."

Hattie shook her head in disbelief. "Haha, no, I just got an email from Galen."

Jayne's nose crinkled in disgust. "Asshole. What does he want?"

"I don't know," Hattie said, rolling her eyes. "I'll read it at some point. From the subject line, it seems like there's some mail for me that hasn't been properly forwarded. Whatever, I'll deal with that later. He can fucking wait."

As they moved from painting their fingers to toes, they chatted about Jayne's work, what Madison and Sophia had been up to, and Jayne's summer travel plans. Hattie heard the front door open. Blaine must be home from his dinner with Eli.

"It sounds like Blaine is home, so I should probably wrap things up. I'm trying to be the model roommate. Plus, I have a vibrator to shop for."

Jayne smiled. "Yes, you do. I'll send you that link right now. Enjoy your little shopping excursion, and enjoy it even more when it arrives," she said with a wink. "I'll talk to you soon. Love you!"

"Love you too." With that, they ended their call. A few seconds later, the link Jayne had promised appeared in her inbox. Hattie looked at the article, opened another tab, and started her search. Grown-ups deserved new toys sometimes, too. She found one she wanted, placed the order, and then checked her email for an order confirmation before closing her browser. Opening up her email, she saw Galen's message once more. *Fine*, she thought, *I'll open the damn thing*.

To: Hattie Renaud
From: glove69@woohoo.com
Subject: Address for Mail

Hey Babe,

Some mail came for you. Let me know where I can forward it. Madison and Sophia won't tell me anything. They're good friends, I guess. I still don't understand why you left the way you did. I miss you. Is there anything I can say to convince you to come home? My life just feels empty without you in it. My days are darker. I love you. Please come home.

-G

The fuck? Where the hell did he get off with that bullshit? *I love you. I miss you. Come home.* How about too little, too late, pal? She was so angry that she slammed her laptop closed, tossed it on the other side of the bed, and headed towards the kitchen. Hattie needed chocolate, more wine, or a cat. Possibly all three.

In her ire over Galen's message, Hattie hadn't heard Blaine go into his room before she left hers. He wasn't in the kitchen, and the bathroom door was open. Grabbing a glass and pouring a slug of red wine into it, she grabbed some dark chocolate from her lunch bag stash and returned to her room, determined to put that bastard's message out of her mind. Popping her earphones in, Hattie opened Netflix on her laptop and resumed rewatching season one of *Bridgerton*. If anything could take her mind off of Galen, it was Simon, the bloody gorgeous Duke of Hastings, and his filthy, flirty eyebrow.

Chapter 16

Blaine

Blaine sat in the waiting room of the therapist's office, his leg bouncing nervously. *You are being stupid,* he thought, *it's just a therapy appointment. People do this all of the time.* After dinner with Eli, he decided that maybe his friend was right. He found an office that wasn't too far away, which currently accepted new patients. When he went to book an appointment, there was one slot available for the next day, a cancellation if he had to guess. Rather than putting it off, he went ahead and took it.

As the appointment drew nearer, Blaine had become increasingly anxious about it. Maybe he should just forget it and go home. Did he really need to be here? Just then, the door opened, and a man who looked to be in his early forties with dark hair and just a touch of silver to it stood there.

"Blaine?"

"Hi," he said, standing.

"Nice to meet you. I'm Patrick." Blaine shook the therapist's offered hand. "Come on in," Patrick said. Blaine followed the therapist into the office and took a seat on the couch. "So, Blaine, since this is our first appointment together, we're just going to cover some basic stuff and then we'll get into the real reason you are here today." Patrick proceeded to tell Blaine about his background and training. After asking Blaine a series of standard questions, he said, "Okay, now that that is out of the way, let's talk about what brought you in today."

Blaine took a deep breath and said, "Well, I... uh..." He wasn't quite sure what to say or how to start.

"Take your time, Blaine. Remember, this is a judgment-free space, so you don't need to worry about anything you say in here. My job is to help you, not judge you. How about, instead, we start with what prompted you to make the appointment to come in and see me?"

Blaine relaxed back into the couch. That was a question he could answer. "I was having dinner with my friend recently, and he said that his cousin had seen a therapist to help him with some eating issues. I don't have an eating disorder, but I can't seem to move past the image of me as the fat kid/young man I used to be. I'm super critical of myself all of the time, especially when it comes to my body. I don't think any woman should want to be with me, that I'm not good enough for anyone. So, I don't know, I guess I'm here to see if you can help with that."

Okay, so apparently it was easier to share than he realized. Once he opened his mouth and started to talk, everything had just spilled out. A sense of relief washed over Blaine after sharing even just that little bit. Maybe there was something to this therapy after all.

"That is definitely something I can help you work on. We're all critical of ourselves, to some degree or another, so you aren't alone there. Committing to coming in and seeing a therapist takes a lot of bravery. I can't promise that it will always be easy, but I can promise that it will get easier over time."

"Yeah?" Blaine smirked.

"Yeah," Patrick said, returning his smile. "There's a name for what's going on with you, Blaine. It sounds like you have what is known as body dysmorphia. Now, there's usually a reason that someone has developed body issues like yours. Sometimes it's from childhood trauma, sometimes it's from something more recent. Our work in here will be to figure out what caused it and to come up with strategies to help you reframe your thinking when thoughts like those that you described do come up, because they will. Is there a moment that stands out to you that might have caused these issues to begin?" Patrick asked.

"No, they've been there for as long as I can remember."

"Alright, let's begin by talking a little about your family and your upbringing."

"I don't think it's anything my family caused," Blaine said.

"I'm glad to hear that, but it will still help me to better understand you. Tell me about your family. Do you have any siblings? Were your parents married or divorced? Those sorts of things."

Blaine leaned back into the couch and began to tell Patrick about his family. He knew he had been lucky to grow up with two loving parents, at least until his dad had died, and a younger sister, who, while they didn't always get along, he was close to and loved very much.

"I was always a little bit pudgy. You know how some little kids are just kind of round?"

"I know exactly what you mean. My brother was that way. I think he was eleven or so before he lost his baby fat, as some people call it."

"Yeah, people used to say that to me. 'Oh, you'll grow out of it, it's just baby fat.' I didn't, though. All growing up, I was always the chubbiest of the boys, and well, kids are assholes, and they would make fun of me for it. Unfortunately for me, I would cope by going home and eating half a package of cookies, which, of course, just added to the problem. I never developed healthy coping strategies, so that became my default for any kind of stress. Kids would bully me, and I would turn to food. My teenage years were particularly tough, not to mention incredibly lonely. I only had a few friends, but they were social outcasts just like me. Girls had no interest in me, or at least not the ones I wanted to. When I got to college, I gained the freshman fifteen, and the cycle continued." Blaine stopped, running his hand down his face.

Memories flashed in his mind of the times he'd been bullied on the playground, the time a girl in his freshman year of high school had pretended to like him only to break his heart and make fun of him. Patrick was right, this wasn't easy, but Blaine wasn't that sad, overweight kid anymore. He had been strong enough to become the man he was today, and he would be strong enough to keep growing so that he could open up his life and heart to someone.

"Looking at you now, it looks as if things have changed. Was there something that happened that precipitated this change?" Patrick asked.

Blaine was surprised when tears started to moisten his eyes.

"It's okay, Blaine. Express yourself however you need to in here. This is a safe space."

Blaine took in a shuddering breath and said, "Sorry, I just didn't expect to react like this." Pulling a tissue from the box on the table next to him, Blaine wiped his eyes and then continued. "My dad… he passed away four years ago. It was unexpected. A heart attack. He was a stocky guy, not overweight like I was, but a solid man. His death shocked my system. If it could happen to him, someone who was way more fit than I was, what would stop it from happening to me? I was determined to make changes to get healthy.

"I started by trying to be more active, cutting down on all the things I knew I shouldn't be having. By virtue of not keeping that stuff around my house, I couldn't turn to it in stressful times. Whenever I wanted to reach for a cupcake, I'd get down on the floor and do some sit-ups. It sucked, but then I started to see results, so I kept going. Then I crashed and burned because I was being so strict. It took me a while, and hearing a lot of people say it, but I realized I could have those calorie-laden treats, but they needed to be just that—*treats*. Not every day, not never. So, I started to introduce things in moderation. Now, as long as I keep an eye on what I eat, how often I drink beer, etcetera, and keep on top of my exercise, I'm able to maintain a healthy body."

"How do you feel when you look in the mirror now?" Patrick asked, crossing his leg at the knee.

Blaine leaned his head back against the couch and said, "That's the thing, isn't it? If I'm in a good mood, if I'm feeling good about myself, then I see someone who has come a long way. If I'm having a bad day, I see all of my failures, past and present."

"We are our own worst critics, aren't we?" Patrick asked, rhetorically. "What about your romantic relationships? You mentioned not feeling good enough for anyone else. Have you had any relationships in the past?"

"Yes. I've had a few. Most of them didn't last too long. Some just weren't a good fit, and others, I got in my own way. I would end them before she could because I would convince myself that she wasn't going to be able to put up with my neediness for being told I was attractive or some other BS like that."

"Self-sabotage is really common in cases like yours. Were these recent relationships?"

"Some were from before I lost the weight, but most have been after. Once I started to see progress, on the days I was feeling good, I would go out and try, but again, they were all short-lived, whether by choice or not."

"You've shared a lot today, Blaine, and I'm proud of you. I said it before, but it takes a lot of courage to take that first step and come into this office, so good for you. We're almost out of time for today, unfortunately. We'll keep working on all of this, but know that it's going to take some time. If I could, I would wave my magic wand and make it all go away, but sadly, I can't do that. Instead, I'm going to give you some homework to start addressing that and your body-image issues as well. We've talked about a lot, and there are many places we can go from here, but we can explore more about what that might look like next time. Between now and then, I want you to do something. Each morning, I want you to look at yourself in the mirror and list at least three positive things about yourself. Start with the ones you can see, and we'll work up from there. Try not to repeat things from day to day. I want you to pay attention to how you feel before taking an inventory, if you will, and how you feel afterward. We'll check back next time on how it goes. How does that sound?"

"Sounds good, Doc."

Patrick laughed. "Just Patrick is fine. See you next time, Blaine."

Blaine felt lighter walking back to his car after his session, which wasn't something he expected to feel. He could do this. He exercised his body, and now he would exercise his mind. He would overcome these feelings of inadequacy and then, finally, maybe he would feel that someone could want him.

Chapter 17

Hattie

It was late afternoon when her vision started to go funny. *Oh no,* thought Hattie, *please don't let this be happening...* It was as if she couldn't focus on what was right in front of her, only seeing clearly on the edges of her vision. It had been a long time since Hattie had a migraine, but the aura was her cue that one was coming. Doing her best to keep working despite the fact that she essentially had a blind spot in both eyes, she waited for the aura to pass. If she was lucky, they only lasted about fifteen minutes. Then at least she would be able to see again and could get home, hopefully before the pain and nausea became too intense.

Hattie grabbed her bag and rummaged through it, searching for her prescription. She was reminded that now that she was here, she needed to find a new primary care doctor to get a refill. She found the bottle and wanted to cry—it was empty. She knew she had more back at the house, but delaying taking it meant that both the intensity and length had the potential to increase.

"Fuck," she said aloud. Hattie messaged her boss to let him know she wasn't feeling well and planned to head home soon. She couldn't leave until her aura subsided, as it wasn't safe for her to drive. Her boss responded with '*No problem. Feel better!*'

Moments later, almost like the lights coming up in a theater, her aura cleared. Hattie grabbed her things and headed to her car, eager to get back to Blaine's.

An hour later, Hattie lay on her bed, curtains closed, in relative silence, when she heard Blaine come in. He bustled around, setting his things down. She heard him greet Marmalade and then start walking down the hall toward their rooms. Hattie had left her door cracked in case Marmalade wanted to come in. As Blaine passed by, he called out, "Hattie, you in there?"

"Yes," she responded weakly.

Blaine pushed the door open a little bit more. "Are you okay? What are you doing lying in the dark?"

"Fun fact," she managed to croak out, arm slung across her eyes to block out the light, "I occasionally get migraines, and today seems to be one of those days."

"Do you need anything? An ice pack or something for the pain?" He sounded really concerned.

"Thanks, Blaine, but right now, just dark and quiet. I took some medicine, so I'm just waiting for it to kick in and its side effects to pass." As if her body heard her talking about side effects, a wave of nausea hit her. With Blaine standing in her doorway, she did her best not to groan.

"Okay, I'll leave you alone then. Let me know if there's anything you want or need, though," he almost whispered.

"Thanks, Blaine." Blaine shut the door behind him, and Hattie drifted off to sleep.

When Hattie woke up, the sun had gone down, but it was still early evening. She was dying of thirst and forced herself to shuffle into the kitchen to get some water. When she rounded the corner from the hallway into the living room, she immediately raised her arm to block the light.

"Hattie, what are you doing out here?" Blaine asked.

"I need water," she responded.

"I could have brought you some," he said, getting up from the couch where he'd been working on his laptop. "Here, let me," he said, pulling a glass down from the cupboard and filling it with cool water.

"Thanks," she managed. She closed her eyes, leaning against the breakfast bar, and slowly sipped the cool liquid. She heard Blaine moving around in the kitchen, but kept her eyes closed to block out the light. Suddenly, she let out a small gasp as she felt a cool, damp cloth laid across the back of her neck. And what was that smell? Was that lavender?

"Would you be okay if I massaged your neck and shoulders? It might help a bit," Blaine said. Hattie murmured her assent. Blaine led her over to the couch and sat her down. Reaching over, he clicked off the lamp he'd been using, darkening the room to a more comfortable level for her. From behind her, he deftly massaged the tight muscles in her back and shoulders. Hattie groaned with relief.

"That feels amazing," she said. "Thank you."

After a few minutes, Blaine stopped. "You good? Is that a little better?" Hattie nodded in response, some of the tightness gone, easing her headache a bit. Blaine replaced the cool cloth on her neck, refilled her water, and sent her back to bed. As she settled into it, Hattie thought about how no one had ever cared for her in such a way when she had migraines before. It was really kind of Blaine to care so much for someone he hardly knew. With that thought, she drifted off to sleep.

Chapter 18

Blaine

Caring for Hattie and massaging her last night felt nicer than it should have. It was the first time that Blaine had really touched her, aside from their initial handshake and a few brushes of fingers as they handed things to each other—not to mention when he nearly grazed her bra-clad breast as he helped free her from her accidental earring entanglement. They were still practically strangers in many ways and hadn't developed the level of intimacy that comes from knowing someone for a while. But based on his body's reaction to his fingers on her skin, even when she was feeling ill, that was probably a good thing. Thank goodness the back of the couch had been between them while he massaged the tight muscles in her neck and shoulders. Otherwise, it would have been pretty obvious how he felt. And that groan! That delicious sound nearly did him in. He fully understood that, at that moment, she felt like shit, but his brain had immediately conjured a very different situation in which he could make her make a very similar sound (preferably while his mouth was on her). Three more weeks. That was all he had to survive, and then she'd be able to move into her new place. Christ, had it really only been a week? This might be the longest three weeks of his life.

Blaine was pouring himself a second cup of coffee when Hattie wandered out of her bedroom. "Morning," she said sleepily.

"Morning. Coffee?" he asked, raising the pot in question.

"Yes, please."

Blaine poured her a cup, getting out the half-and-half she loved so much and handing it to her. After pouring a heavy dollop in, Hattie took a sip, sighed, and smiled. "Oh, that's good."

Blaine returned the creamer to the fridge and asked, "Does the caffeine help with your migraines? How are you, by the way? You seem like you're doing better."

"Between the meds, sleep, some caffeine, and your most excellent massage, I'm doing much better. Thanks for helping me last night. How are you so good with migraines?" she inquired.

"My mom got them really badly," he explained. "My dad traveled a lot for work, so when she had one, I tried to take care of her the best I could. When I was little, the first time it happened, I was worried she would be broken permanently, and Dad would be mad at me for not making her better. I quickly figured out that wasn't the case, and although there wasn't much I could do, what I could was needed and appreciated. That's how I learned to cook. I taught myself so I could take care of my sister, and my mom wouldn't have to get out of bed."

"Wow, Blaine, that's incredibly sweet."

"Mom was never able to figure out what triggered hers, so she could never anticipate when they would come on. Given the unpredictability of that and my dad's travel schedule, it just seemed like the thing to do. I'm sorry you suffer from them—I know that in some cases, that might sound ableist, but, at least in my mom's case, she really did suffer. Do you know what triggers yours? If you don't mind me asking, that is."

"Usually it's stress, but I haven't had one since I moved, and there's been a fair amount of stress, so I'm not sure what brought this one on." Hattie sat, looking at her coffee, seeming to search her memory for anything that might have set her off. "Oh, wait. That son of a bitch," she said angrily.

"What? Who?" he asked, worried.

"I got an email from my ex two nights ago. I shouldn't have read it, but he basically click-baited me, so I opened it. The asshole!"

"I dislike this guy already," Blaine said dryly, leaning against the counter.

"Thanks. After he was all 'I have some mail,' he quickly moved on to 'I love you, I miss you, come home.'" If Hattie rolled her eyes any harder, Blaine was worried she might hurt herself. "I mean, come on, you dick, you've barely tried to reach me since I left, and then you try to pull this shit?" Hattie took a deep breath, clearly trying to calm herself.

"Yeah, that's some bullshit. If you wanted him, you wouldn't have moved literally to the other side of the country and not contacted him for over a month. I mean, you're practically in the Pacific Ocean. You couldn't get much further away from him if you tried."

Hattie looked up from her coffee to Blaine. "Thank you for validating me. For a minute there, I was doubting myself, but I mean, it's not like I've been sending mixed signals. It's been radio silence from my end."

"It's guys like him that give the rest of us a bad name," Blaine said, shaking his head.

"Sorry, I don't mean to dump my problems on you."

Blaine could see Hattie curling in on herself. She was so strong, if only she would let herself see it. It made him furious that someone had made her feel so little.

"Don't," he said. That one word seemed to bring her out of whatever had been going on in her head. He continued, "I asked. I'm just glad that he's not in your life anymore." Realizing how what he just said could be taken, he hastily added, "Taking a break from dating after that guy makes total sense to me." There, that should clear up any confusion his earlier statement might have caused. *Pull yourself together, man!* Changing the subject, he asked, "Are you going in today?"

"No, I was planning on working from home. I won't be in your way, will I?" Hattie asked, looking concerned.

"No, I'm heading into the office here shortly. Why don't I grab dinner on my way home, in case you start feeling bad again?"

Hattie sighed. "That would be much appreciated. Let me know how much I owe you."

Blaine held up his hand in dismissal. "Please, this is my treat. Actually, there is something you could help me with, if you don't mind."

"Anything," she responded enthusiastically.

Picking up his skinny black tie from the counter, he held it against himself. "Tie? Or no tie? If I wore it, I would obviously tuck it into my vest."

Hattie came around to where he was standing and looked thoughtfully at him. "Hmm... let me see it without the tie again." Blaine held the tie off to the side so she could get a better look. "I think tie."

Blaine quickly looped the tie around his neck and tied it. "Look okay?" he asked. Hattie reached up, loosening the knot a bit. Blaine had to work to control his breathing so she wouldn't notice how much she affected him. When Hattie hooked her finger over the top of his collar, he had to stop a groan from bubbling up.

"I'd undo this top button. A bit more rakish that way. Otherwise, it feels really strait-laced," she said, releasing his shirt.

"Thanks," he said softly as Hattie stepped back, reaching across the island to pick up her coffee cup.

"Thank you, Blaine. I truly appreciate everything you've done for me."

"Don't mention it," he said, clearing his throat. "Anything in particular sound good to eat for tonight?"

"Thai?" she suggested with a shrug.

"Thai is always a 'yes' in my book. When Eli and I had dinner the other night, he told me about this new Thai place he went to last week. Maybe I'll check that out. He said they had really good satay."

"I love satay. I think I would die if I ever became allergic to peanuts!" she said. "Speaking of Eli, is he doing okay? The last time we hung out, I don't know, I couldn't quite put my finger on it, but there was just something that seemed off about him, or something. But then I second-guessed myself and told myself I just don't know him that well, or maybe he was just having an off night. Anyway, I wanted to check with you since you two have been friends longer."

"I know what you mean. I don't think you're wrong. I had the same feeling when we had dinner. He was just ever so slightly off, but I couldn't tell if it was in a good way or a bad way. I'll see if I can get anything out of him the next time I see him."

"Let me know if there's anything I can do to help. He's been so kind to me since I moved. I would love to find a way to help him in return."

"Will do." Blaine looked at the clock, taking one last sip of his coffee. "I've got to head out. Enjoy your day working around Marmalade's forced cuddles," Blaine said, smiling.

Work had gotten away from Blaine, and it was almost the end of the day before he remembered to reach out to Eli, asking for the name of the Thai restaurant. Luckily, Eli responded quickly.

After firing off a quick text to Hattie with the link to the menu, Blaine mapped it to see how long it would take to get there. He figured if he ordered right before leaving, it would probably be ready for pickup by the time he arrived. When the map appeared on his phone, he double-checked that he had entered the correct address. The address was right, just in a part of town that surprised him. Blaine salivated over Hattie's choices: massaman curry, cashew stir-fry with rice, and pad woon sen—all three of his favorite dishes. What the heck had Eli been doing to find this place? It was farther than he expected, but luckily, Blaine didn't have to wait long before their order was ready.

Hattie met him at the door, taking the food and two Thai iced teas from him so he could set his stuff down.

"Thanks," he said, toeing off his shoes.

"Oh my," she said, closing her eyes and breathing in deeply. Blaine did his best not to stare at the rise and fall of her breasts. "This smells divine," she said.

"My car is probably going to smell like a Thai restaurant tomorrow, but I'm okay with that. This stuff smells amazing," he replied. "I'm going to go change really quickly. I would hate to get curry on yet another white dress shirt."

Hattie chuckled, raising an eyebrow. "I see there's a pattern with you, then. I'll set everything out while you get settled."

"Great, I'll be right back." Blaine quickly slipped into grey joggers and a T-shirt, doing his best not to think about Hattie's look of ecstasy that crossed her face at the smell of the food. When he reached the end of the hall, Hattie was bent over feeding Marmalade, and blood rushed to his groin at the sight. Her loose shirt had fallen forward as she bent over, exposing her lace-covered breasts. They were the perfect size to fit into his palms. He groaned inwardly. He was never going to unsee that image. Why, why did it have to be pink lace? It was almost as good as the black bra she was wearing when she got tangled up in her sweater. Almost. That image was going to haunt his dreams. Oh, who was he kidding? He would gladly welcome that image in his dreams. In fact, he might even choose to

see it later—in the shower, with his hand wrapped around his cock.
Thank God for coconut oil.

Chapter 19

Hattie

"Wow! This is delicious. Good find, Eli," Hattie said, moaning around her fork. She tried to stop herself, but the food was drool-worthy. "This cashew stir-fry has the perfect amount of spice, salt, and sweet."

Blaine cleared his throat and then agreed. "Sorry, bit of cashew there, I think. It's really tasty. The restaurant was in a weird area, though."

"What do you mean?" Hattie asked, taking another bite.

"Not weird, generally, just strange that Eli would have been there. It was pretty off the beaten path, at least for the places he usually goes. It felt like more of a neighborhood joint. Whatever, I'm not going to dwell on it. I'm not his mother, and even if I was, he's a grown-ass man and can take himself to whatever parts of town he wants to."

Hattie laughed. Blaine was really funny without meaning to be. "You sound just like my friend, Madison, sometimes."

Blaine looked alarmed. "Is that a good thing?"

"Don't worry, it's great. You would love her. It is exactly like something she would say, though. Maybe he was checking out a dance class or some other activity. I know he's been trying to get out and do more things since his sister extended her stay, and she's been helping with Nana. He mentioned there was a new studio he was thinking about trying out. Maybe it was that? I told him I might tag along someday if he'd let me."

"Do you dance?" Blaine asked inquisitively, spearing a piece of curried potato.

"If you can call it that," she said, shaking her head in embarrassed amusement at her own memory. "Before I moved out here, I was taking a Bollywood dance class. I wasn't great at it, but it was a ton of fun. Eli said he thought this new studio might have something like that. I figured it would help me get out. You know, make some friends outside of you, Eli, and work."

"What? We aren't enough?" Blaine teased, pressing his hand to his chest in mock surprise.

"You are lovely, but it might be nice to have more non-work friends who don't have a penis." Hattie meant for that to come off in a joking way, but as soon as it was out of her mouth, she realized she had just talked about Blaine's cock—something she was very much trying, and mostly failing, to avoid thinking about.

Thankfully, Blaine hadn't seemed to notice and replied, "Taking a class is a great idea. Maybe I should try something like that. Not dance, I'm terrible. Eli is always trying to get me to go, but I'm not going to subject myself or anyone else to that. Maybe some other kind of class or club or something. I'm naturally a homebody, so it might be good to push myself a little. I've lived here for almost three years now. It's probably about time I do something more than just hang out with Eli and my cat in my downtime."

"There's a lot to do around here, so I'm sure you could find something. What kinds of things are you interested in?" Hattie asked.

"Other than work and working out, I don't do much, which I'm sure you've noticed. I like to cook, but stick to pretty boring and healthy stuff since I'm still trying to get my body where you want it." Blaine must have immediately realized what he had said based on the look on his face.

Quickly changing the subject, Hattie decided to completely ignore what Blaine had just said and instead asked, "How was work?" Hattie didn't really understand what Blaine did, so she hoped to learn more about him and his work by asking, while avoiding Blaine's comment. A look of relief quickly crossed his face. She imagined he was hoping she hadn't noticed the slip and didn't want him to feel embarrassed for bringing his attention to it, since it was clearly just a slip of the tongue. Dammit, now she was trying not to think about Blaine slipping his tongue into her mouth. First his dick, now this!

"Busy. I've got a bunch of projects right now, including the big one for the Marines, which is a new logistics management system to track their global inventory. We're almost finished with that job, but there's always a flurry of changes at the end before we officially submit things for approval. We're close to that point, so I expect to put in a lot of additional hours soon, since I'll need to balance everything else while getting the Marine Corps stuff finished up. I love the work, but hate the last-minute scramble that seems to come with every project."

"What is it you *do*, though?"

Blaine laughed. "As the Project Manager, I'm responsible for keeping track of everything, making sure the project components are completed on time, dotting the i's and crossing the t's and all that, and then triple-checking everything before we submit it."

"In some ways, it sounds similar to my job, where, because I wear multiple metaphorical hats, I have to keep track of all the different things I do. How did you get into aviation logistics? Maybe you spent your childhood thinking, 'When I grow up, I'm going to be a project manager,' but somehow I doubt that."

Blaine laughed, "That's a very amusing image. I can just see me as a kid making that declaration. Sadly, I definitely did not. I was going to be a superhero when I grew up," he said.

"Obviously," she said, nodding seriously.

"When it was clear that wasn't going to pan out, I decided I wanted to be a Navy pilot. I may have watched *Top Gun* a time or ten the summer I made the decision. Unfortunately for me, you can't be a Navy pilot with hay fever, and I'm basically allergic to the world when it comes to grass and trees."

"Oof, I feel you there. Grass tries to kill me regularly each year." Shifting back in her chair, she said, "Working in the aerospace industry is close to being Tom Cruise, though."

"Please, I wanted to be Ice Man," he said, grinning.

"Not a bad choice, either," she smiled in return. Hattie was not about to admit that she had a fondness for bad boys, purely fictional, of course.

"You're right, though. Aerospace is at least in the realm of fast planes. I'd still love to fly one of those jets, but I'll have to content myself with flight simulators instead."

Hattie could easily picture Blaine in a sexy flight suit with aviators on, maybe a little too easily.

"They are fun to watch. Maybe we could go to the airshow together and see the Blue Angels. It might be fun."

"Sure, yeah. That sounds like fun. I bet Eli would join us. Maybe some of your other new friends, which I'm sure you'll continue to make, can plan to come along too, since it's still about nine months or so away."

"Oh no! I didn't realize it had already passed. I saw a poster for it somewhere but didn't pay any attention to the dates," she said.

"Sorry to be the bearer of bad news. It actually happened right before you moved out here."

Hattie was bummed. It would have been something fun they could have done together. "Well, boo," Hattie pouted.

Blaine gave her a funny look she couldn't quite decipher and said, "Can you please pass me the curry?"

"Sure," she said, handing it over. "Looks like there's enough left over that you'll be able to have some for lunch tomorrow, too."

"Thanks," Blaine said, scooping more curry and rice onto his plate. "So, what about you? Did you have a productive day with Ms. Marmalade over there?"

"We got along great. She mostly stayed off my keyboard, so I consider that a win. I only had to message my boss once to apologize for the weird Teams message, because she decided to jump up and hit send after adding her personal flair of a GIF of one of those blow-up balloon men you see at car dealerships. How she did that in that short amount of time was truly remarkable."

"Yes, she's quite talented, and her best work is definitely reserved for Teams, speaking from experience." They laughed and looked over at the cat in question, who was lounging on the back of the sofa. Clearly knowing she was being talked about, she deigned to half-open one eye and stare at them, not bothering to raise her head off her crossed paws, which just caused the two of them to burst into laughter again.

Blaine set his fork down on top of his plate, pushing it away from him. "How's your head doing?" he inquired.

"So much better! I was really worried the migraine might come back, but thankfully, it seems to be staying at bay. Thanks for asking." Why did he have to be so thoughtful? It made it harder not to want to get involved with him. Hattie silently reminded herself, once again, that she was rediscovering herself—no men allowed!

Leaning back in his chair, he said, "I'm so glad to hear that. Sometimes, my mom's would last three days, occasionally more."

"If that ever happens, I think I might cry." Hattie reached both arms up to stretch, her shirt riding up so that a strip of skin showed. She noticed Blaine's eyes land there and then quickly dart away. He was clearly uncomfortable seeing her body. *See, he's not interested in you*, the little voice in her head said. Lowering her arms, she said, "I'm stuffed, but this was delicious. I want more, but I know I'll regret it, especially since I made dessert."

"You didn't have to do that," Blaine said.

"I know I didn't, but it's one of the perks of working from home, and I figured you were picking up dinner; the least I could do was make cookies." Hattie retrieved the chocolate crinkle cookies she'd made from the kitchen, placing the container on the table between them. "I remember you mentioned that you're not a big sweets guy, and I know you eat pretty healthy generally, but these are mostly cocoa powder, so they're not super sweet, and bonus, not a ton of calories either."

"Thank you, Hattie. It was very nice of you to do," Blaine said, selecting one from the container. Biting into it, he closed his eyes. "That's one hell of a cookie," he said.

Hattie smiled. "My sister loves them. We used to make them at Christmastime and add crushed candy canes, which are also delicious." They ate the rest of their cookies in silence, enjoying the chocolatey treat and their full bellies.

Blaine started to put the lids back on the takeout containers in preparation for clearing the table when Hattie noticed a little bit of powdered sugar on the corner of Blaine's mouth that had taken up residence in his beard. "Blaine, you've got a little spot of something right there," she said, gesturing to her own face.

"Oh, thanks," he said, reaching up and wiping his fingers along the sides of his mouth. "How's that?" he asked.

"It's still there, here," she said, reaching out, brushing it away, her thumb reveling in the softness of his beard on her skin. What would that feel like on other parts of her body? *Thoughts like that are not allowed*, she reminded herself. *Remember, Blaine is not an option. There are no options. The only option is no men.* That and the ultra-quiet vibrator that had arrived today and was currently charging in her room. Thank you, Jayne, for that recommendation. She'd definitely be taking that baby for a spin later tonight, for sure.

"Thanks," he whispered hoarsely.

"Of course," she said. Needing something to busy her hands so she wouldn't be tempted to reach up and stroke Blaine's face again, she picked up their dishes and carried them to the sink, returning to the table to help repack the takeout containers. Hattie was definitely going to hide in her room for the rest of the night. Hopefully, some time with her new toy and a good romance book would be enough to distract her from thoughts of Blaine.

Chapter 20

Blaine

Hattie was going to kill him. Every day with her in his house was both a delight and pure torture. While her fingers were stroking powdered sugar off his beard, he was keenly aware of every spot she was touching him. He knew that if he turned his head a fraction of an inch, he could kiss her palm. If he reached up, he could rest his hands comfortably on the curve of her hip. If he pulled her a few inches closer, there would be no doubt about what she did to him. Instead of doing any of those things, Blaine choked out a quick "thanks," quickly grabbing takeout containers off the table and heading into the kitchen to give himself some space from her before he did something stupid. He also needed to put something between the two of them so that she might not notice what she was doing to his body, his grey sweats doing nothing to hide his growing erection.

With the open fridge shielding his body, he told her, "I've got this if you want to go relax. I imagine you still want to take it easy so your migraine doesn't come back."

"Thanks," she said to his back, "I do. Thanks, too, for picking up dinner and putting everything away."

"Not a problem. See you in the morning, Hattie," he said, glancing in her direction. Hattie waved from the doorway to her room before closing the door. Blaine rested his head on the cold inside edge of the fridge and whispered, "Fuuck…"

Blaine lay in bed, sleep evading him. He'd decided not to take a shower and relieve himself, worried that Hattie might start to wonder why he was showering twice a day since most mornings he took a shower after his run. The hard-on he'd had since dinner hadn't gone away on its own. He'd been lying here, torturously, for an hour. Surely, Hattie was asleep by now, and he could safely take things into his own hands, right? Blaine decided that if he wanted any sleep, it was worth the risk. He reached under the covers and slowly palmed himself over his clothes.

A sound made him pause his explorations. What was that? Blaine listened closely for a moment. There was a very faint buzzing sound coming from somewhere in the house. Blaine lay there, not wanting to get up to figure out where the noise was coming from, when he heard another sound—a gasp followed by a moan. Suddenly, he understood what the buzzing noise was and who was gasping and moaning.

Hattie was getting herself off with the help of a vibrator from the sound of it. He imagined her, turning her face into the pillow to smother her moans as she worked the toy over her center. The thought alone instantly took his cock from half- to full-mast. There was no way that he wasn't jerking off now. He would do his best to be quiet, but hopefully, Hattie would be too distracted to notice. Blaine knew he would have been if he hadn't heard the buzzing first.

Sliding his boxer briefs and pajama pants down to his thighs, Blaine gripped his dick, giving it a tug. Across the hall, Hattie let out another breathy moan. Blaine grabbed the lotion he kept on his bedside table, squeezing some onto his palm. It was his turn to gasp when the cold lotion met his hot skin. He began to stroke himself slowly at first, then faster, listening intently for those delicious sounds slithering through the dark from across the hall. Hattie's moans grew breathier and breathier. The more she moaned, the faster Blaine stroked.

Blaine pictured Hattie on her knees for him, wearing nothing but that lacy pink bra he'd spied the other night. Wrapping her hair around his fist, he pulled back on the ponytail in his hand so that she was looking up at him. "Suck it," he imagined himself saying.

"Yes, Daddy," she replied.

Fuck, why did that turn him on so much? His cock swelled, and his balls started to draw up as he continued his rhythmic stroking. He wasn't going to last much longer, and for his sake, he hoped Hattie didn't either. As if she had heard his thought, Hattie cried out in release, and Blaine's own orgasm unexpectedly hit him. He turned and buried his face as much as he could into the spare pillow to help cover the sound of his own cry, just as he imagined Hattie had. He continued to stroke himself until he'd emptied himself of his release. He had intended to grab a tissue or something like that before he came, but given the suddenness of it, he hadn't had time. Instead, he slid his shirt off, using it to clean up the mess he'd left on his chest and abdomen. After righting his clothes and tossing his cum-covered shirt to the floor, Blaine, feeling sleepy and sated, finally drifted off to sleep.

Marmalade's meowing woke him up the next morning. Shit, he'd forgotten to set his alarm in his distraction last night. It was already seven o'clock. He wouldn't be late for work, but he definitely didn't have time to work out this morning. He opened his door at the same time Hattie opened hers across the hall. Her gaze immediately went to Blaine's shirtless torso. She quickly glanced down at the cat.

"Morning, you two," she said.

"Mind if I hop in the shower first?" he asked. "I forgot to set an alarm, hence my current state," he said, gesturing to his bare chest.

"Go for it," she said, turning toward the kitchen. "I'll start some coffee and feed our soul sister here," she said. Blaine could have sworn there was a slight blush on Hattie's cheeks. Interesting.

For the rest of the morning, they danced around each other, both trying to get ready quickly without getting in the other's way. Blaine buttoned the last button on his vest, rolled up his sleeves, and grabbed his laptop and gym bags.

Blaine was just about to call out goodbye to Hattie when she came out of her room. "Hey, I was just heading out. Since I didn't get to work out this morning, I'll probably go for a run after work, so don't wait on me for dinner."

"Sounds good," Hattie said, taking another sip of her coffee while she tried to slip her earrings in. Blaine tried to ignore how the dress she wore today hugged her curves in all the right ways without being overtly sexy. Maybe he would see if Eli was free tonight. After last night and how she looked this morning, he wasn't sure he could trust himself alone with her. Space, he just needed space. Surely, that would make everything better, right?

Chapter 21

Hattie

Blaine closed the door behind him, and Hattie slunk against the counter, sighing in relief. She'd been a bit of a mess since she saw him in the hall.

Blaine. Had. A. Tattoo.

She never imagined him to be a tattoo guy. He always seemed so buttoned-up, so it had never even crossed her mind that he might have one hidden under his vest and tie. The knowledge of it made her a little weak in the knees.

Until this morning, she'd never seen him shirtless, but there it was in all its glory. Filling most of the right side of his ribcage was the most beautiful angel tattoo. Given its size and complexity, she didn't think it had been the result of a drunken night in college, but rather a deliberate and thoughtful choice. The angel appeared to be hovering, with her wings outspread behind her, her long hair and arms crossed in front of her to ensure her modesty. It was artistic and tasteful, and something about it was just so Blaine. Hattie would love to know what the story was behind it. Maybe someday she would work up the nerve to ask him about it.

Hattie's phone rang, pulling her out of her contemplation of Blaine's inked torso. Jayne was calling. Hattie grabbed her phone and answered with, "Blaine has a tattoo."

Jayne laughed, "Good morning to you as well. I wouldn't have pegged him for a tattoo guy based on what you've told me and that photo you sent."

"Jayne, it was gorgeous, and the muscles, there were so many of them."

"Slow down there, girl. How exactly did you see these muscles?" Jayne inquired.

"It's not what you're thinking. We bumped into each other in the hall; he was running late and wasn't wearing a shirt. Usually, when I see him, he's already been up for hours and is dressed. Even if he's dressed casually, he's always dressed." The words were spilling out of Hattie quickly. "Jayne, he has an Adonis belt."

"Take a breath. You sound like you're about to pass out," Jayne laughed.

"And there was last night..."

"Hang on, what do you mean last night?" Jayne asked accusingly.

Hattie told Jayne about how he had taken care of her during her migraine, and about the powdered sugar on his face, how soft his beard had been, and the direction her thoughts had gone, despite his obvious discomfort when her shirt had ridden up. "I waited awake a full hour after he turned his light off before I tried out my new vibrator—and oh my god, you were right. That thing is remarkable!"

"Well, it sounds like it's going to get a workout as long as you live with him. Listen, we clearly need to talk more, and soon, but I've got to get to a meeting. I was just giving you a quick call to say that I got the new dates off for your move—I'm coming to California, baby! I even bought tickets already!"

Jayne and Hattie both squealed at the news. Marmalade looked slightly freaked out, so Hattie forced herself to calm down. "That's amazing! I cannot wait for you to be here!"

"I'll send you all the deets via email. I'll try to call you later, okay? In the meantime, don't do anything I wouldn't do."

"You realize that doesn't narrow it down too much, right?" Hattie teased.

"Which is one of the many reasons you love me. Love you, babe! Gotta go."

Hattie said goodbye and smiled. Her best friend was coming to visit! They had talked about it for weeks, but now it was official, and Hattie couldn't wait!

Over the next week or so, Hattie didn't see much of Blaine. He hadn't been kidding when he had told her about the amount of work he needed to squeeze in at the end of this Marine Corps project.

She was surprised to find out that one evening, he went on a date. He was pretty tight-lipped about it, though. So, between his early morning workouts and runs on the beach, and late nights working or going out, she barely saw him. But, she wasn't going to let his absence get her down. She had plenty of ways to enjoy her time and her vibrator.

For a "congrats on ditching Galen" gift, Sophia and Madison sent her a year-long subscription to Cumm, an audio erotica app filled with performances by some very talented people (she had a soft spot for the Brits on the app—she blamed her giant childhood crush on Peter in *The Lion, the Witch, and the Wardrobe* film).

Hattie couldn't say if it was the audio erotica that she'd been ingesting aurally, the O's her new vibe was delivering, or the lingering image of Blaine's tattooed torso, but she had been horny as fuck all week. She really hoped he would continue his disappearing act, at least for a little bit this evening, so she could take care of herself.

Hattie breathed in a sigh of relief upon pulling up at the house. Blaine's car wasn't there yet, which meant she probably had time to do what she wanted. No, make that needed to do. She tossed her bag down next to the door, taking the time to re-lock the front door just in case he came home soon. The noise would give her enough time to at least put herself back together like nothing had been happening. Marmalade was asleep on the couch. She gave Hattie a peek through a half-opened lid and then went back to napping in her spot of sunlight.

Hattie pulled up one of her favorite creators on Cumm and hit play on one of the episodes she hadn't listened to yet. Based on the tags, she was going to like this one. She'd specifically chosen the episode because it was one of the shorter ones. She loved the 30-minute-plus listens, but she just wasn't sure she had time for it right now. While it started to play, she changed out of her work clothes, stripping down to just her bra and underwear. She slid her vibrator out from under the other pillow where she had been keeping it (she'd long ago given up on keeping it in the bathroom since she was using it so often). She made herself comfortable on the bed, positioning her phone on top of the pillow next to her. It didn't take long for her to get where she had been wanting to go. Who needed a man when you had technology?

Chapter 22

Blaine

Blaine rubbed his hand over his eyes, trying to wipe away the sleep. He hadn't meant to fall asleep. It had been one of those weeks and one of those days. On his way to work this morning, his car suddenly died. Fortunately, he was almost there, so he just walked and then called the mechanic from his office. At lunch, he got a tow to the shop and then took a rideshare back to his house, where he apparently crashed.

Hattie was listening to something on her phone, from the sounds of it. Her coming home must have been what woke him. What was she listening to? Was it some sort of murder mystery? He thought he heard someone getting slapped and the sound of a struggle. The tone of whatever she was listening to suddenly changed, and male moans filled his ears. What the hell was Hattie listening to?

Blaine crept quietly out of his bed toward the door when he realized exactly what he was hearing. That was definitely not a murder mystery. This woman continued to surprise him—she was listening to porn.

Blaine stood by the door listening as the man in the audio told her to use her toy on herself. He couldn't hear the buzzing, but the little mewls Hattie started to make indicated that she was certainly doing something in there. The sounds she was making caused blood to rush straight to his dick.

Fuck.

He should put his headphones in and give her some privacy, but instead, he stood there like a perv, stroking his cock over his pants. When the audio instructed Hattie to pinch her nipple, she let out a small cry of pleasure. When the mysterious male said, "Come for me," Hattie obediently complied. By this point, Blaine had crept back to his bed to give himself better access to his aching dick.

Blaine's phone started ringing on the bed next to him, volume nearly all the way up. Shit. The mechanic was calling.

Things suddenly quieted across the hall. *Fake it till you make it*, Blaine thought. Sounding sleepy, he answered, "This is Blaine." While the mechanic explained what was going on with his car, he heard Hattie go into the bathroom and then out into the living room. After hanging up with the auto shop, he sat on his bed for another minute, letting his erection flag before heading out to the kitchen. He did his best to look sleepy.

"Hey," he said.

"Hi!" Hattie said from her perch on the couch, sounding a little high-strung. "I didn't realize you were home."

"Yeah, I had car trouble this morning, so I came home partway through the day. I completely crashed out after I got home, though. The mechanic just called, and that's what woke me up. I was dead to the world up until that point. My boss is probably wondering what the hell happened to me." Hattie looked relieved at this bit of news.

"I'm sorry about your car. What's going on?"

Blaine leaned his forearms on the island, keeping it between himself and Hattie, just in case. "Turns out to be nothing major, so that's good. They, of course, don't have the part they need, and since tomorrow is Friday, it's going to be Monday before they can fix it."

"That sucks," she said.

Blaine turned and grabbed a glass from the cupboard, filling it with water from the fridge. "Yeah, at least it's not an expensive fix, so there's that," he said with a shrug. "I don't have any in-person meetings tomorrow, so I can easily work from home. I'll just explain what's going on to my boss. He should be okay with it. Then, on Monday, I'll get a ride in and go pick up my car at the end of the day. It'll be fine." He drained the glass and set it in the sink.

"Did you have any plans this weekend?" she asked. "I haven't seen much of you, so I wasn't sure."

Blaine hadn't thought that far ahead, honestly. He'd been so busy at work the last couple of days that he hadn't thought about how he was going to avoid Hattie this weekend. Honestly, that's what he'd been doing, wasn't it? He'd been avoiding her so he didn't have to deal with his attraction to her. *How's that working out for you, pal?*

"I've been so busy that I haven't thought much about this weekend. So no, no plans."

"If you're up for a little adventure, I was thinking about driving down to Holtville Hot Springs to check out the springs and just get out of town for a bit. If you aren't too tired, would you want to come? Obviously, I would drive," she smiled.

Blaine knew he should say no and continue keeping his distance, but honestly, he was tired, and he liked Hattie. Spending some time relaxing in the hot springs sounded amazing.

"Sounds fun," he finally replied. "Let me see how I'm feeling Saturday morning, but sure, let's do it."

Saturday rolled around, and Blaine still hadn't talked himself out of going. He and Hattie had spent the night before together, eating pizza and watching a movie. The movie was so terrible that it was funny, and they spent the entire time making fun of it. It was a fantastic evening. Blaine couldn't remember the last time he'd enjoyed himself so much. Which was exactly why he should go out there, tell her he was too tired, and then keep his ass home. As he was telling himself all of these things, he pulled on his swim shorts and tied them closed. Who was he kidding? He walked into the hall and grabbed a few beach towels from the linen closet.

"I made coffee!" Hattie said with a smile, holding up two travel mugs. Damn, why was she so adorable? Hattie wore a strappy sundress, underneath which he could see the straps of her bathing suit. *Please, dear lord, let it be a one-piece*, he silently begged.

"You're bright and chipper this morning," he observed.

"What can I say? If I'm properly motivated, I can be ready to do all kinds of things in the morning."

Blaine immediately pictured a variety of activities they could get up to in the morning, which she could probably be motivated to do. *You are a disgusting human. She's made her position quite clear,* he chided himself. "Well, then, let's hit the road. Those hot springs aren't going to relax themselves," he said. *Smooth, man, real smooth.* This is why he should never be allowed around women. He was a danger to himself.

The two-hour drive south went by faster than Blaine expected. He and Hattie listened to a comedy history podcast about Cleopatra, which had them both cracking up. They reached the hot springs without any trouble and found easy parking. After gathering their things, they headed toward the pools.

"I don't know about you, but I'm a hotter-the-better kind of gal," Hattie said.

Internally, Blaine groaned. He knew she was talking about the water, but he couldn't help but think about her. Responding to her comment, he said, "I like it just this side of uncomfortable, so choose a spring, and let's get in."

They found a pool that wasn't too crowded and set their stuff down in the shade nearby. Blaine took off his shirt, set it on top of his shoes, and pulled out the two towels he'd brought for them. When he looked up, Hattie was slipping her dress over her head. Fuck. It wasn't a one-piece. In fact, it was barely a two-piece. It was the world's tiniest red bikini. Blaine's breath seemed stuck in his throat. Swallowing and reminding himself to breathe, he did his best not to ogle Hattie and to hide his growing hard-on. His eyes couldn't help but travel up her body as she folded her dress up and placed it to the side. Her practically non-existent bikini had a flirty little ruffle that ran along the top edge of her low-slung bottoms. As his eyes continued making their way up her body, his breath caught. That same ruffle ran along the fabric triangles covering her perfect breasts.

He was so fucked.

Turning quickly to avoid Hattie noticing the growing bulge in his shorts, Blaine stepped into the hot spring. Sitting back in the hot water, Blaine took a deep breath and slowly exhaled, resting his head against the surrounding rockface. He willed his body to forget what he had just seen. Maybe he could simply keep his eyes closed for the rest of the day. A small sigh escaped Hattie's lips as she joined him in the water. Blaine cursed himself for at least the tenth time for not just staying home.

"This was so worth the drive and the early morning," Hattie said quietly. Blaine let out a small noise of agreement. They sat quietly for a few moments, soaking in the blissful silence. Finally, Hattie spoke again, "Can I ask you something?"

"Sure," he said.

"Well, something I've been wondering about for a while now, ever since that one morning you slept in late..." she hesitated.

"Yeah?"

"Well, um, that was the first and only time before today that I've seen you without a shirt..." Again, she seemed to hesitate, making him wonder where she was going with her question.

"Yeah..."

"Well, it surprised me to see that you had a tattoo."

Blaine laughed. "Most people are when they see it," he said.

"You have to admit that you don't really seem like a tattoo guy," she said.

"I get that," he agreed.

"Is that your only one?" she asked.

"Wouldn't you like to know," he teased. Shit, had he just said that? That almost sounded flirty. *Well, it was, wasn't it, you ass?*

A blush started to creep up Hattie's chest and cheeks, and while it could have been from the hot springs, Blaine wasn't entirely sure.

"Do you have any ink?" he asked, trying to change the subject back to something less flirty. Now, the blush was definitely there and not from the water.

"Yes," she answered, looking anywhere but at him. Intriguing, he thought.

"Dare I ask where?"

Hattie slowly and carefully pulled the right side of her bikini top in just enough that he could see something there, but he did not know what it was. She quickly slid the triangle of fabric back into place.

"What does yours mean? Or, is there a story or anything behind it?" she asked, gesturing at the angel's wings peeking above the waterline. "It just looks like something you thought about rather than getting on a whim."

"You are correct. I contemplated this one for a couple of years. When I was in college, I was in an English lit class, and we talked about symbolism, and the concept of angels came up. The professor said that angels can represent many things and not just religious ones. Of course, angels can represent death, but they can also represent beauty, love, timelessness, frailty, and all of these other things that I had never really thought about. In essence, angels are enigmatic but represent all that we are as both physical and spiritual beings. I thought it was a really beautiful concept.

"The idea for the tattoo came from that experience, as well as my grandfather's death. I'd been pretty close to him, and his death hit me hard. I wanted to get a tattoo to honor his memory. His initials are incorporated into the small heart-shaped stone that hangs from the bracelet on her wrist. I'd been working on what I wanted the design to look like when I saw this one statue in a museum during a trip to Germany. When I saw it, I knew I wanted whatever design I got to be based on it because it perfectly captured the feeling I was looking for. An artist friend of mine from back home was able to render my idea into a drawing, and I took that to the tattoo artist. He was able to translate it into his own style and give it a bit of his own flair, and it ended up being exactly what I wanted and more."

"From what I saw of it, it's gorgeous. Could... would you mind, that is, if I took a closer look?" she asked timidly.

No, just tell her no, Blaine's inner voice urged. "Sure," Blaine said, completely ignoring his own advice. Hattie stood and came closer to where he was sitting. Blaine kept his eyes averted as she crossed over to him. As she approached, he raised himself a little bit more out of the water, raising his right arm behind his head so she could more easily see. Hattie settled down next to him on the natural stone bench, leaning in to take a look at the detail. Blaine's eyes struggled not to stare at her barely covered chest. Instead, he forced himself to watch one of the drops of water slowly slide its way from her throat down toward the valley between her breasts. When it reached the water, he raised his eyes back up and followed another one as it slid its way towards her bosom. He'd been so busy trying not to stare that he hadn't noticed Hattie move her hand through the water. Slowly, she dragged her fingers along the outline of his tattoo. Her touch sent a shiver down his spine, shocking him out of his reverie and sending a jolt straight to his dick. He quickly dropped his arm back to his side, forcing her fingers away.

"Sorry, ticklish," he said in defense. Hattie gave him a gentle smile and moved further away, but not back to where she had been sitting. Hattie closed her eyes and leaned back.

"Beautiful," she said quietly. They sat there like that for a while, enjoying the solitude, warm water, and sun on their skin. Blaine wasn't sure if she was talking about the pools, his tattoo, or what. "Have you thought about getting anything for your dad?" she asked after a while.

Blaine had, but something held him back from doing it. Finally, he replied, "Yes, I think I even know what I want, but I don't know, I just can't seem to bring myself to do it."

"I get that. Your pain is still so fresh."

"It's been four years..."

"That's nothing, though. I have no doubt that you loved your grandfather, but the way that you love a grandparent is not the same way you love a parent. The loss of him is going to leave a wound that is deeper and will take longer to heal."

They were both quiet for a moment. "If anyone understands that, you do," Blaine said. "Thanks, Hattie. I'm sorry that you understand, but thanks nonetheless." She gave him a sad smile. "What about you?" he asked. "Have you ever thought about getting one in honor of your dad?"

"I thought about it briefly, but the thing is, and I don't say this to get pity, I didn't really know him. I was really young when he died. And while I miss him, it's not in the same way as if I had known him my whole life." They sat in quiet contemplation after that, relaxing back into the rocks, letting the healing waters ease their stresses away. Hattie sat with her eyes closed. Blaine couldn't help but let his gaze stray to her.

A voice startled them out of their quiet moment. "Mind if we join you two?" asked an older woman. Blaine tore his gaze away from Hattie and looked toward the voice. Two women, probably in their sixties, stood at the edge of the pool.

"Not at all," Hattie said, "come on in."

The rest of the day passed in pleasant conversation and company. Blaine was glad for the company as it helped distract him from Hattie. After soaking in the pools for a bit, they ate a picnic lunch in the shade of the trees before starting back home in the early afternoon. Blaine offered to drive back since Hattie had driven them there. Hattie fell asleep partway back and slept for most of the ride. Blaine didn't mind. It gave him time to think without potential interruption and without having to fake conversation with Hattie. He couldn't wait for her to move out.

The sooner she was gone, the better. This was absolute torture.

Chapter 23

Hattie

Blaine had spent much of Sunday out with Eli, and then on Monday, it was back to work for both of them. Hattie had really enjoyed their trip to the hot springs. She was glad to learn more about Blaine and to spend some downtime with him.

It felt like something had shifted between them after Friday and Saturday, but she couldn't put her finger on what. Blaine's project had ramped back up again, so she didn't see much of him in the first part of the week. Thursday afternoon rolled around, and Hattie sat in her office, finishing up something for their grant writer. Her cell phone started ringing. She picked it up and saw that it was her future (fingers crossed!) landlord calling.

"Hello?"

"Hi, Hattie, this is Cecilia from Shoreside Apartments."

"Hi," she replied nervously.

"I wanted to call you with an update on your apartment." Hattie braced herself for bad news. "I've got good news! The guys working on the unit think they'll be done sooner than anticipated!"

Hattie let out a sigh of relief. "That's fantastic! What does that mean?"

"So we had you planning to move in on Sunday next week, but the guys think they'll be done by Wednesday, so you could move in as early as next Thursday."

"That's amazing!" she said, feeling lighter already.

"I realize it's only four days, but you've been waiting so patiently, and I know you had a temporary living situation that I'm sure you'd like to get out of."

"Yeah, it would be great to have my own place," she said. But would it? Was she that eager to leave Blaine's? "Honestly, though, I'll probably wait until Saturday since I have a friend who is coming in to help me move in."

"Whatever works for you, just let me know. You can move any time after Thursday, so take your time and let me know. Thank you again for being so patient with us throughout this process. I promise it will be worth the wait, though! The upgrades look fantastic!"

Hattie felt so relieved. When her phone rang, she worried it would be yet another delay. She was finally going to be able to move into her new home! It was going to be strange, though, to live on her own again after living off and on with roommates during and after college, then with Galen for several years, and now with Blaine. Other than those few weeks when she had been cat-sitting, Hattie hadn't lived by herself for over five years. She was going to miss sweet Marmalade... and Blaine. She was going to miss his warmth and laughter. He was always such a comfort to come home to. They got along so well and moved around each other with such ease... but staying with Blaine wasn't an option. He had been very kind, letting her stay with him this long, but she wasn't sure how much longer he would want her around. She imagined he wanted his house back to himself eventually. Besides, she was on a mission to rediscover herself, and it would be easier to do that if she were living alone. She decided to text him:

Hattie: *Hi! Are you around this evening? I've got good news to share!*
    Blaine: *Amazingly, yes. Finalizing project right now and sending it off to Washington by end of day. Sushi?*
    Hattie: *Could we go someplace with less fish?*
    Blaine: *Right, I forgot you moved to live by the ocean but hate fish unless it's deep-fried and covered in malt vinegar.*
    Hattie: *Tacos?*
    Blaine: *Always.*

Hattie set the table while Blaine set out the Mexican takeout containers he picked up on his way home. As they settled in and started to eat, Blaine asked, "So, what is this news you were so excited to share?"

"My landlord-to-be called this afternoon, and I can move in as early as Thursday!"

"Wow, so soon? That's great news," Blaine said. Was that a hint of disappointment? A warm feeling took root in Hattie's belly at the thought that Blaine might miss her when she was gone.

"I figured you'd be thrilled. I'm sure you'd like to have your house back. You've been so kind to let me stay."

"Yeah, no, it's great. Having our own spaces again will be great, I'm sure. In my head, it just wasn't happening so soon," he said.

"I know what you mean. You've been lovely to live with, actually. It's been so easy in a way that even Galen and I never had. You've been my easiest roommate."

"It's because I came with a cat, isn't it? Be honest." Hattie laughed, and Blaine smiled at her. "I would offer to take you out to celebrate tomorrow, but I've got this stupid annual awards dinner thing I have to go to. Actually, I was planning to ask if you wanted to come with me. If you don't mind being bored for the first part of the evening, we could go out afterward and celebrate."

"An awards dinner? What is it for?"

"It's a regional thing for folks in aeronautics. They give out awards for various types of projects, best in career, that kind of thing. My company sponsors a table every year, so those of us in management roles are expected to attend. There's a cocktail hour followed by dinner and awards. It's pretty boring, overall; at least it was the last two times I had to attend. However, I have to go, whether I want to or not. Luckily for us, it's held pretty close to here, so at least we don't have to travel all the way into San Diego or something like that."

"I'm happy to go with you, Blaine. I would feel bad making you go on your own. We can make up stories about the people giving speeches to keep us entertained, if we need to. We don't even need to go out afterward."

"I would feel terrible if I didn't reward you somehow for sitting through what's probably going to be a boring as hell dinner, but hey, at least there's an open bar!"

"Why didn't you lead with that?" she teased.

"Actually, I should have asked if you had anything to wear before asking if you wanted to come," he said.

"What, I can't go like this?" she asked, gesturing to her sweats and long-sleeved T-shirt from her alma mater.

"While I think you look like the height of fashion, I'm afraid the dress code is listed as creative black tie. Do you have something that might work for that? I was planning on a suit."

"Sigh. Men are so lucky," Hattie lamented. "Fashion expectations haven't really changed since the 1800s, aside from minor tweaks in cut and style. But, it just so happens, Mr. Wilson, I have something that could work. I'll need to swing by the storage unit where I stashed the rest of my stuff and grab it, but fortunately, I know which box it's in, so it should be pretty easy to find."

"Well, that's settled then." Blaine smiled at her and then dug into his fish tacos.

The next day, just as Hattie was pulling up to her storage unit, Blaine's name popped up on her phone with an incoming call. "Hey, Blaine."

"Hi, Hattie. I'm so sorry to do this, but something's come up, and I'll be stuck here a bit longer than expected. I brought my suit with me just in case—lessons learned from past years—so I was wondering, instead of meeting at the house, if you're okay with us just meeting at the venue?"

"Oh, that's no problem, Blaine. I'm just grabbing my dress now, and then I was going to head home and get ready."

"Great. Thanks for being flexible. Just grab a rideshare to the hotel, and then I can get us home from there."

"Sounds like a plan."

"Thanks again for agreeing to go to this with me. I usually go on my own and am bored out of my mind. It will be nice to have someone to talk to, and an excuse if I'm dying to get out of there at the end."

Hattie laughed at his comment. Stepping out of her car, she said, "I'm happy to be your escape plan. I'll see you there. Six-thirty, right?"

"Yes. If I get there before you, I'll wait where the cocktail reception is being held."

"I'll plan on the same, then. See you there." Hanging up, Hattie slid the door to the unit open. She stood there for a minute, looking at its contents. This was her life in a metal box. She felt grateful, which made her happy. She had worried that she would open the door and feel regret or remorse or something similar. Instead, she felt a sense of validation—that she had made the right decision. In a few days, she would be moving everything into her own apartment.

She found the box she was searching for and slid her finger under the floral tape her friend used to seal it. Pulling back the flaps, she was thankful that Sophia included this in the boxes despite Hattie's insistence that she would never wear it in her new life. Sophia convinced her that if she was throwing caution to the wind, she might as well go all out, since maybe she'd do something wild that required a stunning gown. Hattie lifted the heavily beaded floral gown from the box and admired it. She just hoped it wasn't too much for this event. Oh well, it was all she had right now, and it would have to do. Plus, she knew how great it looked on her. She couldn't wait to see Blaine's face when he saw her in it.

Chapter 24

Blaine

Blaine glanced down at his watch while waiting in line at the bar. Hattie should be here any minute. She had texted him when she left the house in her rideshare. He placed his order, saying hi to a few folks he knew as they waited. He took his drink from the bartender and moved to stand where he could easily see the entrance to the cocktail reception.

As he raised the glass to take a sip, the most beautiful woman he'd ever seen entered the room. She turned to leave her jacket at the coat check, and Blaine couldn't tear his eyes away from the open back of her dress, which fell all the way to her lower back. He stood there, glass raised halfway to his lips, when he realized, as she turned around, that the woman in question was Hattie.

To say she was breathtaking was an understatement. Her hair was pulled up into a messy chignon. She wore large, skinny gold hoop earrings. Her dress, though... her dress was a work of art. It clung to her body like it was made for her. The floor-length gown was a pale champagne color, covered all over in beaded red and cream flowers nearly as large as her palm, along with beaded leaves. The tiny beads glittered softly under the light of the cut-glass chandeliers. And the damn thing clung to her like a second skin. His breath caught when he realized that not only was the dress cut low in the back, but it was cut identically in the front—the deep "V" nearly reaching down to her belly button. Her breasts peeked out through the inside of the "V," leaving both very little and oh so much to the imagination. Blaine audibly swallowed. Others had noticed her as well, as a number of heads began to turn her way.

Hattie looked around for him, and rather than waiting for someone else to try to swoop in and steal his date, he strode toward her.

"Hattie, you look... wow." *Smooth, Blaine, smooth.*

"Is it okay? I was worried it might be too much," she said, resting a hand on her stomach.

"You look like perfection personified," he managed to say.

"Wow, Blaine," she said, a blush creeping up her chest and cheeks. "You look fantastic, too. Very dashing," she said, stroking his skinny black satin tie. He had to stop himself from shuddering at the contact.

Blaine shook his head in disbelief. "It's all true, Hattie. You are by far the most beautiful woman here. Can I get you a drink?" he offered. "Actually, never mind, you should definitely come with me. I don't know if I trust anyone else around you with you looking like that." His eyes traveled the length of her and back up again. What had happened to his filter? He was saying every thought that came into his head without stopping to think before it came out of his mouth.

Hattie smiled up at him. "I'd love one, thanks." They made their way to the bar, and a few of Blaine's colleagues stopped them on the way to say hi and get introduced. Blaine kept his hand on the small of her back as they maneuvered through the crowd, his thumb resting on her exposed skin just above the edge of the fabric.

"What can I get you?" the bartender asked.

"I'll take a pinot grigio, please," Hattie said. Despite the crowd, the handsome blonde bartender couldn't tear his eyes off Hattie. Blaine stepped protectively closer.

Blaine definitely needed another drink if he was going to make it through dinner with her sitting next to him looking like that. He downed the rest of his Gin & Tonic and said, "Make that two, please." He dropped some cash into the bartender's tip jar, getting a nod of thanks and a wink in return. After stepping away with drinks in hand, Blaine lifted his glass, clinking it against Hattie's, and said, "Cheers."

"Cheers," she responded, smiling softly.

"Do you want to hang out here for a bit, or would you rather head into dinner?"

"Let's stay here for a bit," she said.

They moved to stand next to one of the rounded marble pillars, from which they could see most of the room. He had to hand it to his company; it truly was a beautiful location. The room felt luxurious, with gold and cream colors and accents of light peacock.

"I figure there's probably a lot of sitting in our future," Hattie said, "so why not enjoy the space?" Hattie looked around, admiring the decor.

Blaine chuffed out a laugh. "You aren't wrong there. I'm not a huge fan of this event, but we're more or less expected to be here, so here I am."

"Well, I'm happy that I could help make this year more bearable for you. It's the least I could do, especially after everything you've done for me, someone you didn't even know until two months ago."

Had it really only been two months? Honestly, he couldn't imagine his life without Hattie in it in some way. It was similar to how he had felt when he and Eli had met. Some people were just meant to be there.

Hattie was like a magnet, drawing everyone in the room. Between her beauty and the fact that Blaine always came solo to everything, people flocked to them in droves. Mike came over to say hi. Blaine gave him a quick hug and a back thump in greeting.

"Who is this charming woman you have on your arm tonight?" Mike asked, his interest evident despite the blonde he'd brought with him.

"Mike, this is my friend Hattie, the one who's been staying with me until her new place is ready."

"No wonder you've been keeping her from me," Mike said. Glancing at his date, Mike said, "We'll see you in there, eh?" He gave them a wink and then wandered off.

"Sorry about him," Blaine said. "He's a great guy, but he's kind of a player right now. He just got out of a long-term relationship, and it's like he's making up for lost time or something."

Hattie laughed and replied, "It's okay, Blaine. I can hold my own around the likes of him. He actually reminds me of Galen in many ways."

"Yeah?"

"Definitely. Tall, dark, handsome, and emotionally stunted." Now, it was Blaine's turn to laugh.

"That pretty much sums him up," he said with a smile. "But, he's a great friend to have, and he's fantastic at his job, which is good since we end up working together a lot."

They chatted with a few more of Blaine's coworkers and colleagues, but finally, it was time to head into the ballroom for dinner. They found their table and took their seats. Mike and his date sat across from them. Blaine leaned over to whisper something to Hattie about the man sitting to her left and nearly forgot what he was about to say. In the press of people in the cocktail reception, he failed to notice how good she smelled. Like roses and something else floral, maybe geraniums? He had to stop himself from rubbing his nose along her neck and inhaling deeply. Blaine was regretting his decision to invite her tonight. Her presence, in that dress, smelling the way she did, was only going to make an already torturous night even worse.

In his hesitation, Hattie turned her face toward him. Their mouths were mere inches from each other. Hattie's pupils dilated as she took in Blaine's presence so close to her. Instead of pulling away, as he suspected she might, she leaned in and whispered in his ear, her lips brushing the shell of his ear, "Isn't this better than on your own?"

Blaine swallowed and replied, "So much better." He was going to need so much more wine to get through this event. Luckily, bottles were already on the table. He picked up the bottle of white and offered some to Hattie, who accepted another glass.

By the time the event finally ended, Blaine remembered his promise to take Hattie out to celebrate the news about her apartment. If he were honest with himself, he shouldn't drink anymore and definitely shouldn't drive. He would just leave his car here, and they could ride-share to wherever. Then, he would come back tomorrow and grab his car.

"I promised you a celebration. Where would you like to go?" he asked.

"Honestly, thanks to that open bar and the wine on the table, I'm feeling pretty good. Plus, this dress isn't just an anywhere dress," she said, gesturing up and down her body.

"No, it most certainly isn't," he replied. Unconsciously, Blaine reached up and fingered the delicate beading along the inside of one of the shoulder straps. Hattie's breathing picked up as his fingers played with her dress, ever so slightly caressing her skin in the process.

"What if," she stuttered, "what if we just went home and celebrated there instead?" Blaine's fingers moved of their own volition along her collarbone and up her neck before he realized what he was doing. He pulled his hand away, ready to apologize, when he looked at Hattie, her eyes hooded with lust.

"That sounds like a perfect idea," he said. "Let's go home." Blaine reached out for her hand, and she took it as they made their way to the exit.

Chapter 25

Hattie

Hattie ran over the events of the evening in her mind, going back over and over them to make sure that she wasn't making any of it up. She had retrieved her coat from the coat check and leaned against one of the smooth marble pillars while Blaine chatted with the concierge to arrange a ride home. No, Blaine had definitely been throwing 'I'm interested' signals at her all night. She may need to write Sophia a thank-you note for making sure to pack this dress. And Blaine, oh boy, was she interested in return.

Or at least for tonight.

Had she been too forward in suggesting they continue this party at home? They'd both drunk a lot, but not so much that either of them was impaired in making serious decisions, as evidenced by the fact that Blaine had opted to leave his car here rather than drive them home in it. But lord, did she want that man to strip her down and have his way with her. His suit looked as if it were custom-fit, accentuating some of her favorite features of his. Just to make sure they were both on the same page, she decided she'd test the waters while they were in the car on the way home.

Blaine returned to her side. "The car should be here in just a few minutes."

"Thanks for getting one for us," she replied.

"Of course," he said.

"I know you said you don't usually like this event too much, but I had fun. Some of those speeches could have been a wee bit shorter, but other than that, I enjoyed it," she said. "It was nice to meet some of the people I've heard you talk about."

"This was definitely my favorite year," he said, giving her a soft smile. "Thanks for coming with me. You made it much more enjoyable." One of the hotel employees waved them over, indicating their car was there. "Shall we?" he asked, gesturing for her to go ahead.

Blaine held the door open for her and waited until she and all of her dress were in before shutting it. He slid in next to her on the other side, and their driver set off towards their destination.

They were uncharacteristically quiet. Blaine kept his eyes forward as they journeyed home, his hand resting on the seat next to him. Hattie casually set hers on the seat as well and slowly inched it closer until their hands were a finger width apart. Reaching out with her pinky, she stroked her finger up and down the length of his. Blaine turned to look at her, surprise and lust filling his eyes. He hadn't pulled away or freaked out, so she took that as a sign to continue. Ceasing her stroking, she set her palm on his thigh and gently curled her fingers to rest on his inner thigh. Blaine's breath hitched, his pupils growing wider in the dim light of the car.

Not wanting to put on a show for the driver, Hattie leaned over and whispered, "I have an idea of how we can celebrate when we get home." Blaine's chest rose and fell as he looked to be trying to control his breathing. She pulled back just enough to be able to look at him and found that his gaze had wandered to where her breasts were pushing together since she had twisted her body to whisper in his ear.

"Hmm?"

"I might need your help with my dress, though."

Blaine's breath stuttered as he leaned back in the seat and closed his eyes. He sat forward again, turning to look at her. Blaine opened and closed his mouth several times before finally giving up and nodding. Hattie turned back to face the front of the car, but left her hand on his thigh. Blaine made no move to remove it. The rest of the ride went by quickly, and soon they were pulling up in front of Blaine's house. Hattie didn't wait for him to help her out; instead, she gathered up her dress and stepped out of the car. Blaine was shucking off his coat as she came around to his side.

"Shall we?" he asked, gesturing to the front door.

"Let's," she said as they made their way up the steps. Blaine held the door open for her and followed her inside. He shut the door and leaned back against it.

"Hattie..." he started, a bit breathlessly.

"Blaine," she interrupted, "I'm going to be bold here and say something that might not sound like me. But I've been trying to find the old me again, the brave me again, and so I'm just going to say it." Hattie paused and took in a deep breath before continuing.

"I'm tired of dancing around how I feel about you. You are a very sexy man, and I'm really hoping you'll agree to fuck me tonight. But if we do this, it can only be tonight. I'm still not interested in a relationship or ruining the friendship we've built, but I'm not going to lie—I've wondered what your skin tastes like and if what's below your belt is as impressive as what is above it. Based on what I saw in the hot springs, as well as right now, I'll say it looks like it is." She had rarely been this direct with a man, but she couldn't deny that she wanted Blaine.

Hattie took a tentative step towards Blaine and noticed that his breathing became more rapid. "But," she continued, "if you aren't interested or don't want to risk it, just say so, and I'll go to my room, change into my sweats, and just go to bed." She took another step towards him, and he made no move to stop her. Another step. Another. Hattie was close enough now that their bodies were separated by mere inches. "So, Blaine, what will it be?" she asked, tilting her head slightly to the side.

In a flurry of movement, Blaine's lips crashed into hers. He spun her, pressing her back into the door where he had just been, pinning her arms above her head. He trailed kisses up and down her neck. *Well*, she thought, *that's one way to answer the question.*

Chapter 26

Blaine

Blaine didn't care if it was only for one night. He had to have this woman. In his bed. On her knees. On his face. Whatever the way, he just needed her. When she'd touched him ever so slightly in the car, he thought he was going to instantaneously combust. That was before she put her hand on his thigh, inches from his dick that had been semi-hard all evening long. Thank god the car had been dark; otherwise, the answer to her unasked question would have been quite evident, much to the chagrin of their driver.

Her teasing had driven him crazy. And that mouth! Hearing Hattie express what she wanted, and to do so explicitly, had taken him by surprise, but he loved it. It was incredibly sexy. Now, she was finally in his arms, where she belonged. She tasted like the apricot of the white wine they'd been drinking mixed with the whipped cream of the dessert they'd eaten. He could easily kiss her all night long. If tonight was the only night he was going to get with her, though, he wanted to get his mouth on as much of her as he could. He could already tell that it was never going to be enough.

He was going to want her forever.

Knowing that should have made him stop, but he didn't care. He'd rather have her for one night than not at all.

"This dress," he started, tracing the deep V with one hand while using his other to keep her hands pinned against the door, "has been driving me crazy. All. Night. Long." He continued to trail his fingers down over the swell of her breast, pausing to slip one finger under and drag it over her hardened nipple. Hattie moaned, and he continued his exploration of the body he wanted to touch so badly for weeks now. Taking a half-step back so he could more easily look her in the eyes, he said, "Tell me what you want first, Hattie, because I want it all, and I can't decide where to start."

Hattie let out a breathy moan as he leaned back in and nibbled on her ear, kissed her neck. "I..." she gasped, "I want your tongue on me," she finally managed to get out. Almost before she had finished speaking, Blaine had dropped to his knees, sliding his hands up and under her skirts. Her skin was silky soft, just like he imagined it would be. Picking up first one foot, then the other, he slid her heeled sandals off, setting them aside. Pushing her skirts up around her hips, he groaned when he saw that she had on a lacy, petal pink thong. If he had to put money on it, he bet it matched the lacy pink bra that he had spied on her that one night when she was bent over feeding Marmalade. This woman knew how to drive him to the absolute edge without even trying. Not bothering to remove the garment, he shoved the lace aside and slid his tongue into her folds. Another groan escaped him at how wet she already was. Hattie sucked in a breath as the vibrations hit her clit.

"Blaine," she panted.

Blaine was determined that very little, short of her telling him to, would make him stop now that he had this woman's taste on his tongue. He needed her to come undone on his mouth. Sliding one of her legs up, using his shoulder to support her, gave him better access to her body.

"Oh, Blaine," she whispered breathily. She cried out as he slid first one finger, then another into her, working them in and out, curling them toward him in a beckoning motion. "Blaine... oh, I'm, oh, god, I'm going to come! Blaine!" Hattie's body tensed, then shuddered as her climax hit her. Blaine reached up his free hand to help support her now shaky body, even as he continued to coax the last of her orgasm from her, determined to wrench as much pleasure from her body as he could. Slowly, he slid his fingers out of her body and stood. She looked dazed as he stuck his glistening fingers in his mouth and sucked them clean. A breathy moan escaped her at his actions.

"You taste like honey, and it's so damn good. I want more, Hattie." She giggled, sounding a little delirious from her release. Leaning in, he kissed her more slowly but not any less passionately than he had before. "I need you, Hattie," he said, his voice strained with desire.

"You are too good to be true, Blaine," she whispered.

"Oh, trust me, the feeling is mutual," he replied.

"Then take me to your room, unless, of course, you want to give the neighbors a show. In that case, bend me over the back of the couch and take me right now."

If Blaine could have gotten harder, he would have at her words. He liked mouthy Hattie almost as much as he liked telling mouthy Hattie what to do. Blaine slowly slid his hand from behind her head and gently placed it around her throat.

"Hattie, I'm going to take you to my room and strip this sinful dress off of you. Then, I want you to get on your knees for me. I want you to suck my cock like the good girl I know you are, and when I decide it's time to stop, I'm going to take my time fucking you until the sun rises. If this is the only night I get to spend with you, I'm going to make it one you'll never forget. I plan to give you at least two more orgasms before morning, maybe more, if you earn them." Hattie stood there with her mouth open in an "O" shape. Blaine had clearly surprised her. While he was pretty easygoing in life, more often than not, he definitely liked to take charge in the bedroom. That didn't mean he couldn't be a good boy from time to time when he felt like it.

Taking Hattie's hand in his, he led her back to his room, flicking on the lights as they entered. He wanted to see every inch of her perfect body, especially that tattoo she'd teased him with at the hot springs. Caressing the bare skin of her back, he slowly slid his hands up and down her exposed flesh. A breathy gasp escaped her at the touch.

"Now tell me, Hattie, how the fuck does this dress come off? Because I'm about two seconds from ripping it off your body, and

I'd hate to do that because it really is beautiful." Blaine slid his hand up to her nape, gently pulling her head back so that he could more easily kiss her throat.

"There's... there's a hidden zipper on the side," she managed to get out, gesturing with her right hand. Sliding his hands down to her waist, he found the zipper and slid it slowly open. The gown visibly slackened with each tooth that was released. Blaine ran his hands along the tops of her shoulders and gently pushed the straps down. With that small amount of weight released, the heavy beaded fabric pulled the rest of the dress down into a puddle on the floor. Other than her lacy thong, Hattie was nude beneath the dress. Blaine sucked in a breath.

"Take it off," he demanded, his voice deepened with arousal. Hattie slowly bent and slid the lace down her thighs, letting it fall to the ground, joining the dress. Blaine took a deep breath in as he gazed up and down Hattie's body. "You are gorgeous, Hattie. I know I saw a lot of you at the hot springs, but seeing you completely bare for me... you are perfection, that's all there is to it."

Blaine undid the buttons on his suit shirt, quickly tossing it to the side and stripping off his undershirt so he could resume touching her. Hattie must not have minded being told what to do too much as she continued to stand there, waiting for Blaine's next instruction. Blaine took a seat on the edge of the mattress, the edge dipping with his weight.

"Come over here," he commanded. Hattie came and stood between his spread thighs. "On your knees." Never breaking eye contact, Hattie sank slowly to the floor. Blaine reached out, remembering how much she seemed to like her nipples being played with earlier, and flicked his thumbs over her erect buds. She closed her eyes, moaning. She really liked that, he noted.

"I want to touch you, Blaine," she said huskily.

Blaine liked being bossy in bed but wasn't a true dominant, so she could touch him as much as she wanted, which he hoped was a lot. "I want that too, Hattie. Touch me whenever, wherever you want. I have very few limits, and if you hit one, I'll tell you to stop." With that, she reached out, sliding her hands up his thighs.

"Did you mean what you said earlier?" she asked.

"About what?"

"That you wanted me to get to my knees and suck your cock like a good girl."

Blaine's dick thickened at those dirty words coming from her mouth. He nodded. "Do you want to be a good girl?" he purred, brushing his thumb across her lower lip.

She nodded, never letting her gaze stray from his. "I want to be such a good girl for you tonight."

"Then take my dick out and suck it."

She slid her hands up the front of his slacks, stopping when she reached his waistband. She moved her hands to lightly caress the skin of his abs. Blaine couldn't help but groan. Her touch straddled the line between pleasurable and ticklish, and it was driving him mad. She traced the trail of hair that led from his belly button down below the band of his pants. Pulling the end of his belt out, she unbuckled it, sliding it free and tossing it onto the floor behind her. Slowly, torturously, she undid the hook and bar closure and slid his zipper down. His cock felt like a steel rod at this point, and it was dying to be freed from his boxer briefs. Blaine lifted his hips slightly so that she could slide his pants and briefs down, and finally free his aching cock. Almost as soon as it sprang free, Hattie's mouth was on him, sucking and licking.

"Easy there, girl," he grunted out, "Otherwise, this isn't going to last long, as turned on as you have me." This woman knew what she was doing when it came to giving head. He'd always enjoyed getting it, but Hattie was top of her class, for sure.

Blaine placed his hand on the back of Hattie's head, guiding her in a way that he knew he liked, but while letting her take the lead at the same time.

"Damn, you're really good at this," Blaine groaned out, "I really don't want to say this, but I'm gonna need you to stop now." She popped off of him and licked her lips like she had just finished a four-course meal. That was an image that would live rent-free in his brain from now on. Gripping her chin lightly, he pulled Hattie into a deep kiss. Sliding his arms around her, he brought her up and onto his lap. He could feel her wet cunt sliding against him as she settled against him. His cock twitched at the contact. Hattie gasped as she slid over him, gently rocking her hips back and forth. Blaine hissed, doing his best to restrain himself.

"Hattie, I know I said I was going to take my time with you—and I will—but I'm not sure I can or want to this time. I need to be inside you, and I'm not sure I'll be able to hold myself back once I'm seated inside you. Instead, I want to take you hard and fast and then take my time with you. If I promise to make you come at least three more times, instead of just two, can I please just have you now?" he asked, nearly begging.

"I said it earlier, Blaine. I want you to fuck me. If that means hard and fast now and gentle later, so be it. I want you to get your cock inside me now." Blaine didn't need to be told twice. He rolled Hattie so that she was beneath him and lunged for the bedside drawer that held a box of condoms. Pulling one out, he tossed it to her and said, "Put it on me and then get on all fours."

"Yes, Daddy," she purred, and Blaine nearly came on the spot.

"Fuck, why do I like it when you say that?" he said as he rubbed his cock against her throbbing clit, turning her giggle into a moan. She started to push her hips up. "Uh, uh, uh, I thought you said you were going to be a good girl for me tonight? On your knees," he said, sitting back so he was kneeling above her. Hattie flipped over and came up on all fours. Slowly, she pushed her hips back, begging him to sink into her. His breathing became rapid as he lined himself up at her entrance and paused there.

"Fuck. Me. Blaine," she grunted out, and that was all the permission he needed.

Chapter 27

Hattie

Hattie hadn't felt this good in a long time. She would have never pegged Blaine as the dominant type, but she was here for it.

Her college boyfriend had been super into BDSM. While she had been willing to experiment with it, and she found that she enjoyed parts of it, it generally wasn't her scene. This version, what she came to think of as BDSM-lite, she found she really enjoyed.

There was something about a man she wanted taking charge. Being in a safe space like this allowed her to just let go and relinquish control, something she rarely did in life. But if this man didn't stick his dick into her soon, she was going to flip the tables on him. A woman could only take so much, after all.

Fortunately, telling him to fuck her was all it took. He slid swiftly into her dripping cunt. Hattie gasped with pleasure as Blaine began pistoning his hips into her. When she reached her hand up to rub her clit, Blaine leaned forward and swatted her hand away. "Mine," he growled, replacing his hand with hers. Between her earlier orgasm, Blaine's possessiveness, and the fact that his cock was hitting her G-spot with every thrust, it wasn't going to take much for her to come a second time.

"Oh, Hattie," Blaine gritted out.

"Give it to me, Blaine," she said. Blaine leaned forward, gently biting down on the soft flesh where her neck and shoulder met as he came. The action surprised and aroused her. Hattie's own release followed quickly. Together, they collapsed onto their sides on the bed, panting, Blaine still buried inside her.

"Hattie..." Blaine growled. The sound sent little flutters to her core. Her inner walls squeezed together, and Blaine sucked in a breathy gasp.

"Damn, woman. I could live between your thighs."

That dirty mouth! That was another surprise tonight. Blaine definitely seemed more like the boy next door than the bad boy at the bar, but behind closed doors, he was a totally different man. He gently kissed the red mark he'd left on her shoulder as he slid out of her. They both groaned at the loss of contact. After tying off and tossing the condom into the bedside trash, Blaine settled back onto the bed behind her, where Hattie continued to laze on her side.

Blaine rested his head on his bent elbow, slowly stroking from her hip to just below her breast and back again. "You're incredible, Hattie." Brushing his fingers across the mark he'd left on her shoulder, he asked, "I didn't hurt you, did I? Sorry, I lost control of myself a little there." In the moment, Hattie felt like Marmalade—if she had the ability to purr, there was no doubt in her mind that she would have.

Hattie rolled onto her back and smiled at Blaine, easing some of the worry from his face. "I don't know if you noticed this, but I quite enjoyed it," she replied. Blaine grinned down at her.

"I do believe that was the moment you squeezed my cock like a vice and soaked my balls with your cum."

Once again, Blaine's dirty mouth left Hattie nearly speechless. On the one hand, she couldn't have Blaine wandering around the house talking to her like that after tonight, but on the other hand, she wasn't sure she wanted him to ever stop.

"Well, there's no guarantee that it will happen again, so we may need to test it." The look Blaine gave her told her that, if she had been wearing clothes at that moment, they would have quickly been tossed to the floor.

"Hattie, I promised to take my time with you next time. If you keep saying things like that, I can't guarantee I'll be able to restrain myself." Gently, he stroked her arm. Quietly, he said, "Tell me what you like, Hattie." It wasn't a demand but rather a request. He genuinely wanted to know. Hattie thought for a moment, then started to laugh. "What?" Blaine asked, looking perplexed.

"You've been such a surprise tonight. Everything you've done has been both unexpected and divine. I could tell you what I like, but honestly, I think I'd rather just enjoy seeing what you do next."

"Mmm, carte blanche, huh?" he mumbled, kissing her shoulder, making his way down to her nipple, and sucking it into his mouth.

She loved the way his tongue swirled around it. She reached up and tangled her fingers in his silky hair.

"Mmm, yes, definitely, especially if you keep doing that," she panted out, arching her back slightly.

Blaine continued his attention to her nipple and then moved to her other side, his fingers whispering along the underside of her breasts, making her skin even more sensitive. He brushed his fingers across the Hindi script of her tattoo and asked, "What's the story with this? Or is now not a good time to tell it? I'm wickedly curious how you decided to get a tattoo, just here," he said, kissing the area of her breast in question. His one hand lazily played with the nipple on her opposite breast.

"If you want me to answer anything, you are going to have to stop doing that, and I'm not sure I want you to."

"What if I ask nicely?" he said, flicking his tongue across her pert nipple, causing her to squirm under his touch.

"Mhm-mm," she responded.

"What if," he began, biting and tugging, "I call you a good girl and do this?" he said, sliding his finger into her folds and then bringing the glistening digit back to his mouth, slowly licking the taste of her off his finger. Hattie's breath hitched as he sucked his fingertip, not breaking eye contact the entire time.

"Blaine..." she moaned as he rolled away. Hattie had expected him to start kissing his way down her body, but instead, Blaine lay back on the bed, fully removing himself from touching any part of her.

"So, Hattie, what's it going to be? Are you going to be a good girl and tell me what I want to know?" he asked, his voice like rough silk.

"Blaine!"

"Uh, uh, uh. You haven't answered my question."

Damn, Blaine and his dirty, domineering mouth. Why did it have to be so sexy? She was a little embarrassed to tell him about her tattoo, which is why she hadn't offered up the story at the hot springs.

"Do I have to tell you? It's not very sexy..." she started.

"I don't want you to do anything that makes you uncomfortable, Hattie. If you really don't want to tell me, then don't. It doesn't have to be a sexy story, Hattie. Mine certainly wasn't. I'll just continue to be in suspense as I trace the symbols with my tongue. I'm just curious, but... I'll reward you either way." He slowly traced the characters with his finger, his touch featherlight. Hattie arched her back slightly at his caresses.

"It's Hindi and is supposed to mean, 'I'll keep you safe.' My best friend, Jayne, has the other half, which says 'I'll keep you wild.' It wasn't a drunken decision, but it was a youthful one. If I did it now, I would still get it, but likely would choose a different location. She was the one who convinced me that getting it on the side of my boob was a good idea. At the time, we might have been a little tipsy, so of course, her argument made total sense. Once we decided, there was no changing her mind."

"I like that. And I love the location; it gives me an excuse to do this," he said, swiping his tongue along her tattoo. Hattie gasped at the feeling of his expert tongue on her body.

Hattie needed more. Despite initially being hands-off, once she started talking, Blaine gave in to both their needs for contact. He had been teasing and touching her the entire time she was telling him her story. Now, it was time for him to make good on his promises. "You told me that if I told you about it, you would reward me."

"Mmm, good girl, I did, didn't I? How would you like to be rewarded?" he asked, his voice growing deeper with desire as he rolled on top of her.

"I want your mouth on me again. I want you to be a good boy and take me apart and make me come all over your face." Blaine's cock twitched against her leg, so he must have liked that idea.

"That I can do," he said, slowly kissing his way down her belly to the apex of her thighs. Blaine lightly nipped her inner thigh, making her jump, spreading her legs in reaction. Hattie suspected that had been his plan all along, given that as soon as she had moved her leg to be out of reach of his teeth, he attacked her clit with such ferocity she didn't know if she could take much more. As if sensing she was reaching some sort of limit, he released her bud and languidly stroked his tongue through her slit, circling her sex, and back again. She groaned when he added two fingers. As he continued to work his fingers in and out, Hattie let out a breathy moan. Give the man a gold star or a Nobel Peace Prize or something. He deserved it. How in the hell was he single when he could go down on a woman like this? Clearly, the women who had dated him in the past were complete and utter fools.

Placing his shoulders under her thighs, Blaine moved up the bed slightly, giving him even more access. Oh god, was he using both hands and his tongue? Hattie wasn't sure, but suddenly, the sensations overwhelmed her as she came hard and wet. Blaine waited for her orgasm to pass before sliding out from between her thighs, beard glistening with her cum, and coming to rest beside her. Hattie attempted to speak, to thank him for his service to humankind, or something, but the man had literally made her come to the point of being speechless.

Chapter 28

Blaine

Blaine couldn't stop touching Hattie. She was like an addictive drug, and he couldn't get enough. He knew her body was extra sensitive after her orgasm, but he needed his skin against hers however he could get it. He lightly stroked his fingers up her torso, down her arm, over and over, pressing just hard enough not to tickle but light enough to tease rather than soothe. He knew she would need a few minutes before she'd be ready for more, so despite his cock's protestations, he just lay there with her.

Slowly, she turned her head toward him and looked at him. "What?" he asked, a small smile on his lips. Part of him still couldn't believe this was really happening.

"Bla... I... wow," she settled on. Blaine couldn't help himself and chuckled.

"I'll take that as a compliment," he said, brushing a strand of hair off her face. "Are you cold?" he asked. They hadn't bothered to move the covers aside, and while the house wasn't too chilly, she was naked.

Taking the opportunity to drink her in, he slowly looked her up and down. One hand rested against her cheek, the other on her stomach. Her thighs and patch of dark hair between them glistened with her arousal and his saliva. That thought made his dick start to harden again. He moved his perusal down her shapely calves to her toes that were painted almost the same baby pink as her lacy underwear had been. Slowly, he dragged his gaze back up her body, stopping on her breasts, where the hand that had been resting on her stomach now lightly pinched and rolled her nipple. A low growl unexpectedly ripped from his throat. He sat up, scooting back against the headboard. "Come," he commanded.

"Oh, I think I just did," Hattie sighed, stretching her arms over her head.

"I think that you more than think it. I think you'll be feeling it until next Sunday. Now, get over here and ride my cock."

Desire flashed in her eyes, and instead of some sort of snarky comeback, Hattie rolled over and crawled her way up the bed, settling over his thighs. He nodded toward the condom box on the bedside table, indicating that she should get one out. She pulled a foil packet out and started to hand it to him when he said, "Put it on me." Blaine could have done it, but he loved the feel of her hands on him. But telling her what to do went beyond just the touch. Hattie was often in her head, and by commanding her, she was able to let go of control and simply enjoy. It was one way he could help take care of her. She spent so much time taking care of everyone else—like when she texted her friends just to check in, making extra food for him so he would have lunch, sending care packages to a little boy she used to babysit who was now off at college—caring was in her nature, but no one ever cared for her in return, at least not in the way that she deserved.

Hattie tore the packet open and rolled the condom down his shaft. She bit down on her lower lip as she worked it down his length, and the sight was beautiful. Once it was fully on, she looked up at him expectantly. Blaine leaned forward, capturing her lips in his in a searing kiss. Breaking the kiss, he leaned his forehead against hers, whispering, "Ride my cock, Hattie." Hattie lifted her hips, sliding along Blaine's sheathed length. When she reached his tip, she lined their bodies up and sank torturously slowly onto him. He could have lifted his hips to get her there faster, but he had promised to take his time with her this time around, so he was willing to cede control to her at this moment.

"You're in the driver's seat, darling," he said when he could sense both her hesitation and desire to move. Hattie let out a sigh and slowly started to rock her hips. Blaine captured one of her nipples in his mouth, using his fingers to tease the other one at the same time, like she had just been doing a few moments before.

"Blaine..." his name came out like a moan. Never had his name sounded so seductive. He hadn't thought he could get any harder, but having his name moaned like that proved him wrong. He added that to the list of things he would be replaying when he was on his own and his hand was firmly wrapped around his cock.

"I... my legs are jelly, I can't..."

Blaine understood what she was trying to say, flipping them over while staying seated inside her. After getting them settled with Hattie on her back, Blaine thrust deeply into her.

"Is this better, baby?" Blaine asked, throwing one of her legs over his shoulder. Hattie groaned as he slid in and out of her again. "I'll take that as a yes," he said. Blaine was suddenly overcome by an emotion he couldn't quite name: adoration, lust, longing, and loss, all rolled into one. He knew that when he had said yes to tonight, it wasn't going to be enough. Again, he thought to himself, if this was all he got, he was going to make it count and make sure that Hattie had no doubt about how much he was loving every minute of being with her. Leaning down, he poured everything he was feeling into kissing her, all while thrusting in and out of her slick heat. Bracing himself on one arm, he used his free hand to whisper touches across her arms and chest. Hattie's breathing grew more and more ragged, and Blaine could tell she was close to coming again. Increasing his pace, he groaned with his own impending pleasure.

"Oh, Blaine," she breathlessly moaned his name again, "I'm so close." Blaine rocked his hips faster and faster until she came apart around him. He quickly followed her over the edge, collapsing into a panting, boneless heap next to Hattie. Gently, he placed a kiss on her bare shoulder.

"That was... wow."

"Yeah," she agreed.

"Stay here," he said. Hattie gave a soft laugh.

"If you think I could move right now, you are sorely mistaken," she said, eyes closed. Blaine retrieved a warm washcloth. Hattie stirred lightly as he gently swiped it along her skin. He loved being able to care for her like this; it was an urge he hadn't had with other partners in the past. He liked taking care of them, but with Hattie, he felt an overwhelming sense to protect and care for her.

Blaine returned to the bathroom and quickly cleaned himself up. He considered taking a shower, but decided he would rather curl up next to Hattie. When he returned from the bathroom, Hattie lay with the covers draped across her waist, dozing soundly. Blaine slid into bed, pulling the blankets up around them more. Hattie slept through it all.

Blaine lay next to Hattie, fighting off sleep of his own, knowing that once he gave in, the night would be over. He was spent and needed to get some rest, but he also didn't want this moment to end. He sensed that if Hattie were awake, she would bolt if he pushed her to stay, so instead, he drowsily watched her sleep. Hattie was everything he had hoped for and more, but he knew that tomorrow they would be back to being temporary roommates and "just friends." Would it be possible to be around her as simply a friend after tonight? He knew that's what they had agreed to, but that was easier said than done after the experience they shared tonight. He rubbed his thumb back and forth across her stomach, half-hoping to rouse her from sleep. Instead, all he managed to do was get her to curl into his side. There was no way he was going to be able to stave off sleep with Hattie snuggled up against him like this. Instead of fighting it, he tucked her closer into his side and drifted off. No need to dream when the woman of his dreams was already in his arms.

The next morning, the sun began to stream through Blaine's window. Since his bedroom was on the back side of the house, he hadn't worried about closing the blackout curtains last night. He'd been more focused on getting Hattie out of that dress. Hattie... Blaine wasn't entirely surprised to see she was no longer in the bed. The sinful dress in question was also no longer in a puddle on his bedroom floor. He wasn't surprised she was gone, but he was disappointed. If he hadn't been dying of thirst and needing to pee, he would have stayed in bed longer, replaying last night. As it was, he pulled on some shorts, assuming that they were back to roommate rules, and dragged his sorry ass to the bathroom and then into the kitchen. Hattie was either in her room or had gone out. Regardless, she'd made a full pot of coffee, for which he would be forever grateful. He poured himself a cup and shuffled back to his bedroom, not quite ready to start this day.

Chapter 29

Hattie

The sun warmed Hattie's skin as she sat on the shore. She had woken up in Blaine's bed, his arm comfortably draped across her waist. Nearly every part of her was begging her to stay, except for the part that was in a complete panic over what might happen if he found her still in his bed. She managed to slide out of bed without waking him and crawled back to her own room to get some more sleep. When she came to a few short hours later, she quickly threw on some clothes, made coffee, and left before Blaine stirred. Last night had been... indescribable. Blaine was so much more than met the eye.

After walking along the beach for a while, Hattie still felt panicked, so she made the call she both knew she needed and might regret. Jayne answered on the second ring. She gave Jayne a brief version of everything that had happened last night and her mid-night panic.

"So, you just went back to your room and what? Went to sleep?" Jayne asked.

"Pretty much. I was worried that if I stayed, it might confuse things in the morning light."

"So let me get this straight, you had the most amazing night of sex—in your life—and then you snuck out on him in the middle of the night, determined never to sleep with him again, despite the fact that you currently sleep across the hall from him."

"Pretty much."

"Okaaay... and why, again? Please remind me why you don't want to have a repeat with a guy who is super nice, seems to more or less have his shit together, and can give you mind-blowing orgasms?"

"Because, Jayne, I don't want to date right now. Blaine isn't the kind of guy you carry on a carefree, no-commitment relationship with. He's the kind of guy you bring home to mom. So, no. No repeats. I'm finally starting to remember who I was, and that needs to be my focus right now."

"Uh-huh, and yet, you've had the hots for this guy basically since you met him, you've been living together quite peacefully for the past several weeks, and he gave you at least three world-record orgasms in a single night. Oh, and let's not forget that his freak flag meets where your freak flag flies in the sky."

"Yeah."

"Hattie Elizabeth Renaud..." Jayne sucked in a breath. "Sometimes, you just confound me!"

"Sorry," Hattie said with a little laugh. Part of her agreed with Jayne and had wanted nothing more than to crawl back into bed with Blaine after getting up to use the bathroom in the middle of the night, but for so many other reasons, she needed to distance herself from him. They still had one week of living together, and then she would be able to be in her own space and figure out who she was. After all, figuring out who the hell Hattie was on her own was part of the reason for this move. She had always gone from serious relationship to serious relationship, and after what happened with Galen, she was afraid to get into another relationship right now. Hattie was still untangling the damage he had done to her, whether it was intentional or not.

"But hey, at least you'll be able to have this view when you come yell at me in person!" Hattie said as she flipped the camera and panned the beach for Jayne.

"Yeah," Jayne sighed blissfully. "As mad as I am at you right now, I cannot wait to see you!"

"Same."

"So what will you do for the rest of the week? Are you just going to avoid him?" Jayne asked.

"No, I just needed a little space this morning, but we're both grown-ups, and this is what we agreed to, so it should be fine. We'll see each other the usual amount, and then I'm moving out next week. If it's weird, I can always move out any time after Thursday. I don't need a bed for a few nights. If things are really awkward, I'll just load up my car with the stuff at the house and move into my new place. I'm sure it will be fine, though." Hattie had her fingers crossed that it was the truth and things would be okay. She just had to get up the guts to go back to Blaine's.

"For the record, I think you should ride that train as often as he'll let you…"

"Jayne!"

"…but, I'll support your decision. For now," she said, giving Hattie a wink.

"Alright," Hattie said, "time to grow a pair and head back. Talk to you soon."

Hattie hung up but didn't make a move to stand. After some more ocean gazing, Hattie decided it was time to go back and face whatever the music was. Standing, she brushed the sand off her butt and began the walk back to the house. When she opened the front door, Blaine was sitting in the armchair reading.

"Hey," she ventured.

"Hi," he returned. "You must have been up early this morning. Thanks for making coffee," he said, raising his cup in a toast.

Hattie breathed a sigh of relief. Blaine wasn't acting any different. Fingers crossed, it would stay that way. "I had to use the bathroom and didn't feel like I'd be able to fall back asleep, so I decided to head down to the beach for a bit. You were right; there's hardly anyone down there early in the morning. It was nice," she said.

"After all that wine last night, running was not going to happen this morning, but I might try to at least go for a few miles this evening if I can muster the energy. That's later's problem, though. For now, I'm just going to read and take it easy. I made some biscuits, by the way, if you want any. They're in the fridge. Help yourself," he said, picking his book back up.

See, totally normal. Everything was going to be just fine.

Hattie showered and got dressed. Deciding to take Blaine up on his offer of biscuits, she headed into the kitchen. Blaine was in the kitchen filling up his coffee cup when she entered. Hattie pulled down a plate, and when she closed the cupboard, Blaine was standing closer to her.

"I know that we said last night would be last night, but I just had to do this," he said, crashing his lips into hers and kissing her deeply. He lifted Hattie up, setting her on the counter, kissing her the whole time. Finally, he broke the kiss, leaving both of them breathless. Blaine picked up his mug and wandered down the hall to his room, leaving Hattie perched on the counter, panting and wondering what the hell had just happened.

Chapter 30

Blaine

You are officially an asshole, an idiot, or both, Blaine chided himself. He had promised himself that he would respect Hattie's wishes and that last night would stay in the past. Then she walked out wearing lounge pants and a strappy little tank, wet hair leaving damp spots on her top, and he lost all resolve, which is why he was now sequestered in his bedroom in a forced timeout. That kiss had been hot, but it must be the last time. He willed his dick to understand that, despite its protestations.

He was going to owe Hattie an apology later, but first, he needed a shower where he could rid himself of his erection. After a few minutes, he could hear her moving around the kitchen again (his dick congratulating itself on the fact that it had taken her time to get over the moment), so he made his way into the bathroom.

Hattie was sitting at the kitchen table working on her laptop when he came out. "Sorry," he said before she could say anything. "I shouldn't have jumped on you like that. I really wanted to do that one more time last night, but we both fell asleep. So, anyway, I want you to know that while I don't regret it one bit, I am sorry at the same time. You made your boundaries very clear, and I plan to respect them from here on out."

Hattie looked slightly shocked at his admission. Giving her head a small shake as if to clear it, she said, "Wow, Blaine, thank you. That was very mature of you. I'm honestly a little blown away by how you've handled crossing the lines that we did last night."

"I promised you, Hattie. You aren't looking for something, and honestly, even if you were, I'm not exactly in a place where I would be a good partner for you. I just started seeing a therapist, and there's a lot I need to unpack. But... can I say one final thing about last night, and then I swear I will never mention it again?" he asked.

Hattie looked at him for a moment, then nodded.

"Last night was incredible. I'm not sure... I've never had a night quite like that. I didn't want you to be in any doubt that no matter what Galen or anyone else in your past said, you are a phenomenal woman in so many different ways. Thank you for sharing yourself with me in such a special way." *Seriously, Blaine, shut your mouth now.* "I'm going to head back and pick up my car, and then I'm going to run and do a few errands. How about I pick up some pizza on the way home, and we can just have a chill night? Maybe watch a movie? I'm not truly hungover, but I definitely drank more than usual last night and think I'll take it easy today."

Hattie cleared her throat and responded, "Sure, that sounds great. Thanks, Blaine."

Blaine didn't really have errands to run. He just needed to get out of the house before he said or did something stupid. He called a rideshare and headed to the hotel to retrieve his car. Fishing out his keys, he slid into the driver's seat and started the engine. He began to drive without a specific destination in mind.

Almost on autopilot, as if heading to work, he pointed his car north when he hit the 101 and kept driving. As he approached San Juan Capistrano, he saw a sign for the historic mission. Deciding it would be as good a place as any to spend some time, he turned on his blinker and took the off-ramp. While Oceanside has its own mission, he hadn't yet visited it for some reason. It had been decades since his last visit to one of the missions. One summer, when he was a kid on a family road trip, he and his family stopped at the mission in Carmel, one of the twenty-one Spanish colonial outposts. Since then, he'd been fascinated by the California Missions' history and, even though he wasn't Catholic, enjoyed all of the iconography as well.

After parking and paying the meager admission fee, he took the offered brochure and started to wander the grounds, beginning with the soldiers' barracks. Hattie would love this place, he thought. He wondered if she had ever visited the Oceanside mission. If he could find a way to bring it up without admitting he'd driven all the way up here, he would suggest she check it out.

When he finally reached the chapel, Blaine was ready to take a break. He sat down in one of the pews and drank in the quiet. For the past hour or so, he'd been avoiding thinking about anything other than what was right in front of him, but now, sitting in this silent church, he could no longer ignore the thoughts that had been lurking.

Blaine meant what he said to Hattie—last night was some of the best sex he'd had in his life, and she was a phenomenal woman. He was sorry it had taken her ex being such an ass for her to come out of her shell and embrace who she was. The glimmers and hints he'd seen told him he'd be lucky to keep her in his life, even if only as a friend. And he'd only had a few sessions with his new therapist, but Eli was right; Blaine clearly had more to deal with and get over than he'd realized. Every day, he looked at himself in the mirror, listing all the good things about himself. Whenever a negative thought tried to creep in, he pushed it away and replaced it with a positive thought. It was small, but even that little bit, on top of his sessions, had helped him realize that no, he was, in fact, not the fat kid he once was. It gave him the confidence to go for it with Hattie last night. If he were being honest with himself, the time limit also helped give him courage. She couldn't reject him if it was just for the one night.

The bench creaked as someone else sat down near Blaine. He looked up to see an older woman sitting there. She glanced at him and smiled. She reminded Blaine so much of his grandmother that it was uncanny. "You look troubled, young man," she said without any preamble.

Blaine huffed out a laugh, "And here I was thinking I was doing so well."

"There is an aura of conflict about you," she said, "assuming, that is, that we're allowed to talk about auras while sitting in a church," she said, gesturing around them. It was her turn to give a small smile. "I'm Emma, by the way."

"Hi Emma, nice to meet you. I'm Blaine." Blaine reached over and offered her his hand, which she shook in greeting.

"Oh, that's a nice strong name for a strong young man. Oh, no need to be embarrassed," she said as Blaine started to blush. "I'm sure you know that you're a good-looking kid."

"Ironically, that's a little bit why I'm sitting here," he said.

"What's got you troubled, Blaine?"

Blaine sighed. Did he really want to divulge his troubles to this complete stranger? He couldn't explain why, but he did. Perhaps it was that Emma reminded him so much of his grandmother, but he felt safe and comfortable with her.

"It's complicated," he began.

"Isn't it always?" she replied with a little laugh.

"Seems to be the case, yeah. There's a girl, a woman... she's smart and beautiful and funny, and everything I want in a woman, but she doesn't want to date—not just me, anyone. On top of that, I have a host of self-esteem issues I'm trying to work through. I wasn't always this handsome," he said with a wink, to which she replied with a grin. "It's as if... as if we're the perfect pieces that fit together, but we belong to different puzzles. To make things more complicated, she's temporarily living with me, and last night, we crossed some lines, both of us willingly, with the understanding that today we would uncross them. Only, after the fact, I wish we didn't have to. So I'm just sitting here trying to reconcile how I feel with what I know I need to do in order to still be friends with her, because I can't imagine my life without her in it. The idea of that is unimaginable... it would feel like living in a world where suddenly all the art was black and white. Does that make sense, Emma?"

Emma reached over and squeezed his hand. "It does. It may not be that you belong to different puzzles; rather, you are both in the wrong part of the puzzle. Give it time, and the universe may yet move your pieces around. By then, you will have either moved on and be happy that she's your friend, or you can decide to cross those lines you spoke of again. Life is complicated, but let me tell you something, I had an incredibly uncomplicated life for a number of years, and you know what?"

"What?" he asked.

"Blaine, I was so bored I was losing my mind. That's how I ended up here," she said, gesturing around the mission. "Complications make life worth living."

"Thank you, Emma." She reached over and gave his hand another squeeze. Blaine looked toward the front of the church again, taking a moment to process everything Emma had said. When he turned to say goodbye to her, she was already gone. *That's strange*, he thought. He was surprised she hadn't said goodbye. Upon further reflection, he hadn't heard the bench creak or feel it shift when she stood up either. Goosebumps erupted on his skin, and the hair on his arms stood on end. Blaine decided it was time for him to head back out into the warm California sun.

Chapter 31

Hattie

Blaine had returned Saturday evening, just as he promised, with pizza in hand. They slipped back into their comfortable routine easily, as if nothing had changed. It was Blaine's turn to pick the movie, and he chose *Road to Bali*, with Bob Hope and Bing Crosby. Which was one of the things Hattie loved about him. He would probably never admit it, but Blaine had a soft spot for old films, especially musicals.

Sunday had been just like any other Sunday they'd spent together. Eli and Blaine had worked out together. Hattie did her laundry, called her mom and her sister, and made some homemade protein granola bars she thought Blaine might like.

Monday rolled around, and she just needed to get through the next couple of days and then she could move. Hattie couldn't believe that in just a few days, she would finally be able to truly settle into her new life. She planned to pick up the keys to her new place on Thursday after work. Most of her stuff was in the storage unit she was renting, including the second-hand items she'd bought to furnish the place. Instead of moving anything in sooner, she decided to wait until Saturday. Eli and Blaine had both agreed to help her with the bigger items, and Jayne was coming on Friday, so she would have plenty of help.

Hattie and Blaine seemed poised to have a perfectly normal week. So, what the hell was her problem? Hattie had been so worried that Blaine wouldn't keep his promise, but he hadn't mentioned their night together or tried to kiss her again. It was like it had never happened. The voice in her head reminded her, *That's what you wanted, remember?* Hattie had become increasingly jumpy around Blaine, and every time her phone pinged with a message or rang with a call, she startled, wondering if it was Blaine. Could it be that he was past their night, but she wasn't?

Hattie was making breakfast when Blaine wandered out of his bedroom, buttoning up what she assumed was his favorite vest, considering how often he wore it. "Morning," she said. "I'm making scrambled eggs, half egg whites. You want some?"

"That would be great. Thanks, Hattie. I'm definitely going to miss having hot breakfasts ready after my run," he said, smiling.

"There's fresh coffee, too, as I'm sure you can smell," she said.

Blaine grabbed a mug from the cupboard and filled it up. He leaned back against the counter, blowing on his hot coffee. After taking a sip, he said, "So, I was wondering, since this is your last night here and all..."

"I'll still be here tomorrow night unless you kick me out," Hattie said.

"Yes, well, I assumed you'd probably spend tomorrow evening with Jayne after picking her up from the airport." Blaine had offered to let Jayne stay at the house on Friday night, but Jayne had opted to get a hotel for the night. Hattie still thought it was really sweet that he'd offered.

"You're right. Huh, I guess that does make this my last night really here," she said, feeling a little sad at the thought.

"Anyway," he resumed, "it's not like we'll never see each other again, but I was wondering if you wanted to do something kind of special to mark the end of the era, if you will. It doesn't have to be anything too fancy. I was just thinking we could go down to that Mexican place by the water that you like so much. My treat."

"Blaine, that's really sweet of you. I'd love to do something special with you. You've been so kind to me, someone you didn't even know, and it truly means a lot to me that you let me into your life like you did. I'll always be grateful, and I'm thrilled that we get along as well as we do and that I'm lucky to now count you among my friends."

"Great. It's a date, then," he said. "I'm going to go finish getting ready. I'd love some of those eggs when they're done. Thanks again for making them," he added, coffee in hand as he headed back down the hall.

"They should be ready in about two minutes. I'll plate some up for you."

"Thanks!" he called back down the hall.

Hattie resumed stirring the eggs. When they were done, she divided them between two plates, and topped them with spinach, tomatoes, and cotija cheese. Blaine came back and sat down in front of one of the plates.

"Thanks again, Hattie. This looks delicious."

You look delicious, she thought. Doing her best to ignore that thought, she smiled at Blaine.

"This might seem like a random question, but have you ever been to the mission here? I only ask because your new apartment is closer to it than my place, and I was just curious." Picking up his fork, he took a bite of the eggs she had cooked.

"I haven't yet, no. It's one of the things I've been wanting to do."

"That might be something fun for you to do while Jayne is here, you know, if you need a break from unpacking and assembling things, that is," Blaine commented.

"That's a great idea," she said. "I assume you've been?"

Blaine let out a small chuckle. "No, actually, I haven't. Isn't that funny since it's right there? But I've been to a few of the others. I went to San Juan Capistrano a while back, and I visited some others while growing up. I always thought they were pretty interesting. I remember one trip as a kid when we went to the mission in Solvang and then stopped at some European bakery to get cream puffs. It was the first time I remember having a cream puff, so that memory really stuck with me." Blaine wore a dreamy smile.

"I can see why. I love cream puffs, but hardly ever eat them. Once for work, we ended up with an extra container of the little bite-sized ones left over from some fundraising event. I ended up taking the whole thing home and demolishing them all in about four days." Hattie laughed at the memory.

"Oh god, those things? I can't buy them ever again. I have zero self-control, or at least I did the last time I tried. I ate them all in a single day. Needless to say, I didn't feel so hot the next day." Blaine grimaced at the memory.

"Oof, I can only imagine," she replied. "I know how I felt plowing through them in the short time I did, and I can only imagine that feeling compacted."

Blaine scraped the last bit of egg into his mouth. Taking another swig of his coffee, he said, "Thanks again for breakfast, Hattie. I'll see you later for tacos and margs." Blaine stood, took his dishes to the sink, and, after brushing his teeth, he was gone for the day.

Hattie found herself standing in the kitchen, holding the now-empty frying pan and wondering how she could stop these thoughts of Blaine. She was overcome by a sense of sadness. As much as she looked forward to moving into her new place, she knew she would miss living here. She hadn't missed how Blaine had called it "my place" instead of the house, as they'd begun calling his home while they had been living together. But the sadness wasn't just about the comfort of living with Blaine; it was about Blaine and what appeared to be her unreturned and unexpected feelings for him.

Chapter 32

Blaine

Blaine wasn't sure what had possessed him to offer to take Hattie to dinner. A final roommates' dinner, he reminded himself. *Sure, buddy, you keep telling yourself that.* He had done so well this week hiding his warring feelings. Anytime he started to struggle, he reminded himself of what Emma, the older lady in the church, had told him: that he and Hattie were puzzle pieces that might come together at some point, but only if and when the universe was ready. The older woman's presence had soothed him on Saturday when he had needed it most, but he was still a little weirded out by how she had seemingly disappeared.

When he realized that tonight was Hattie's last night with him, he wanted to do something. While he was confident they would see each other again, it would be different with her living in her own place. It was going to be strange going back to just him and Marmalade. She was going to miss Hattie, too.

Hattie pulled up to the house at the same time Blaine did. "Hey," he said as he climbed out of his car.

"Hi! How was work?" she asked.

"Work was work. Not a bad day, just one of those ones that felt long. I'm for sure looking forward to street tacos, assuming you still want to go, that is." Part of him was hoping she would say no, while the other part of him desperately wanted her to say yes.

"Are you kidding? I've been thinking about tacos all day! I was trying to finish up some stuff I know you won't use, so I ended up with a really bizarre lunch. All I could think about while I was eating it was the promise of tacos later. And, I know I can't have more than one since they're so strong, but I definitely want one of their margaritas too—they are so good!"

Blaine gave a slight smile and laughed. "Maybe I'll have one too. It's a celebration of sorts after all. Why don't we get a rideshare down there if that's the case?" he asked, unlocking the door. Marmalade darted out to greet them, winding her body in and out of both of their legs.

Hattie bent down and gave the cat a scratch on the head. "Hey, Lady M. We missed you, too."

Walking in and setting down their bags, Blaine said, "Whenever you want to go, just let me know and I'll call a rideshare."

"That sounds great. I'm just going to change quickly, but I'm happy to head down anytime after that."

"I'll go ahead and feed Marmalade while you are getting changed."

Hattie caught Blaine snuggling his cat when she came out of her bedroom. "Oh, Marmalade, I'm going to miss you!" she said, leaning over the back of the chair Blaine was sitting in to pet her. The action caused her face to be right next to Blaine's, her loose auburn hair cascading down over his shoulder and chest. Blaine took a deep breath in, relishing and hating being this close to Hattie all at once. She always smelled like roses. That was another thing he was going to miss. Maybe he should look into getting a rose-scented candle or something. *It wouldn't be the same,* he thought. Man, he needed to get a hold of himself. Suddenly, his emotions were all over the place.

"Ready?" Hattie asked.

"Yeah. Let me call a ride." Blaine was doing his best to pull himself together.

"Let me, please!" she said. "If dinner is your treat, the least I can do is pay for a ride there and back."

"That would be great. I'll just run in and use the bathroom quickly while we wait." Blaine displaced a now grumpy Marmalade and stood. He didn't actually need to use the bathroom; he just needed an excuse for some space. Blaine was experiencing a lot more feelings tonight than he could afford to. He just needed a minute to collect himself and resurrect the walls he'd been so good at hiding behind this week.

Closing the bathroom door behind him, Blaine leaned against it and took several deep breaths. There was an ache in his chest, and he knew it was because Hattie was leaving. Moisture began to gather in his eyes. He silently wiped away the tears before they could fall.

He took in another long, shuddering breath. Forcing himself to pull himself together. He could do this. He could sit across the table from her and simply enjoy their last evening together. For the sake of appearance, he flushed the toilet and washed his hands just as Hattie yelled down the hall that their ride would be there in two minutes.

"Great," he said, coming out and plastering a smile on his face. "Tacos and margs, let's go!"

After placing their orders, margaritas in hand, Blaine said, "I would like to propose a toast. I already said something along these lines, but I'm glad you dropped into my life the way you did, Hattie. I needed a little bit of a shakeup, and that came in the form of you. You've been a fantastic roommate and an amazing addition to my collection of friends. It's going to be a little strange not seeing you all of the time, but I have no doubt that we'll see each other often enough, starting this weekend when I help you move heavy objects." The last bit was said with a smile. "So, cheers to being blessed to have you in my life."

"I'm not sure I'm worth all that praise, but thanks for being you, Blaine. Especially for helping me move heavy objects this weekend." They both laughed at that and clinked their glasses together.

"Now that you will be totally settled, what will you do?" he asked.

"I know! I'll have all this free time instead of stressing about where I will live. Honestly, I don't know. I came out here to get away from Galen and figure out who I am, and while I've been doing some of that, the stability of being in a place that's mine and mine alone will be good. I think I am going to start going to that Bollywood dance class. I don't know. Maybe I'll start crafting again. I used to do a lot of crochet and things like that, but stopped. Once upon a time, I used to do some writing; maybe I'll start that again. Or maybe I'll do something entirely new! I'm sure there are plenty of things out there that I would enjoy but haven't tried yet. Carly and her friends, who meet monthly, were talking about maybe doing a sip and paint thing that sounded kind of fun."

"You'll be great at whatever you set your mind to," Blaine told Hattie sincerely. *Ease up there, buddy.* This was starting to feel a little bit like a flirty friend date, and that was not what he had intended. Remembering the pep talk he'd given himself in the bathroom, changing topics, he said, "Eli's birthday is coming up in a few weeks, and I was thinking about throwing a small get-together for him."

"Oh! That's a great idea. I'd love to come."

"I thought we could just do it at the house with our close mutual friends. The weather should still be nice enough to do it in the backyard."

"One of the perks of California over upstate New York at this time of year for sure," Hattie said.

"Now that our friend Thomas has finished filming *Wings of Justice*, he said he and his girlfriend Jessie would be able to come down. I'd love to surprise Eli with both Thomas and the party. He loves surprises but is often hard to surprise. I was hoping I might be able to get your help with part of it."

"Anything. Eli has been a lifesaver since I moved, especially while you were gone."

"Awesome. Maybe you can invite him out the night of the party and then ask if you can stop by on your way to pick up something you forgot that I just happened to find. We can sort out those details later."

"That's a great idea, Blaine! I'm sure he'll love that," she said.

They easily fell into conversation afterward, and Blaine was truly glad he had asked Hattie to do this. It was good practice for whatever this new relationship between them was. His brief emotional outburst from earlier seemed to have passed, which he was happy about.

As they were waiting to pay, Hattie got an uncomfortable look on her face. "Are you okay?" he asked.

Hattie sighed. "Yes, I... I have a question that I probably should have asked sooner, but well, I didn't." She began nervously picking at her drink napkin. Blaine hated to see her so uncomfortable.

Doing his best to put her at ease, he said, "Hattie, you can ask me anything. If it's something I don't want to answer, I'll just tell you."

"You are so much better at that than I am. Boundaries, what a concept," she said with a shy smile. He wasn't entirely sure that was the truth, but he kept that to himself.

"What is it?" he urged.

"Are we, that is, maybe you have already, but, um..." she huffed out a breath. Looking up at the ceiling, she blurted out, "Does Eli know that we slept together? And if not, should we tell him? I realize he's your best friend, and you may have already told him, and that's fine if you did. I would just like to know if that's the case."

With that seemingly innocent question, pictures of their night together flooded Blaine's brain, presumably since all of the blood that should have been in it shot to his crotch. "Um," Blaine started hoarsely. Clearing his throat, he continued, "I haven't told him, but we should probably tell him, just in case it comes up at some point. I don't want him to think we've kept anything important from him."

"Okay, I just didn't want to accidentally slip and say something, so I actually think it's the right call. So, do you want to tell him, or should I?"

"Why don't you let me? He and I were going to meet up for breakfast while you're getting the truck and things like that on Saturday. I can tell him then."

"Great. Sounds good."

Chapter 33

Hattie

Hattie was all packed and ready to go. She just needed to load her suitcases into her car and pick up Jayne from the San Diego airport. Unfortunately, Jayne's flight had been delayed multiple times already, which meant she would arrive ridiculously late that night. With nothing productive to do without unpacking something, Hattie started to deep clean Blaine's kitchen.

The front door opened, and Blaine laughed when he saw her standing on a stool in the kitchen, wiping off the upper cabinets.

"What are you doing?" he asked, smiling. "I assumed you would already be on your way to San Diego. I was surprised to see your car still here when I pulled up."

"Sadly, Jayne's flight keeps getting pushed back. She was supposed to get in at 6:25, but right now it's looking like it's going to be closer to eleven at this rate."

"That sucks. I'm sorry she's been delayed so much. I know you were looking forward to spending some time with her tonight."

Hattie's phone chimed with an incoming message. Hattie climbed down from the stool and picked up her phone. Glancing at the screen, she said, "Fuck!" before letting out a huge sigh.

"Delayed again?" Blaine guessed.

Hattie nodded. Several more chimes followed in quick succession. Hattie picked up her phone again and read Jayne's messages:

Jayne: Plane now arriving at midnight.

Jayne: I'm getting in so late, I'm going to just take a cab to the hotel.

Jayne: You should stay at Blaine's tonight.

Hattie quickly typed out a reply.

Hattie: Don't be silly. I will come get you.

Jayne: No, don't. We'll both just be exhausted for your move tomorrow, and no one needs that. Get some sleep and some last-minute kitty snuggles. Come find me in the morning.

Hattie: But you're coming all this way to help me. I feel bad.

Jayne: Hattie.

Hattie: I'm still coming.

Jayne: Hattie.

Jayne: Elizabeth.

Hattie: Don't you dare, Jayne!

Jayne: Then don't make me.

Hattie: Fine, I'll stay at Blaine's tonight!

Jayne: I thought you might see it my way.

Hattie*: I'll see you in the morning, you bitch.*
Jayne*: Love you too.*
Jayne*: Bring me coffee.*

Blaine was watching Hattie with a look of amusement when she finally glanced up.

"Everything okay?" he asked.

"Jayne's insisting that I get some sleep, and she'll take a cab to the hotel, whatever time she gets in. So, I guess I'm staying here tonight, assuming that's alright with you, that is."

"Of course. You still live here until tomorrow," he said. Blaine was too nice sometimes. Hattie ignored the little pang of emotion in her chest.

"I guess this means we get a bonus last night together, unless you had other plans?" She really hoped he didn't have plans. The last thing she wanted to do was sit alone in this house right now.

"Nope," Blaine replied. "I was probably just going to watch a movie or something like that and try to take it easy since tomorrow is going to be a busy day. Wanna join me one last time for old times' sake?"

The thought of one more quiet, easy night with Blaine warmed Hattie. Given all the stress of getting ready to move, sitting quietly with Blaine and just relaxing already had her shoulders dropping from where they had hiked up with stress.

"That sounds lovely," she replied.

"I picked last time, so it's your turn to choose," he said.

Hattie thought for a moment before smiling and said, "I think the only way to end this is to finish how we started—with Lady Marmalade. I think we should watch *Moulin Rouge.*"

Blaine laughed. "A perfect bookend," he said, returning her smile. "Let's have dinner and then we can air pop some popcorn and settle in."

She was going to miss this, the easy camaraderie, the laughter. Forcing those thoughts away, she smiled and said, "Sounds like a plan. Let me just put this cleaning stuff away."

"Thanks for doing that, by the way."

"You're welcome. I needed something to do with my hands to keep busy, so I decided to do some deep cleaning since no one ever has time for that."

"I'll go change while you put things away, and then I'll make us some dinner. There's some chicken that I was going to use to make chicken salad, so it will be quick to pull together."

Blaine queued up the movie and made popcorn while Hattie quickly made short work of the few dishes that were there. They settled into what had become their respective ends of the couch, with the bowl of popcorn sitting between them. As if she sensed they were watching 'her' movie, Marmalade sauntered out of wherever she had been taking her evening catnap and graced them with a show of her flexibility, appropriately timed to the can-can scene. They both laughed, which apparently insulted Marmalade's ego, so she wandered off elsewhere in the house.

Hattie was disappointed not to see Jayne until tomorrow, but she was also glad to have this unexpected chance to spend a little bit more time with Blaine. She reached over to grab another handful of popcorn at the same time as Blaine. Their fingertips grazed each other, and Hattie had to hold in the shudder that wanted to wrack her body. The touch brought memories of their night together flooding back. Doing her best to act naturally, she pulled her hand out at a normal rate and ignored the feelings racing through her body.

When the movie ended, they cleaned up and started to get ready for bed. Hattie was just stepping out of her room as Blaine was heading into his. He stopped just before closing his door.

"I don't know if I ever told you this or not, Hattie, but you've been a great roommate. Thanks for making what could have been a really strange situation an awesome one instead. I'm... I'm glad I met you," he said. "I just wanted you to know that. Goodnight." Before Hattie could respond, he shut the door.

"Goodnight," she said to the closed door, fighting off all the emotions that were threatening to force their way to the surface. Hattie crawled into bed and dreamt of all the things that could never be with Blaine.

Chapter 34

Hattie

In the morning, Hattie pulled up to the hotel Jayne was staying at, coffee and breakfast in hand. Knocking on the door to the room number Jayne texted her, the door slowly cracked open, revealing a sleepy-looking Jayne. When she saw it was Hattie, Jayne threw open the door, wrapping her arms around Hattie in a fierce hug as they both squealed in delight. Hattie was grateful for the little plastic stoppers on the tops of the to-go cups; otherwise, they likely would have been splashing hot coffee all over each other.

"You're here! You're actually here!" Hattie exclaimed.

"I know!!" Jayne responded just as enthusiastically. "Oh my god, is that coffee? I love you so much," Jayne said as Hattie handed her one of the cups as she walked into the room.

"I got breakfast sandwiches, too," Hattie said, setting a paper bag on the little table by the window.

"You are a godsend," Jayne said, opening the curtain to let in the morning light.

"I figure it's the least I can do since you came all this way just to help me move in." Hattie smiled at her friend, her heart lighter at seeing Jayne in person after so long and after so much had happened.

"Correction: I came because I love you, and I'm happy to help you move in. Mostly, I came to see this hot man you have been living with for the past month get all sweaty lifting heavy things." Hattie tensed when Jayne said that last part. "Ooh, what was that look?" Jayne examined Hattie and gasped, "Oh my gosh, you're jealous!"

"No! I just..." Hattie started, looking at the floor, unable to finish what she had begun to say.

"Oh, hun... did you catch feelings?" Jayne asked, in all seriousness. Hattie shrugged and hung her head. Jayne reached out and gave her a side hug. "Tell Auntie Jayne all about it." Hattie chuffed out a laugh at that. With an arm around Hattie, Jayne lowered them to a seated position on the side of the queen-sized bed.

"The thing is, I..." Hattie started, surprised to find tears welling up in her eyes, "I am the one who suggested the one-night rule, but now, now I wish there could be more nights. More days. I want all of it."

"But Blaine doesn't feel the same?" Jayne asked, setting her coffee cup down on one of the nightstands.

"I don't know. The morning after, he gave me the most intense kiss I've ever received in my life. I mean, we are talking molten here, Jayne! After kissing the hell out of me, he promised he would respect my wishes and never mention it again. I literally couldn't get off the counter for a solid couple of minutes because my legs couldn't support me. Ever since then, he's been a total gentleman and hasn't said or done anything else. I feel firmly friend-zoned."

"Ouch," Jayne said, cringing.

"Yeah, ouch," Hattie said, brushing a few tears from her cheek. "We both agreed on just one night for certain reasons, so even if he wanted to, I don't think he would because, see previous reasons."

"But you've changed your mind, so maybe he could, too?" Jayne got up and grabbed the box of tissues from the hotel bathroom, handing it to Hattie.

"Maybe, but I don't want to risk asking him in case it's not how he feels. I don't need that humiliation on top of everything else. I also need to remember that I had valid reasons for only wanting it to be one night." Hattie softly blew her nose and wiped away her tears with the tissue Jayne had given her.

"Are you sure, though?" Jayne asked, sounding a little frustrated. "Hattie, do you really think you don't know who you are without a man?" Hattie hesitated, unsure of what to say. "Because, if you ask me—I've known you a long time now—you have always been you. Yes, when you were with Galen, your flame was dimmer, but it was still there. You were still fundamentally Hattie. Since you moved out here, I've seen your flame shine as brightly as it used to. You are thriving out here, even though it's only been a few months. You've got a job that challenges you and that you enjoy. You've made friends. You've tried new things. You get to see the ocean every damn day if you want. If you need another analogy, you were like a dirty penny, and now you've gone and gotten yourself all shined up. Part of that, I think, is due to Blaine, but most of the credit goes to you for simply being brave enough to take the step of seizing what was left of your life and leaving Galen to pick up his own damn dry cleaning." By this time, tears were falling steadily from Hattie's eyes, both from her feelings about Blaine and the kind, fierce words her friend had just spoken.

"I love you, Jayne," Hattie said, wiping more tears from her cheeks. Jayne wrapped her arms around Hattie in another hug.

"I love you too. You don't have to decide what to do about Blaine right now, but think about the reasons you're not willing to try and what you could lose if you do or if you don't. And don't make me yell at you again. Now, I was promised a breakfast sandwich and the chance to get all sweaty. Is that something you can help me with?" Hattie laughed, wiping her eyes.

"That is most definitely something I can help you with," Hattie said, handing her friend one of the egg sandwiches from the bag after giving her another hug.

Blaine

On Saturday, Blaine picked up Eli and drove them to their favorite crepe place. They didn't want to eat too much or take too much time before helping Hattie move, so crepes were perfect. They ordered and then took a seat by the window. The sun streamed in, warming their table. Blaine unzipped his grey sweatshirt and pushed up the sleeves. He had dressed for getting hot and sweaty, but the morning was still chilly, or at least chilly for Oceanside, so the sun felt nice. Eli slid into his seat across from him. Blaine had been trying to figure out how to tell Eli about him and Hattie. He honestly wasn't sure how to bring that sort of thing into conversation, so he decided to come right out with it.

"So, I have something to tell you."

"Have I had enough coffee for this?" Eli asked, suspiciously raising one eyebrow.

"Probably not," Blaine laughed. "Hattie and I slept together." Eli nearly spit out the sip of coffee he had just taken.

"You should warn a person with more than just 'probably not' before you say shit like that," Eli said, coughing. Blaine pulled a few paper napkins from the dispenser on their table and handed them to Eli.

"Sorry. I just wasn't sure how else to tell you."

Eli finished wiping the rogue drips of coffee off his face and tossed the crumpled napkins onto the table. "I don't know, maybe ease into it a little? Jesus. So, are you two an item now?"

Blaine huffed out a derisive laugh and rolled his eyes. "No," he said without any mirth.

"Hmm." Eli looked skeptical.

"We agreed it was just for the one night," Blaine forged on. "We just wanted to let you know so you aren't surprised if one or the other of us mentions it."

"And... you're okay with this?" Eli asked, wrapping both hands around his mug.

Blaine paused before responding, "Yes, I don't love it, but yes. Neither one of us is in a place where we can do the relationship thing, so this is better for everyone."

"Uh-huh," Eli said cocking his eyebrow again.

"It's fine, really. We're still going to be friends."

"That look that just crossed your face tells me there's more to this than you're willing to admit."

"It is what it is, and this is how it's going to be," Blaine said firmly, picking up his mug and taking a sip of his coffee.

"Damnit, man. You are stubborn. Can I ask, knowing that I have zero interest in sleeping with Hattie, how was it?"

"You may not," Blaine said adamantly.

"Wow, so it was that good, huh? Interesting," he said, picking up his mug and taking a sip. Blaine shot him a withering look. Eli laughed. "That's what I thought," he said.

"Just shut up and eat your crepes so we can go move some heavy shit for *our friend.*"

Chapter 35

Hattie

Hattie and Jayne pulled up in front of the storage unit just as Blaine and Eli arrived. Jayne let out a long, low whistle.

"Which one is Blaine? Because they are both fine as hell," Jayne whispered as they exited the car.

"Shh," Hattie whispered as Eli and Blaine stepped closer.

"Hi," Blaine said.

"Mornin'," came from Eli.

"Hey, guys. Eli, Blaine, this is my dearest friend, Jayne. Jayne, this is Eli, whom I know I've told you about…" she said, gesturing to Eli, who, despite the cool weather, was dressed in basketball shorts and a sleeveless shirt, showing off his impressive biceps. Blaine, on the other hand, had opted for athletic pants and a dark tee.

"All good things, I'm sure," Eli said, holding out a hand to shake.

"…and this is Blaine." Blaine stepped forward to offer his hand as well.

"Jayne, it's so great to finally meet you after everything I've heard about you."

"Not all good things, I'm sure," Jayne said, laughing.

"There may have been a few stories," Blaine said, smiling.

"Alright, muscles, as much fun as all this chit-chat is, sadly, Hattie's stuff isn't going to move itself. Let's get this sweaty show on the road," Jayne said as Hattie unlocked the unit and slid the door open.

"I'm not sure how I feel about being reduced to man meat," Eli said playfully.

Blaine patted him on the shoulder and said, "You'll get over it."

Jayne gave Eli an appreciative glance up and down and said, "You, my dear man, are scrumptious, and if I wasn't already coupled up, I'd pack you up in my suitcase and take you home with me."

"Jayne!" Hattie exclaimed, shocked. Meanwhile, Eli looked both embarrassed and smug.

"It's okay, Hattie, when you've got it..." he trailed off, and Blaine playfully smacked him upside the head.

"Come on, Scrumptious," Blaine said, "let's get that loveseat out of the way first."

For the next hour or so, they worked to load the furniture, boxes, and flat pack that Hattie had managed to acquire during her short time here. After the truck was full and the storage unit empty, Eli offered to drive the truck to Hattie's new apartment, which she was extremely grateful for. She hated driving the moving truck. It was big and boxy, and she wasn't confident doing it. So, instead, Eli followed behind as Hattie led the way to her apartment with Jayne riding shotgun. Blaine brought up the rear of their little moving caravan.

If Jayne had any further comments about Hattie and Blaine, she kept them to herself. Instead, she asked Hattie about some of the things they were seeing and fun activities they could do around town, either on this visit or another time. Hattie recalled Blaine's suggestion of visiting the mission, and Jayne agreed that it could be interesting.

"And now the fun part," Eli said, looking up at the three-story complex that was to be Hattie's new home. "Please tell me your unit isn't on the top floor."

Hattie smiled. "It's not. It's on the second floor." Eli let out a groan.

Blaine patted him on the back and said with a grin, "It could be worse! Aren't you glad you've been taking all those dance classes?"

"Shut up, man. Come on, let's start with the big stuff first."

They spent the next several hours lugging boxes and furniture up the stairs to Hattie's new apartment. Eli and Blaine entered the unit and set down the three boxes they'd each been carrying. Because of their friendly yet competitive natures, they pushed each other and, as a result, carried several boxes each trip, making the move go even faster.

Eli leaned back, stretching out his back, and said, "That's it, Hattie, that's the last of it."

"Wow, really? That's incredible! You guys are a godsend. Thank you so much for your help! This would have taken Jayne and me all day on our own. So, thank you. I genuinely mean it. Now, I know

I promised you pizza and beer if you helped, but what do you guys think about showers, instead? Then I can buy you a nicer dinner later tonight. There's no way I'll have this place sorted in time to be able to make any sort of food tonight, so since I'll be eating out, I can at least repay you with more than just Domino's and Dos Equis, not that there's anything wrong with that. I just feel like you deserve more. Unless you have other plans, of course," she said.

"Honestly, as good as pizza sounds, a shower sounds so much better right now," Blaine said. He lifted the hem of his shirt to wipe the sweat off his face, and Hattie couldn't help but glance at the exposed flesh of his abdomen, with its tantalizing Adonis belt and treasure trail of hair. She quickly looked away before either man noticed. Jayne looked at her as if she knew exactly what Hattie had been thinking about.

Eli pulled his phone out of his pocket and tapped on it. "Yeah, looks like I'm free, and I agree. Some cold water and a hot shower sound amazing right about now. If we offer to take the moving truck back for you, would that earn us dessert, too?" Eli asked, brows waggling.

Hattie laughed and shook her head. "Definitely," she said. "Now, I would hug you, but you're both disgusting right now. So go earn that dessert, and we'll see you later. How about six at London's? You guys always talk about that place, but I have yet to go."

Eli let out a little moan and gave an odd smile. "They've got the best fries."

Blaine laughed but agreed. "He's not wrong; they do. They even have Brussels sprouts," he said with a wink in Hattie's direction.

"Perfect, we'll see you guys there. Thanks again, and for taking the truck back, too." The guys waved and headed out.

Hattie ran to the bathroom, and when she came out, Jayne was staring out the window, a bottle of water in her hand. "You good, Jayne?"

"Oh, I am. You're right. He definitely doesn't seem like a tattoo guy." Hattie joined Jayne at the window and saw her watching Blaine and Eli, who were chatting by the moving truck. Blaine had fully taken off his shirt and was wiping sweat from his neck with it, his tattoo on full display. Memories of her kissing up his inked skin flashed in her mind.

"Uh-huh, yeah, and it's much more beautiful up close." Blaine poured water over his face and hair. Heat surged to her belly at the sight, and Hattie had to force herself to look away. Before the guys could glance up and see her and Jayne creepily staring at them, Hattie stepped away, turning toward the mountain of boxes, and asked, "So, where should we start?"

Chapter 36

Blaine

"So I'll go ahead and drive this beast back to the rental place, and you can meet me there?" Eli asked. They stood next to the moving truck after taking a minute to rest and drink some cold water.

Blaine pulled his shirt over his head, wiping the sweat from his face, neck, and torso. "Sure, sounds good."

"I don't know about you, but I think a shower now and dinner later sounds more than fair for the work we did."

"Yeah, it wasn't too bad. It would have been a bitch for those two on their own. Not that I doubt they could have done it! They're feisty enough, especially with their powers combined, to do anything they want to," Blaine said, smiling.

Eli chuckled at his remark. Blaine splashed some cool water on his head, wiping it back through his hair.

"You doing okay with all of this? I can tell it's been a little weird for you today," Eli said.

Blaine shrugged one shoulder. "Like I said this morning, it is what it is, and it will be fine, somehow or another. Thanks for checking in, though."

"Anytime, man. That's what friends are for, right? Alright, let's get this over with and get to that shower. Hang on, that sounded wrong..."

Before Eli could try again, Blaine said, "Please just get in the truck now and stop talking. You'll only make it more awkward if you keep going." Blaine shook his head with amusement as he turned and walked toward his car.

Hot water flowed in rivulets down his body as Blaine stepped into the shower, groaning at how good it felt. He had always loved showers. They were the one place where, no matter the chaos in the world or his house growing up, he was guaranteed peace and space to think. Naturally, his mind drifted to this morning and the woman he couldn't stop thinking about. He knew he had to push all thoughts of her aside, but it was easier said than done. Hattie had shaken up his life, so maybe he needed to find a way to shake things up again to get her out of his head.

Blaine felt more human after his shower. He tossed on a pair of jeans and a black T-shirt. Running his hands through his hair to style it, he decided it was time for a haircut. Would he have time to get one this afternoon? He was definitely going to try. It wasn't much, but maybe even that small thing would help his thoughts move on to something else.

Blaine grabbed a bottle of sparkling water from the fridge and sat on the couch, flipping through a magazine that had come in the mail. Marmalade sashayed out of Hattie's room... wait, no, not Hattie's. It wasn't hers anymore, and he needed to stop thinking of it that way. It was simply the guest room slash his sometimes office. Seemingly, sensing that he needed her, Marmalade hopped up onto Blaine's lap, sitting herself down right on top of his magazine.

"Sometimes you are such a cat," he said, shaking his head as she kneaded biscuits on the glossy pages.

"Meowr," Marmalade chirped in return

"You're a good cat, though. Are you going to miss Hattie?"

"Meowr," she replied as if she understood his question. He stroked her back, her presence once again giving him comfort during a time when he needed it.

"Me too, Miss Marmalade. Me too," Blaine sighed. "But there's nothing to be done about it. Rules were made for a reason. She's gone, and we just have to accept that. It's not like she's gone from our lives forever; she just won't be a daily fixture in them." He sat petting her, enjoying her rumbling purr. Blaine needed to take his own advice and accept the situation, not just sit here and wallow in it. At that moment, he decided to do something he'd been too chicken to do for a long time.

"Right, well, sitting around here moping isn't going to accomplish anything, is it? I'm off to get a haircut and then dinner. I'll see you in a bit," he said, stopping to look back at the cat, who was now licking the inside of her leg as evidence of her displeasure at being moved from his lap. Maybe he should cut back on the talking to the cat... *Pull yourself together, man,* he thought. Hattie had only been gone a few hours, and he'd already devolved into a man having imaginary conversations with his feline companion.

Blaine pulled up to the barber shop, crossing his fingers that they'd be able to get him in this late in the day on a Saturday, and on short notice. Blaine pulled the door open and was greeted by the energetic sounds of Green Day's "American Idiot."

"How can we help you?" the guy behind the counter asked as Blaine strode into the shop.

"I don't have an appointment, but I was hoping for a cut this afternoon if you've got time." Normally, Blaine was a lot more structured with his planning, but the last month with Hattie had thrown him off a bit.

"It's your lucky day. I can get you in right now. My three o'clock just canceled."

"Fantastic," Blaine said.

"Come on over." Blaine followed him to a black swivel chair and took a seat. The stylist spun him around so he was facing the mirror and said, "My name's Charlie."

Using the mirror to look at the stylist, he replied, "Hi, I'm Blaine."

"Nice to meet you. So, Blaine, what are we doing? Same thing, just shorter?"

Blaine looked at Charlie in the mirror and said, "Actually, I'd like to do something different. I want to shake things up a bit."

"Ooh, I like the sound of that. What are you thinking?"

"You ever seen *Avengers: Endgame*?" he asked, feeling slightly dorky.

"Sure have. I'm a huge comic book geek, so I've seen all the Marvel movies," Charlie said. Blaine had lucked into the right guy at the right time.

"I was thinking Hawkeye, post-Ronin, you know, with the super short sides?"

"Aw yeah, that'd be a great look for you. Let's do it! Come on back to the bowl, and let's get started."

Blaine ran his hand through his shorn hair, glancing at himself in the review mirror. Well, this was definitely different for him. Edgy was not how anyone had ever described him, but this haircut definitely was. Charlie had more or less left the top alone, just cleaning it up a little and slicking it back, but he shaved the sides close, all the way along the back of his head. He wondered what his coworkers would think of his almost mohawk come Monday. On that note, he wondered what Hattie would think. Eli, he knew, would give him shit for it, but he didn't care. After all, that's what friends are for. It was time to debut his new look. He slid his keys out of the ignition and headed for the door of the restaurant.

Blaine heard Hattie's laugh as soon as he walked in. Funny how he could zero in on that sound despite the noises of the restaurant, after such a short time. He spotted the booth where the three of them were sitting, signaling to the server that his friends were already there. He took a fortifying breath to steady himself and headed to their table. Eli was the first to notice him.

"Damn, man! I leave you alone for a few hours unsupervised, and you come back looking like a parakeet." Eli grinned the whole time he was saying it, so Blaine knew that he secretly liked the look. Eli dropped his arm from the back of the booth so that Blaine could slide in next to him.

Jayne piped up next, saying, "Hawkeye is my favorite Avenger, too," with a wink. Hattie sat there in silence, her mouth slightly open.

"How did the unpacking go this afternoon?" Blaine asked as he took his seat next to Eli.

Hattie appeared to find her voice again. "Good. I'm realizing just how much stuff I still need to buy."

"Like a coffee pot," Jayne piped in.

"Yeah, like that. So, some shopping might be in order tomorrow, but we got sheets on the bed and at least found the coffee mugs, so we can drink coffee once we finally get a coffee maker."

Blaine couldn't help but offer, "If there is anything you need in the meantime, feel free to borrow some of my stuff."

"Does that include the coffee pot?" Jayne teased.

"You can pry that out of my cold, dead hands first," Blaine said with a smile.

Hattie laughed, that beautiful, musical sound of hers. "Yeah, you don't even want to joke about that. You haven't seen this guy before coffee and running. I only saw it once, and it wasn't pretty."

But you are, he thought.

"Ugh, you're one of those, aren't you?" Jayne asked.

"One of those what?" Blaine asked, bemused.

"Those people who get up early to exercise. Blech, no thank you."

"Yeah, I'm more of a PM yoga class kind of guy myself," Eli said. "Despite that, he's always trying to get my sorry ass out of bed and come with him. I did it once, and I swore never again."

"Twinkle Toes over here does the same thing to me, in reverse, begging me to stay out all night dancing or going to dance classes," Blaine said, gesturing towards Eli.

"Hey, the ladies like a man who knows how to move his hips," Jayne said with a little wiggle.

A little distractedly, Eli said, "Yeah, that's true."

Marcus, the server who often helped them, brought over a basket of fries and some fried pickles. "We went ahead and ordered some apps. We were starving and couldn't wait to try the fries you were raving about," Jayne said as Marcus slid the baskets onto the table.

"Can I get you anything to drink?" Marcus asked Blaine. "The rest of your drink orders should be right up," he said, nodding to the others.

"Can I get a Hendrick's gin and tonic, extra lime?"

"Sure thing. Anyone else need anything?" They indicated they were all set for now. Marcus left and came back a few minutes later with a tray laden with drinks. They ordered their entrees, and then their conversation shifted back to Blaine's haircut.

"So, why the change, man?" Eli asked.

"It's something I've been thinking about doing for a while now. I just hadn't pulled the trigger. After my shower this afternoon, I decided I needed to get a cut, and while I was there, I just thought, 'what the hell' and went for it."

"Well, I think it looks great, dare I say, sexy even?" Jayne said.

"Yeah," Hattie quietly agreed next to her. She hadn't said much all evening, but Blaine just assumed that was because she was tired from the move and all the stress of the day.

"So you get a sexy haircut and think that gives you the right to manspread beyond your half of the booth?" Eli said, nudging his thigh, laughing.

"Me? You want to talk about manspreading? You're the king of it!" Blaine fired back. Beneath the table, they started jostling each other's thighs with their knees.

"Boys," Jayne said, giving them an admonishing look, "there's an easy fix to this. Blaine, stand up," she commanded. Based on her tone, this was no brooking argument, so he stood. Jayne slid out of the booth, pointed to where she had been sitting, and said, "Sit." She smoothly slid into his vacated seat, reached across the table, pulled her drink closer to her, and simultaneously pushed his to the opposite side of the table.

Blaine stood awkwardly next to the booth. "Well, are you going to sit down, or what?" Jayne asked innocently. He figured he didn't have much choice and slid in next to Hattie. He did his best to make sure she had space in what now felt like a cozy booth. Every now and then, their thighs would touch, and heat would flare up from where their bodies had met. Somehow, sharing the bench with Hattie made the booth feel smaller than when he'd been sitting next to a six-foot-two Eli.

Marcus returned a while later with their entrees and an entirely different attitude. Where before he'd seemed like his usual chummy self, at least based on Blaine's past experiences with him, he now appeared almost frosty.

"How's your shift going?" Eli asked, obviously sensing the change in their server as well.

"Just fine, thank you," Marcus responded in a clipped tone, avoiding looking at Eli.

Blaine was worried that maybe someone had been rude to Marcus. He wouldn't say he knew him well by any stretch of the imagination, but he'd always seemed like a perfectly nice, friendly guy. He was an attentive server when they'd been in and always got their orders right. "Hope your other tables are treating you okay tonight," he said.

Marcus looked at Blaine and said, "They've been fine," and more gently, "Thanks for asking." At that moment, Marcus seemed to deflate slightly. "Is there anything else I can get you?" Blaine could have sworn he saw a strange look flicker across Eli's face. Glancing at Hattie, he saw her looking at Eli, too, before turning to look at him. She gave him an almost imperceptible nod, as if to say, *'Yeah, I saw that too.'*

Eli only ate about half his food and then declared he was full. In Blaine's experience, Eli always finished his whole meal, sometimes eating part of Blaine's as well.

"You okay, Eli?" Blaine asked.

"Yeah, just tired. All that heavy lifting wore me out," he said with a wink toward Hattie. "Mind if I get by, Jayne? I need to use the little gentleman's room. Be back in a jiffy."

After Eli walked away, Blaine turned to Hattie and asked, "Does something seem slightly off to you?"

"Yes," she replied, "but again, I'm not sure I could say what." Blaine felt exactly the same. For the past month, Eli had been busier than usual and was always a little cagy when Blaine asked him what he was up to. He had a suspicion that it might have something to do with Marcus, but he couldn't say for sure. Sometimes, Blaine wished Eli didn't keep things quite so close to his chest. What the hell was going on with Eli?

Chapter 37

Hattie

A few weeks later

Hattie was finally beginning to feel at home in her new place. She and Jayne had gone shopping the day after she moved in and bought most of what she still needed. She now had a small set of matching dishes, a couple of pots and pans for cooking, a cozy reading chair, and her one splurge—compliments of Jayne—a fancy coffee maker/espresso machine. Jayne had said that this way, Hattie could spoil her with homemade lattes whenever she visited. Needless to say, Hattie loved her housewarming gift. A few pieces of art hung on the walls, and framed photos of her with Jayne, and with Sophia and Madison, rested on top of the ladder bookcase she'd bought, the little figurine of Marmalade that Blaine had given her in the center. She had even picked up a few houseplants and had managed to keep them alive so far. For the first time in a long time, she was in a space that felt safe, comfortable, and fully hers.

Galen had tried to reach out again. Hattie simply responded with her P.O. Box address, which she had decided to keep for a few more months, and ignored everything else he'd said. From what Sophia and Madison told her, it wasn't like he was sitting around waiting for her to come back—he'd been drowning his supposed sorrows in plenty of ample bosoms. Why he continued to bother her, she would never understand, nor did she care. That part of her life was officially over.

In addition to unpacking and occasionally hanging out with Carly and some of the other friends she met through her monthly ladies group, Hattie had started taking a weekly yoga class at the same place Eli went, although they'd only gone together once. She was developing a routine that suited her. Hattie's boss had recently complimented her on her job so far. While she had never pictured Oceanside as a forever home before moving here, it definitely felt that way now, and she couldn't imagine not living here or at least very close to it.

Hattie pulled the door to the restaurant open and saw Carly standing by the host stand, typing out a message on her phone. Carly looked up when she approached.

"Hattie, hi!" she said, giving her a quick hug.

"I'm so glad you were able to meet for dinner!" Hattie said. Hattie and Carly ate lunch together most days, but due to the upcoming exhibit opening, Carly's workload had been intense, and more often than not, she had ended up eating lunch at her desk. Hattie was glad to have the chance to catch up with her when she didn't have to rush back to her office.

The host returned to show them to their table. As they settled into their seats, Carly said, "I'm so sorry it's taken so long for me to have a free night. Things have just been extra busy lately."

"I bet you'll be glad after opening night. I'm busy working on programming, but my work feels like it's more of a steady pace, unlike your job, which has these periods of concentrated production."

They scanned the menus and decided on dinner and drinks. After the server came and took their orders, Carly continued their earlier conversation.

"I actually love the rush that comes once the doors are finally open, but it can be a ton of work to get to that point. But we're almost there! Then I can have my days and nights back, at least until the next big opening. My boyfriend will probably appreciate that, too."

"Speaking of, how's Mario?" Hattie asked with a wry grin.

"He's great, thank you." Carly blushed.

"I'm so happy that it seems like it's really working out between you two." Carly was the one female friend she had grown closest to since moving to Oceanside. She had little bits of Jayne, Madison, and Sophia's personalities all rolled into one. While no one could ever replace her friendships with those women, Carly was a great addition to the list.

"Me too. I really like him. I think I might even love him," she said, a dreamy look on her face.

"Oh, Carly! I'm so happy for you."

"Aww, thank you! He really is the sweetest…" The server returned with a glass of Cabernet Sauvignon for Hattie and an IPA from a local brewery for Carly.

Carly sipped her beer and then said, "Enough about me, how are you?"

"I'm good. I'm pretty much unpacked at this point. I'm still finding things that I need, so I'm slowly acquiring those. But so far, I've been happy with my apartment and the management seems really responsive, and blessedly I hardly ever hear a peep out of my neighbors," Hattie quipped. Carly laughed heartily at that, knowing Hattie's experience that led her to live with Blaine in the first place.

"Fingers crossed they stay that way. How's your friend, Jayne, doing? I was so glad I got to meet her when she came out to help you move into your new place."

Hattie smiled warmly. The two women seemed to easily hit it off when Hattie had introduced them briefly during Jayne's visit. "She's good. She's always busy with teaching and research, but she makes time for me when she can. Even if we don't talk to each other often, it always feels like it was just yesterday," she replied.

"Those are the best kinds of friends. Speaking of your move, how are things going with Blaine?" Carly asked. Hattie had confessed to Carly what had happened between her and Blaine one night after they had too many margaritas.

"They're not. We're just friends, remember?" That familiar ache of longing settled in Hattie's chest at the mention of Blaine. She swirled the garnet liquid in her glass before taking a sip.

"You say that, but you always seem a little sad about it," Carly remarked.

Hattie sighed. "Yes, well, that doesn't change the fact that things are the way they are. And who needs a real man when I have a whole host of book boyfriends to choose from?" she asked, doing her best to lighten the mood.

"Speaking of perfect, fictional men," Carly said, "I was thinking we should start a smutty book club."

Hattie laughed.

"No, I'm serious! Between you, me, the monthly ladies, and a few other folks from work, we definitely have enough people to pull off a book club. Come on! A little wine, a little smut... it would be a great time!"

"Are you sure you have time for that?" Hattie asked.

"I would make time for smut club," Carly said emphatically. "I love spending time with Mario, but sometimes a gal needs a night off, you know?"

"I can understand that. Well, if you're serious, I would definitely be down for smut club. You know I love me a good romance novel. What should we read first?"

They proceeded to dive into their current reads and the miles of books that sat on both their TBR lists. Hattie heard a familiar laugh and looked up to see Blaine and a woman she wasn't familiar with being led to a table. Her stomach sank a little at seeing him.

Carly, noticing her watching him, asked, "Do you know him?"

"That's... Blaine." And he looked good. He looked really good. He was wearing fitted gunmetal grey slacks, a light-colored button-down with the sleeves rolled partway up, his favorite vest, and the skinny black tie she had advised him to wear that one morning. She didn't fail to notice that he had left the top button undone and the tie a little looser just as she had suggested. A black leather jacket was slung over one arm. That was new, or at least she hadn't seen it before. The host led them around the corner, and they disappeared from Hattie's view.

"Oh! No wonder you wanted one night with him!"

"Carly!"

"I'm just saying, if I had been in your situation, I would have done the exact same thing, Hattie."

Hattie sat quietly for a moment.

Carly, clearly sensing that Hattie didn't want to talk about Blaine, returned to the topic of their burgeoning book club with the question, "So, tell me, have you read any tentacle porn?" The question was just the right thing to pull Hattie out of her thoughts and into a very interesting discussion about monster and alien romances and some very creative writers.

As they were getting ready to leave, Carly asked, "Are you going to stop by and say hi?"

"Oh, I wouldn't want to interrupt," she said.

"If he saw you, he might think it was a little weird that you didn't say hi," Carly reasoned.

"I suppose that's true..."

"Come on, we'll just swing by on our way out." They gathered up their coats and purses and walked over to the booth Blaine was in. He glanced up when they approached and did a bit of a double-take.

"Hattie! Hi! How are you?" he asked, standing and giving her the briefest of hugs.

"Hi! I'm good," she replied. "Carly and I were just having dinner and saw you so I wanted to stop by before we left to say a quick hi."

"I'm glad you did. Carly, good to meet you. I've heard a lot about you, so it's nice to finally have a face to put with the name. Sorry, I'm being so rude. This is Tabitha," he said, gesturing to the dark-haired beauty sitting on the opposite side of the booth.

"Hi!" she said with a friendly little wave.

"Hattie was my temporary roommate not long ago due to some apartment issues she was having," he said by way of explanation. While it was the truth, it felt like a knife to the gut.

"Well, we don't want to keep you from..."

"Oh, don't worry, I'm an easy date, so I don't mind. It's great to meet one of Blaine's friends," Tabitha said.

The knife had returned, hot and searing. Date. Blaine was on a date. With another woman. Not that he shouldn't be. It's not like he and Hattie were together. What should she care? He should date. He deserved happiness. She needed to get out of here before she started to cry.

"Well, we'd better get going," she said. "I'm supposed to video chat with Jayne in a bit, and I was hoping to get a shower in before I do. It was great to see you, Blaine. Nice to meet you, Tabitha."

After saying goodbye to Carly, Hattie managed to hold herself together until she walked through her front door. Once the door shut behind her, she burst into tears, sliding down the door to the floor. She wasn't even sure why she was crying so much. He'd moved on. She needed to do the same. That didn't change the fact that it still hurt like hell to see him with someone. She wanted to call Jayne, but knew Jayne would just tell her to tell Blaine how she felt. But how could she, especially now?

In the middle of her Saturday morning cleaning routine, Hattie's phone pinged with an incoming text. She set down her rag and pulled her phone from her back pocket. She saw there was a message from Blaine. There was that small twinge in her chest every time his name showed up on her phone. They had exchanged a few messages since she moved out. On the one hand, it was not as many as she would have liked. On the other hand, she hoped their limited communication would help her distance herself from her feelings for him.

Blaine: *Nice to see you the other night. You still good to help with surprising Eli for his birthday?*

Hattie: *Absolutely! How can I help?*

Blaine: *Might be easier to discuss in person?*

Hattie: *Today?*

Blaine: *If you have time.*

Hattie: *Sure. You're welcome to come to my place, or we could meet for coffee? Or whatever, really. No fixed plans today.*

Blaine: *Coffee and beach walk?*

Hattie: *This is why they pay you the big bucks.*

Blaine: *You know it.*

Blaine: *Meet you at Deja Brew in an hour?*

Hattie: *It's a date.*

Shit, she hadn't meant to say that. Ugh, he'd already seen it, so she couldn't delete the message now. Blaine was responding, dots starting and stopping, when his reply finally popped up.

Blaine: *Coffee date with a friend and a walk along the beach? Score for me!*

The hurt from the other night flared to life again thanks to that single word, *friend*. Blaine saw her well and truly only as a friend. He had made that much clear. Doing her best to ignore the way her heart was aching, Hattie picked up her rag again and went to clean the bathroom, wiping stray tears off her cheeks as she did.

Blaine

Blaine had to reread Hattie's message several times before her meaning sank in. Hattie obviously didn't mean a date. Blaine scrambled to formulate a reply, which was hard when his brain was short-circuiting at the idea that she could have meant a *date,* date. *Obviously not, you ass.* He typed something and hit send. Only afterward did he realize what he had written. Smooth, Blaine, real smooth. Hopefully, she would forgive him for sounding like a complete and total idiot.

Blaine finished his planned workout for the day and hopped into the shower. Naturally, his thoughts drifted to Hattie, as they so often did. Before he knew it, his hand was again wrapped around his length, and he was moaning her name. He really needed to stop doing this if he ever wanted a real chance of moving on. He'd tried to stop thinking about Hattie, mostly unsuccessfully, especially when he was in the shower. He attempted to go out on a date with Tabitha, another friend of a friend, and while he enjoyed his time with her, that spark he had with Hattie just wasn't there. Still, at least he was putting himself out there and trying to follow the advice of the mission lady, Emma: if it was meant to be, it would be. Until then, he wouldn't sit around pining for her. Try, try again, as the old adage went.

After his shower, Blaine got dressed and headed to Deja Brew, one of the many cafes near the beach, this one a particular favorite of the locals. After stepping through the doors, he scanned the crowded, bustling room for Hattie. He didn't see her in line or at any of the tables, so he must be the first to arrive. Blaine stood just inside and debated whether or not he should wait for her or get in line. His instincts urged him to wait for her to arrive before ordering, but that seemed like date-like behavior and, as he reminded himself for the millionth time that day, this was not a date. It was simply two friends getting together on a Saturday morning. If this were Eli, there wouldn't even be a question—he would simply get in line. Friends didn't necessarily wait for each other to order.

After far too much internal debate, Blaine stepped forward and into line. It was fairly long, so he used the time to calm himself down a bit before Hattie arrived. He hadn't realized just how wound up he was until he walked into the coffee shop. If she came in now, it would be obvious that something was off with him, and that would not do at all. It was a good thing they planned to walk along the beach. That would help calm him further, especially in Hattie's presence.

Blaine pulled out his phone to check for any missed messages, but he had none. While slowly shuffling forward in line, he looked at the specials. Usually, he stuck to one of two drinks, both low-calorie and boring, but kind of like his haircut, he had been trying to break out of his routine. He decided to go for the most lavish option on the menu—in this case, a white chocolate peppermint mocha with whipped cream, peppermint pieces, and white chocolate drizzle. It was definitely much more exciting than his usual fat-free latte.

Being a little more out there was difficult, but the rewards had been worth it—he had a growing group of friends, he was feeling more confident, and he was starting to feel more settled in his new skin—so he planned to keep pushing himself. Blaine was still meeting regularly with his therapist and gradually working through his self-esteem issues. It took working with a professional to realize that kids were often mean and would put others down to hide their own feelings. No wonder there were so many bullies out there. Some kids would lash out; however, Blaine had been one of those who turned to food for comfort. Knowing that, he reflected on other stressful times in his life and recognized he had done exactly that. Being aware of it made it much easier to challenge that behavior and stop it before it started. Was it easy? No, but it was becoming easier. The exercise routine he had established helped. Living in a place he loved helped. If he was being completely honest, loving Hattie had helped, too.

Chapter 38

Hattie

The bell over the door of the coffee shop rang as Hattie pushed it open. Quickly scanning the space, she found Blaine standing in line, waiting to order. This was the first time they had seen each other in person since she moved into her new apartment, other than their brief interaction at the restaurant. Hattie was equal parts happy and nervous to see him. She reminded herself that they were there to talk about Eli and that she needed to push her lingering feelings for Blaine aside and focus on their friend. Hattie walked over and stood next to him, feeling a bit unsure of how to greet him.

"Hi," she said.

"Hey," he responded, turning and giving her a quick hug, just like the other night at the restaurant. When he pulled back, Hattie could have sworn his lips ghosted her cheek. *Wishful thinking, you horny cow.*

"How are you?" she asked, doing her best not to stare. Blaine looked really good. Maybe it was his new haircut, or maybe she just hadn't seen him in a while. Whatever it was, he looked and smelled wonderful.

"Good. How about you?" he asked, tucking his hands in his coat pockets.

"Same," she replied as they moved forward in line.

"How's the moving-in going? Do you have everything you need now? The offer still stands. If you need something I have, you're welcome to borrow it."

"Except for the coffee pot."

"Except for the coffee pot," he smiled.

"Well, never fear! Jayne bought me a really nice one as a house-warming gift, so your coffee pot is safe from me."

"That's a relief," he said, wiping imaginary sweat from his brow. Hattie nudged him playfully on the shoulder. She had missed this, being playful with him. She could do this—she could be just friends with him.

They were next in line to place their order. Hattie ordered a chai latte while Blaine surprised her by choosing the most froufrou item on the menu. After placing their to-go orders, they moved to the end of the counter to wait for their drinks. While they waited, Blaine said, "Thanks for meeting up. It's nice to see you. The house has been a little quiet since you moved out."

"I wasn't that noisy of a roommate, was I?" Hattie said, laughing.

"No, I just got used to having someone to navigate around, you know?" Blaine responded.

"I imagine it must have been odd for you to be on your own for so long, then to unexpectedly have me there and then gone again."

"It was, but it was also nice."

Blaine had clearly maintained his new sexy haircut, as it looked like he had recently shaved the sides and back again. "Do you still like your new haircut?" Hattie's fingers itched to reach out and rub against his freshly shaved sides. *But friends don't stroke friends*, she reminded herself.

Blaine reached up and ran his hand along the side of his head. "Actually, yeah. It took a little bit to get used to it, but now I like it. Have you ever known that there was a part of you that you just never shared with the world, but that was always in you?"

Hattie nodded. "Boy, do I ever," she said, quirking her lips into a small smile.

"I guess you do, don't you? Well, that's what this feels like, and now that it's out there, people are getting to know that part of me. The reaction from my coworkers was really interesting at first, but now they all seem to have adjusted. I actually have better relationships with a few of them now since it opened up conversations between us."

"How do you mean?"

"We're a pretty large office, so there are a lot of people that I only sort of knew or that I would see in passing. We were always friendly, but our conversations never went past more than a 'hi, how are you?' The haircut made them stop and comment, which led to questions of why or what inspired it, and so on. It turns out that a lot of us have more in common than we realized, simply because we never really talked to each other. I've been hanging out with a few of them after work since Eli's been busy lately. It's been nice."

"Huh, I would have never expected that, but it makes total sense," she said. The barista called out their names. Grabbing their to-go cups, they headed toward the door. They were both quiet as they made their way to the beach. Hattie slipped off her ballet flats, enjoying the feel of the cold sand as she dug into it, wiggling her toes.

Blaine was watching her, a soft smile on his face. "It never gets old, does it?" he asked.

"Moving here was the best decision I ever made." Hattie didn't for a second regret her somewhat impulsive move. Sure, there were things she missed about New York, but Oceanside felt like home in a way she hadn't expected. Now, if only she could get Sophia and Madison to move out here, too.

They began walking along the beach. It was a chilly morning by Southern California standards, but Hattie didn't think it was too bad, especially compared to early November weather in New York, where it was currently about twenty degrees colder. Despite the breeze, Hattie felt comfortable in her knit hat, sweater coat, and long-sleeved tee she'd tossed on.

"Shall we?" Blaine asked, gesturing towards the waves.

"Come on," she said, and they headed toward the surf where the sand would be a little easier to walk on.

They walked for a few moments in silence. As they edged onto the damp sand, Blaine said, "I'm glad that you are still up for helping surprise Eli. Have you seen him since you moved out?"

"Only once. We went to yoga together, but we didn't really spend quality time together. I had a virtual hang with Sophia and Madison that night, so I couldn't stay afterward, unfortunately." Hattie had been running late that night and had barely had time to say hi before unrolling her mat and starting class.

"I was hoping you had been able to get something out of him. Whatever we noticed is up with him, it's worse now. I don't know if you noted any difference when you saw him or not."

"No, like I said, we basically just did yoga, and then I had to go. I felt bad because I wanted to check on him. On the outside, he looked okay, but the sparkle in his normally bright eyes was definitely dimmer."

"I've noticed that too. I've tried to get him to talk to me about it, but he just clams up or avoids the conversation whenever I ask him about it. I'm hoping this party will lift his spirits."

"It's really kind of you to want to do something for him, and I'm happy to help however I can. Eli was really my first friend here, so I want to do what I can for him. So, what do you need me to do?" Hattie sipped her chai as Blaine explained how she could help.

"I've come up with a plan," he said, "and as long as everyone executes their part, it should work. I've made sure that he's available on Saturday night. His Nana loves me like one of her own, so she will help us out, too. He thinks he's helping her for the night, but in reality, she is just making sure he is free. She is going to send him on an errand to pick up something for her from the drugstore. That is where you will meet him. She will call him while he is there and tell him that her friend came over, so he should go do whatever young people do these days. She will also tell him that unless he wants to hear two old ladies reminiscing all night, he should not come home until much later, or something to that effect. I'm leaving the details up to Nana—that woman is scary brilliant sometimes."

Hattie laughed. "I've always wanted to meet his Nana. She sounds like a firecracker."

"That she is," Blaine confirmed. "After he talks to Nana, you can offer to take him to get cheesecake. The man has a serious weakness for desserts and will be unable to resist. On the way there, I will call you and tell you I found, I don't know, your mom's missing earring. Then you can ask to swing by on the way since you're so desperate to have your family heirloom back. Again, we can work out the details later. Then you arrive, and we all yell 'surprise.' Hopefully, we can then sit back and enjoy the party."

Hattie laughed. "Wow, you're really good at this whole deception thing. Are you sure you aren't a spy, not just a project manager?" she teased.

"I promise. Those guys are way cooler than I am," he said with a wink.

"It sounds like a great plan, Blaine. I will execute my part to the best of my abilities." Hattie gave him a little salute.

"I have no doubt you'll be fantastic," he said, smiling.

"You mentioned that your friend, Thomas, the one who's on that show, might be able to come down. Is he going to be able to make it?"

"He is! I talked to him yesterday and he said that he and Jessie will plan on heading down here from L.A. after lunch, so they'll be here in plenty of time for the party."

"That's awesome! I'm sure he'll be glad to see them."

They continued walking for a while longer. Blaine filled her in on how Marmalade was doing, the progress of some of his work projects, and his failed attempt at making a soufflé. Hattie told him about her transition into being a successful plant mother, a funny thing that had happened when she was out with Carly at their monthly gathering, and about her trip to the mission with Jayne.

"You were right, and it was really interesting to learn about what life was like for someone living there. Not having grown up on the West Coast, it was never something I even considered. Thanks for suggesting it. Actually, one of the exhibits reminded me of an upcoming exhibit we have opening at the museum. I was wondering, we have an opening party for it coming up. Would you be interested in coming? I will be there, but I'm not officially working."

"Sure, it's not very often I get to see where my friends work," Blaine said.

Right, friends. Hattie tried not to show her disappointment at the reminder. It wasn't as if she had been asking him out on a date, so she shouldn't be bothered, but she was. As much as it hurt, she needed to get over him. She had clearly been friend-zoned. It was time to fully snuff out the flame she had for him. Maybe seeing him more often was what she needed to help her move on. Avoiding him had not gotten him out of her system, so maybe she needed to try the opposite approach and spend more time with him as friends. Ask him about his dating life. Go bowling. Whatever else friends do when they do friend things.

"I would love it if you could come. I will put your name on the list, and if you are able to make it, great. If not, maybe next time." There, that sounded like something a friend would say, right?

When their drinks were nearly finished, they headed back toward the cafe. Hattie threw her now-empty cup into the trash can along the edge of the beach. Blaine took a final sip of his and did the same.

"Can I say something?" she said. "I'm honestly surprised that you ordered that. It doesn't seem like you."

Blaine pointed to his hair and said, "Hidden depths," then gave her a wink. "I gotta go. See you soon. I'll be in touch about next Saturday," he said, pulling her in for a hug. Hattie tried to memorize the feel of it, breathing in his scent of pine, spice, and something she could never put her finger on. The hug ended sooner than Hattie would have liked. Once again, she reminded herself they were friends, and friends didn't hug for long periods, pressing every inch of air between them out, tangling their fingers in the hair at the nape of their necks. Friends. Friends. Friends. Maybe if she repeated it enough, her body and heart would finally get the message.

The following week, Hattie and Blaine were ready to implement their plan. Eli's grandma, for her part, was ready to go as well. As soon as Eli left the house, Nana texted Hattie that he was on his way to the store. Hattie stationed herself behind a shelf where she would be able to see him come in, but he wouldn't likely see her. She saw him heading to the tea aisle. Hattie fired off a text and made her move.

When she saw he was suitably distracted, Hattie turned casually into the aisle and said, in mock surprise, "Eli! Hi! How are you? I wouldn't expect to run into you here on a Saturday night. I would have thought you'd be out dancing or something like that."

"Hey, Hattie! I'm just helping Nana out tonight, and she asked me to come get her some of this," he said, holding up the box of ginger tea.

Hattie reached out and squeezed his bicep. "That's nice of you. How is she doing?"

"She's good. She was insistent that she needed some ginger tea or she wouldn't be able to sleep tonight, and demanded that I go get it before the store closed. It had to be this brand, which only *this* store carries, and that's why I'm here now."

Almost as if on cue, Eli's phone began to ring. He pulled it out of his pocket and glanced at the screen.

"Sorry, this is her calling, actually. I should take it. Nana? Everything okay?" Hattie couldn't hear what Nana was saying, but could tell she was chiding her grandson nonetheless. "Sorry, Nana. You know I worry about you." Eli playfully rolled his eyes. Nana took over the conversation on the other end of the line. "Are you sure? Oh, uh, yeah, I don't want any part of that. I'll be fine. I'll find something to keep me occupied for a bit and then head home." Their plan was working perfectly. "Yes, yes, I have it here in my hands. I won't forget to bring it home. Love you too, Nana." Eli shook his head, hanging up the phone.

Hattie smiled at him. "Your Nana seems like quite the character, and I only heard one end of that conversation," Hattie laughed. "Maybe one of these days, I'll get to meet her."

"She is a formidable woman. Apparently, I'm no longer needed and have been kicked out of my house for the evening. Some of her friends came over and surprised her with poker. I was told that unless I was set to play while bunions and other old lady ailments were being discussed, I should find someplace else to be. I guess I'll go to a coffee shop or something." On the inside, Hattie smiled maniacally.

"Well, you could... or would you want to hang out with me? I don't have any plans tonight. It's been a while since I got to spend some time with you, so I wouldn't mind if you want to. We could go somewhere and get dessert... maybe some cheesecake?"

"That would actually be really nice. You're right; it has been a while since just the two of us hung out. Plus, I'm a sucker for baked goods." Thank you, Blaine, for that little tidbit. "Let me just get this stuff, and then we can head out, assuming you're done?"

"Oh yeah, they didn't have the lotion I was looking for, so I was just about to head out when I saw you."

Eli paid for the few items he was picking up, and then they were ready to go.

"Do you want to just drive together? This is on my way back home, so I could drop you off later," Hattie said.

"Sure," Eli responded.

"Do you want coffee, too? Or is this more of a dessert and drinks situation?" Hattie asked.

"I could definitely use a drink, just not London's. Been there too much lately." Interesting, thought Hattie.

"There's a French bistro that just opened. Want to try there?"

"Let's do it," he said. "Let me just drop this stuff in my car, and then we can go." While Eli was doing that, Hattie texted Blaine. A few minutes later, they were settled into Hattie's car, and her phone started to ring. The caller ID showed that it was Blaine.

"That's odd," she said. "He almost never calls. I wonder what's up. Would you mind if I took this?"

"Not at all. Go for it."

"Hey, Blaine! Guess who I have in the car with me?"

"Hey, man," Eli said.

"Hello to you both!"

"Everything okay? I was a little surprised that you were calling instead of texting," Hattie said, making sure concern was laced into her voice.

"Everything is fine. I wanted to let you know as soon as I could that I found the earring you were missing. I think Marmalade may have been playing with it. I found it under the front entry table when I was cleaning."

Hattie let out a sigh of relief. "Really? Oh, that's wonderful! I was so devastated when I thought I had lost it." For Eli's benefit, she explained, "When I was unpacking, I only found one part of a pair of earrings that my mom had given me when I graduated from high school. They were given to her by my grandmother for her high school graduation."

"Let me know when you want to come get it. I'm home right now if you want to swing by, but I don't want to ruin any plans you two might have."

Hattie turned to Eli. "Would you mind terribly if we stopped by Blaine's? I've been so worried for weeks that I might never see it again. I'd just like to have it back as soon as possible."

"Sure. Sounds good. I can't go home anyway, remember?" he said with a laugh.

To Blaine, she said, "We were just heading to get some dessert and maybe a cocktail, but we'll swing by your place quickly and then head out."

"No problem. I'm home. See you soon."

"Okay, bye!"

The light changed, and Hattie started to accelerate. "Thanks for being willing to make a quick stop at Blaine's. Like I said, it's been stressing me out. I thought maybe I'd lost it in the move somewhere along the line."

"It's really not a problem. I'm glad he found it for you." Hattie couldn't say what made her do it, but she felt like she needed to check in on Eli. That feeling was still there, and she couldn't shake it. She figured he was more likely to open up if it was just the two of them.

"How have you been, Eli? I feel like the last few times I've seen you, I don't know, your energy is off or something."

Eli took a moment before answering. "I've been dealing with some personal stuff. I'm... I'm not sure I'm ready to talk about it." Her heart ached to hear the sadness in his voice.

"Well, I'm here, and I promise I'm a judgment-free zone," she said. "I just worry since you look a little worse for wear tonight. I've never seen you with bags under your eyes before."

Eli sighed. He didn't say anything, and Hattie remained silent as she drove. Eventually, he said, "Maybe I should talk about it... I... I've been seeing someone. It's been a little rough between us lately. I hadn't told anyone about the relationship, and then last night, it ended."

"Oh, Eli! I'm so sorry to hear that."

"Yeah, me too. I really liked... him," he said, slightly choked. Hattie did her best to hide her surprise and keep her features schooled so he didn't get the wrong impression. Now all of his secrecy made sense. From what he told her, he was straight. No wonder he'd been so secretive about the relationship.

"I didn't know you were bi," she said.

"Yes, well, neither did I," he said. "I don't really know what to do with that information."

Reaching over, she squeezed his forearm. "Eli, it's okay. It doesn't matter who you love as long as they're kind and treat you well. Do you want to tell me about him?"

Eli looked out the window as they drove. She could tell he was thinking. After a moment, he said, "Do you remember our server from the night we moved you?"

"Yes, he was cute."

"He is, and so much more. His name is Marcus. And he's awakened something in me that I didn't know was there. I've never liked a man or loved a man before. I had never even thought about one romantically before, and then there he was, all flirty and funny. When his finger brushed my skin, it felt like someone had burned me, but in a good way, and it made me wonder why. We started hanging out, and then one day he kissed me, and... and I didn't hate it. Quite the opposite, in fact. I really, really liked it," he sighed. "So we started dating in secret, and at first, he was okay with it. But as time went on, he's gotten frustrated with it. I've never felt this way about a man before, so am I bi? I don't know. If I'm not, and this is just a one-off thing, then I don't want to announce it to the world. I'm just really confused about who I am, what it means, everything. Anyway, last night, it all came to a head, and he told me he was tired of being my dirty little secret." Eli grew quiet for a moment. Out of the corner of her eye, Hattie saw him wipe away a tear. "The thing is, Hattie, I think I might love him. Marcus is so bright and beautiful and makes me feel like there is hope in the world just by his existence."

"Did you tell him all of those things?" she asked quietly.

"No, and now, it's probably too late. And I still don't know if I'm ready to be someone else to my friends, my family, the world."

They sat in silence for a few moments at the stoplight. Hattie wasn't sure whether a surprise party would help him right now or not, but she didn't have a way to get in touch with Blaine without Eli overhearing. Plus, if Eli wasn't sure he wanted to tell his friends about what was going on, not showing up would only cause them to ask more questions.

"Thanks for telling me, Eli. Change can be really hard, especially when it's something like your sexuality. Change can also be good, though. I mean, look at me. If I hadn't been willing to make a change, I would likely still be living miserably with Galen in New York. But you have to do what's right for you. I won't tell anyone what you've shared, I promise, but can I make a suggestion that you tell Blaine, too? We both noticed that you've been kind of off and have both really worried about you."

"Thanks, Hattie. You guys are both good friends, and even though I've only known Blaine for a few years, he's quickly become my best friend. You're right, and I should have shared with him, at least in some form. He would have understood and been kind, helping me through all of this. I just wasn't sure in the moment, you know? Hindsight is 20/20 and all that."

"Boy, don't I know it. He'll be there to support you, Eli, no matter what you do. Who you love doesn't define who you are. I've only known you for a short time, but I can see that you're like the brother he never had."

"The older, better-looking brother, you mean," Eli said, some of his natural spark returning.

"That goes without saying," Hattie replied with a smile.

Chapter 39

Blaine

Blaine finished shoving all of his friends into the backyard, begging them to be silent for the next few minutes. He had just come in from the back when he saw Hattie's headlights pull into the driveway. Blaine was feeling excited and hoped they would actually be able to surprise Eli. Blaine puttered around his kitchen as if he hadn't noticed them arrive. He heard Hattie's laughter as she exited the car. The sound sent blood rushing straight to his dick. Taking a few breaths and imagining sitting on a giant ice cube, he urged his burgeoning erection to deflate. A knock sounded on the door. Glancing down, Blaine found he was in the clear and moved around the kitchen island toward the door.

Pulling the door open, he said, "Hey, guys! Come on in. Can you stay for a few minutes? I don't want to keep you from your friend time, but it's been a while since I've seen you both."

Hattie glanced at Eli and said, "It's hard to say no to, but I'll leave it up to Eli."

"As long as I get buttercream frosting at some point tonight, I'm good to stay for a bit," he said with a grin.

"Great! The weather is nice enough that I was sitting outside," Blaine said. He didn't wait to ask if it was okay since he needed to get Eli into the backyard. Instead, he headed toward the door and pulled it open. Hattie set her stuff down, letting Eli follow Blaine. A cheer went up when Eli stepped onto the porch. "Happy birthday, man," Blaine said, clapping Eli on the shoulder.

A confused expression flickered across Eli's face. Turning around, he faced Blaine and asked, "You did all this for me?"

"Of course! I know how much you love parties, cake, and your birthday, not to mention surprises, but man, you're one of the hardest people to surprise! Hattie and your Nana helped make it happen, though."

"Nana!" Eli said, throwing his hands up in the air. "That's why she has been so extra lately. Thanks, man," Eli said, hugging Blaine, then turning and giving a much gentler hug to Hattie.

"Go forth and enjoy, Eli," she said. A look passed between the two of them that Blaine couldn't quite decipher.

"Cupcakes are over there, next to Thomas," Blaine said, pointing to a table across the yard.

"No fucking way!" Eli exclaimed. "You even got Thomas here? You're the best, Blaine." Eli gave Blaine another thumping hug before stepping off the porch and into the party fray. There were about twenty people who had all gathered to celebrate their friend.

"This is great, Blaine," Hattie said as they stood together watching Eli chat with friends and eat more than one cupcake, for sure.

"Um, I promised Eli I wouldn't say anything, but he's got something to talk to you about. When you hear what it is, it will make the past few months make sense."

Blaine looked at Hattie, the glow from the string lights highlighting the auburn notes in her hair and turning her skin almost golden. Her beauty completely distracted him from what she had just said. How had she grown more beautiful in their time apart?

"Blaine?" she asked.

"Sorry, yes, got it. Hopefully, he'll feel like he can open up to me soon." Clearing his throat and attempting to clear his thoughts away, he said, "Let me introduce you to the rest of our friends who are here."

Blaine led Hattie around, introducing her to different groups of people who were busy drinking, chatting, and wishing Eli well. Eventually, they made their way over to where his friend Thomas was standing with his best friend-turned-girlfriend, Jessie.

"You must be Hattie," Thomas said in his charming British accent. "I'm Thomas."

"I've heard so much about you! It's good to finally meet you," she said, extending her hand to him.

"This is my girlfriend, Jessie," he said, looking adoringly at the woman beside him. Blaine felt a pang of jealousy at their new closeness. He was absolutely thrilled they had finally realized how perfect they were for each other. Eli and Blaine had a bet on how long it would take them to fall in love. Eli had won that one. Blaine had thought it would take them at least another year.

"Nice to meet you, Hattie," Jessie said, offering her hand as well.

"Eli and Blaine have both talked a lot about you, so it's great to finally meet you both in person."

"I'm not surprised," Thomas said, "we are pretty awesome." Blaine playfully punched Thomas in the arm. Jessie just laughed at their antics. Blaine had been able to spend some time with Thomas and Jessie before the party. It was great to catch up with both of them while they prepared for the evening.

"I think you know this," he said to Hattie, "but Thomas is an actor and audiobook narrator."

"I didn't realize you were a narrator too. How fun! I hope you don't mind me saying this, Thomas, especially since I heard there was quite a bit of drama with the director constantly changing his mind and needing to reshoot, but I've really been enjoying *Wings of Justice*. I especially like your character. He's really relatable, despite the fantastic setting."

"Thank you. It's nice to hear that people are liking it, especially as you said, with all of the drama."

Jessie said, "Blaine told us that you work at the art museum doing programming, among other things."

"I do! You're a grant writer at one of the museums in L.A., right?" Hattie asked. Hattie came alive whenever she talked about museums. Thomas gave him a knowing look when Jessie lit up as well.

"Museum geeks," he whispered to Blaine, shaking his head as the two women started to talk about their chosen careers. He smiled at his friend in return.

"For now," Jessie continued, "I'm hoping to make the switch to being an author, but we'll see."

"You're going to be great, love," Thomas said, kissing Jessie softly on the cheek. Feeling like he was intruding on a private moment, even though it was in public, Blaine looked around at the rest of the party, taking a quick visual inventory of the food table.

"I should go in and grab some more cupcakes from the fridge. Looks like they've been a hit with more than just Eli," Blaine said, gesturing with his chin toward the mostly empty tray.

"Let me," Hattie said, "Why don't you stay out here and enjoy the party? They're your friends too, after all."

"Thanks, Hattie, that's really nice of you."

Hattie gave him a soft smile.

"I'll come help you, Hattie," Jessie said, "I was going to head in and use the restroom anyway." The two women wandered back to the house, already appearing as if they were thick as thieves.

"Introducing those two may have been a mistake," Thomas said.

Blaine laughed. "So... Jessie as girlfriend. How's that working out?"

"I always knew she was amazing, Blaine. I'm not sure why I never saw it before. I love her more than I can possibly describe."

"You two seem pretty happy," Blaine said.

"I've never been happier, mate. I hope you can find someone who makes you just as happy as Jessie makes me. Mark my words, I'm going to marry that girl someday."

"I will. Someday," Blaine said as he watched Hattie exit the house with a platter laden with cupcakes. A cheer went up from the nearby group when they saw Hattie set down the fresh tray.

A few hours later, Eli sat in one of the patio chairs that had been pulled over to the fire pit. He was holding a beer in one hand and resting his head on the hand holding the bottle. If Blaine had to guess, Eli was a little tipsy. Blaine said goodbye to the last of the party guests, aside from Hattie and Eli. Hattie, despite his protests, was helping clean up and was currently inside, putting leftover food away and, he suspected, doing the dishes as well.

Blaine grabbed a beer from the ice chest and headed over to the other chair by the fire. Eli sat watching the flames dance. Blaine leaned over, beer bottle in hand, and said, "Cheers, buddy."

The gesture snapped Eli out of his staring. Tapping his nearly empty bottle against Blaine's, he said, "Thanks for doing this, man. It's been really good to see some folks I haven't seen in a while. I've kind of been in my own world for the last few months."

"It's my pleasure, Eli. I'm thrilled that we managed to surprise you—not an easy feat to pull off, I might add. So, birthday boy, how are you doing?"

"I'm okay... actually, that's not totally true. I've been keeping something secret, and, well, it's kind of big." Blaine sat patiently waiting for Eli to continue, giving him the space he needed to tell Blaine whatever it was. "I, uh... I've been seeing someone...." Eli stopped to clear his throat and run a hand down his face. "This is harder than I thought it would be to tell you. Okay, here it goes. It's Marcus. From London's," he added for clarification.

Blaine wasn't sure what he had been expecting, but it wasn't this. At the same time, he wasn't entirely surprised. There had been several moments over the past few months when he wondered if something was going on between the two of them, even though Eli had never indicated he had any interest in men. Blaine hadn't been entirely sure how to approach Eli about it and figured he would when he was ready, if that was the case. On top of it all, Blaine had been dealing with his feelings for Hattie at the same time. In hindsight, he could fully admit he hadn't been a great friend lately.

"I'm so happy for you, man," Blaine said, reaching over and squeezing Eli's forearm.

"Don't be. I should say that I was seeing someone. Past tense. He broke up with me last night." Eli leaned back and resumed staring at the fire.

"Are you doing okay?" Blaine asked, even though he thought he knew the answer.

"Honestly, no. The party helped take my mind off it a little bit, though, so that was nice."

"What happened, Eli?"

Eli proceeded to lay everything out for Blaine. How he'd met Marcus a few months ago, before Blaine went to DC. How they had started as friends—at least in his mind—and then became more. How they had made out in the back hall one time. How he was scared and confused about who he was now. How he was devastated that he might have ruined everything with Marcus. Throughout it all, Blaine sat, patiently listening as Eli talked and rid himself of months of secrets that had clearly been weighing him down.

"The thing that kills me, man, is that I see you and Hattie making the same damn mistake, too."

"What do you mean?" Blaine asked, glancing toward the house.

"Get your head out of your ass, man. The two of you have been dancing around each other since that girl moved into your house."

"Yeah, but she…"

"No! I'm tired of the same stupid-ass excuses that the two of you have been pushing. She likes you. You like her. Now fucking do something about it!" At this point, Eli had started yelling. Eli stood and turned to leave, and Blaine saw Hattie standing there, one hand on the doorknob as if she had just come out and hadn't let go during Eli's tirade.

"I'm heading home. I'll get a rideshare, so don't worry about me, Hattie. Thanks, doll," he said, giving her a kiss on the crown of her head. "This was a great early birthday."

Eli took the door from Hattie and closed it behind him as he entered the house. Blaine and Hattie stood there, staring at each other across the yard. Blaine slowly started walking across the yard.

"So…" he said.

"So…" she replied.

"I assume you overheard what Eli said?"

Hattie laughed. "Yeah, I think the whole neighborhood did."

Blaine smiled. "He did get a little loud there." Blaine stood in front of Hattie, about an arm's length separating them. "Thing is," he began, swallowing. Trying again, he said, "The thing is, he's not wrong, Hattie. As much as I've tried to forget the night we had together, I can't. I love spending time with you because you are an amazing woman, but it's getting harder and harder to fight how I feel about you. When I'm with you, all I want to do is pull you to me and brush my lips across your skin, to run my fingers through your hair. When I'm alone, I imagine doing just that and so many other things that friends just don't do with each other."

Hattie let out a shuddering breath and looked directly at Blaine, tears beginning to well up in her eyes. "I thought I was the only one who felt that way," she whispered.

Before he could think twice about it, Blaine stepped forward and crashed his lips onto Hattie's, kissing her like she was oxygen and he had been holding his breath for the past month. She returned his kiss with equal intensity, her tongue slipping along the seam of his lips, seeking permission to enter. Blaine could never deny Hattie anything she wanted and willingly let her in further. She was already buried in his heart, and he would willingly give her his soul if she asked for it.

Chapter 40

Hattie

Hattie pulled back from Blaine's unexpected kiss, both of them panting, chests heaving. Blaine pressed his forehead against hers, cupping her face in his hands, wiping away the tears that were falling freely with his thumbs. He wanted her—Blaine wanted her. The flame she had worked so hard to snuff out these past few weeks roared back to life at his declaration. She couldn't stop the happy tears if she tried. She didn't care about anything other than the fact that Blaine wanted her. The constant ache in her chest whenever she was near him exploded into joy, racing through her body. Hattie wrapped her hands around Blaine's biceps, savoring how good it felt to be this close to him again. Blaine let out a feral-sounding growl, sending shivers through Hattie's body.

"I know," he gritted out, "that we have so much to talk about, but right now, I really want to kiss you again. I want to take off your clothes. I want to make you come around my fingers. Then, after all that, I want you to come around my cock while you scream out my name." Lord, how she loved that dirty mouth of his. Blaine tilted her head, giving him greater access to her neck, where he proceeded to feather kisses up the column of her throat to her ear, which he gently sank his teeth into and tugged. "Or we can, you know, just talk. Your choice," he said.

Thoughts and feelings swirled inside Hattie, pulling her in every direction. They needed to talk. She had so much she wanted to say. So many questions. She couldn't think clearly with Blaine touching her, kissing her, and running his fingers over her collarbones.

"Blaine," she whispered huskily.

"Mmm," he replied, running his nose along the edge of her chin.

"Stop." With that one word, Blaine immediately ceased what he was doing, dropping his hands and stepping back from her. As soon as he did, Hattie had her answer. She didn't want space. She didn't want to talk right now. She wanted his hands, his tongue, his everything. The fact that he had respected her enough to distance himself from her when he very evidently desired her was sexy.

"We should talk first," she said, Blaine's shoulders slumping some at the suggestion, "but, I don't want to. I want what you want. Now take me inside," Hattie said. Desire flashed in Blaine's eyes.

"Are you trying to tell me what to do? I thought you were a good girl," he purred, his hands back on her, slowly making their way up her arms.

"I'll show you what a good girl I can be... Daddy."

Blaine spun her around, pressing her back to his front. One hand slid its way up and across her collarbone until it was loosely resting on her neck. Meanwhile, the other hand slid along the top of the waistband of her jeans, teasing the sliver of skin that was exposed when Hattie had raised her arms up and brought them behind her, around Blaine's neck. "Go inside," he commanded, his voice deep with desire. "Undress down to your bra and underwear. Get comfortable on my bed."

"What about you?" she asked as he licked the line of her jaw.

"I'll be in after I put this fire out. Gotta put one fire out to start another." With that, he let her go and gave her a gentle shove towards the house. "Oh, and Hattie, I don't want to find you've touched yourself while waiting for me." When she didn't move, he swatted her on the ass. "Go," he growled. Hattie had forgotten just how much she liked bossy Blaine, and like it she did.

Hattie didn't hesitate this time to do what Blaine had asked her. She kicked off her shoes by the back door and walked down the hall toward Blaine's bedroom. She opened the door and took a deep breath. It smelled a little like his bath products, but there was a hint of something else, too, something quintessentially Blaine. She peeled off her jeans, folded them up, and placed them next to the nightstand. Her sweater and shirt were next. She balled up her socks and tucked them into one of the pockets of her pants. Hattie headed to the bed and lay down on her side, on top of the covers. She was just getting comfortable when Blaine opened the door and stepped in.

Blaine stripped off his clothes, discarding them on the floor as he stalked toward the bed. There was no better way to describe his approach. By the time he reached the edge of the bed, he was down to his jeans and boxer briefs. Hattie sat up and undid the button on his jeans.

"Naughty girl. Don't you remember what I said?" he asked, leaning down onto the bed so they were face-to-face. "First, kissing. Then, fingers. Then, cock." Blaine gently pushed her back onto the bed again.

"There's no reason you can't do any of those things naked," she panted.

"That's where you are wrong, Hattie. There's no way that I am not going to be inside you the second my clothes come off, so the pants stay on for now." Hattie nearly melted into the bed. Blaine climbed onto the mattress, kneeling between her thighs. Hattie spread them a little wider to make room for him. Blaine brushed the back of his hand up her stomach and over her breasts.

"I thought you were going to kiss me," she said, breathlessly as she gazed into his coffee-colored eyes.

"Aren't you the demanding one?" he teased. "Maybe just for that, I'll make you wait longer."

Hattie reached out and ran her hand along the outline of his hard length. Blaine groaned. "Are you sure you want to do that?" she asked, quirking one brow.

"Why are you so fucking irresistible?" he breathed out. Lowering his head to her breasts, he feathered kisses and occasional nips along the swells of her breasts, her collarbone, and her neck, finally reaching her mouth. This time, when he kissed her, it was slow and sensual, not like the kiss they had shared in his backyard. Hattie sighed at how delicious it was.

Hattie let out a gasp as Blaine's fingers slid beneath the waistband of her panties and found her clit. "You are already so wet," he groaned.

"I'm always wet for you, Blaine."

Blaine groaned again, shoving her underwear to the side. Hattie lost her ability to speak as Blaine went to work, sliding his fingers through her slick folds, making small circles around her clit, finally sliding first one finger and then another into her. They might have only had one night together, but Blaine obviously paid attention to what Hattie liked, and he was doing it all right now. Hattie was teetering right on the edge of her release when Blaine lowered his mouth to her sex, sucking and licking.

"Oh, Blaine, I'm going to come!" she cried out. Blaine flicked her clit, and it was enough to push her over the edge. Hattie arched her back, crying out his name as her orgasm consumed her. She slowly came back to herself, her body relaxing back against the bed.

"Seeing you fall apart, crying out my name, is the most beautiful thing in the world," he said, shaking his head, seemingly in disbelief. "You are really here. You are *really here* in my bed again," he looked at her with adoration in his gaze.

"I am," she said, "now give me that cock."

Blaine playfully slapped the side of her ass. "Topping from the bottom, are we?" he asked, sliding her underwear off. If she'd known she was going to end up here tonight, she would have opted for a lacy pair instead of boring white cotton. "Take your bra off," he demanded, retaking the control they both wanted him to have. Happily, Hattie did as she was told. "Undo my zipper," he said.

Again, she did what he told her to. Blaine stood and slipped his boxers and jeans to the floor, joining the random trail of the rest of his clothes. Grabbing a condom from the bedside table, he tossed it next to her as he crawled back onto the bed, positioning himself between her spread thighs. "Put it on." Again, Hattie was more than happy to oblige him.

Blaine notched himself at her entrance. Not breaking her gaze, he slid slowly, achingly into her. They both gasped at how good it felt.

"My turn," Hattie said as she flipped them over so she was on top.

Chapter 41

Blaine

Hattie managed to take Blaine by surprise when he suddenly found himself under her. She grabbed his hands and placed them on her breasts as she started to swivel and rock her hips.

"Fuck, Hattie," he gasped out. While he liked being in control, he liked it just as much when she took what she wanted. Seeing her take her pleasure by using him was one of the hottest things he had experienced. Despite the fact that she had just come, she rode him hard and fast, both of them crying out with their release within minutes.

Coming down from her orgasm, Hattie fell forward, resting her head on Blaine's chest. He ran his fingers up and down her spine, loving the softness of her skin, the tenderness of this moment. Unlike last time, he could hold her without fear or without protecting himself from future hurt and just be with her. Hattie slid off of him and onto the bed next to him. He didn't want to get up, but at the same time, he needed to. They lay across from each other, each taking the other in.

Eventually, Blaine couldn't wait any longer. He whispered, "I'll be right back," and headed into the bathroom. He disposed of the condom and grabbed a warm washcloth for Hattie. She let him tend to her and wipe her down with the cloth despite the fact that she hadn't actually gotten that dirty. He loved that she was letting him take care of her. After getting up and tossing the washcloth into the hamper, he lifted the covers and slid in. "Join me, won't you?"

Hattie smiled at him and slid under the sheets with him. She watched him silently for a moment. "So, kisses, fingers, cock, talk?"

Blaine chuckled. Only Hattie could make that sound sexy, serious, and silly all at once. "Yeah. I'm happy to stay here, but if you think this conversation would be better had with clothes on, I won't be happy about it, but I would deign to get dressed for you."

"I think this can be a clothing-optional conversation," a smile flitting across Hattie's face. "The thing is, I don't really know where to start."

"Me either," he admitted, running his hand through his hair. "I suppose the beginning is as good a place as any. If I am being completely honest, I have been attracted to you since you answered my Craigslist ad. My attraction to you only grew from there. The more I got to know you, the more I liked you. Then there was that night your earring got caught, and instead of helping you, I wanted to press you up against the wall and have my way with you, which I did, in my mind, directly after. I thought I might die the night I heard you using your vibrator or that day I heard you listening to that delightfully dirty Englishman make you come."

"Oh my god, you did hear that!" she said, covering her face in embarrassment. Blaine pulled her hand away, kissing the back of it, and continued.

"I absolutely did, and I was jealous that it was him, not me, making you moan like that. Then you agreed to be my date for my work event and showed up, outshining every other woman there. All evening, I dreamt of lowering my head between your breasts and dragging my tongue up them. It was three hours of pure torture. When we got home, you offered me one night, and I couldn't say no since it was all I had been thinking about for a month. That night was everything I had hoped it would be, but I woke up the next morning wanting to keep you and knew I couldn't. It wasn't just the physical that drew me to you. You are kind and thoughtful. You are funny as hell, sometimes so subtly that it takes me a minute to realize you just cracked a joke. Marmalade honestly prefers your lap to mine. Every day you have been gone, it has been too quiet in this house. I miss the joy you brought to it. The joy you brought to me." Blaine reached up, tucking wayward strands of hair behind Hattie's ear. "I've been seeing a therapist to work through my body issues and my lack of self-worth, which were two major things standing in my way of feeling ready for a relationship. It hasn't been long, and I still have a long way to go, but I know I have things to offer and that I am good enough for you, even if I don't always feel that way. So, that's where I'm at," he finished.

Hattie was quiet for a moment. Finally, she said, "Blaine, I don't know what to say. That was the most beautiful thing any man has ever said to me. I resisted my attraction to you as well, and on one hand, I'm glad I did because it allowed me to get to know you outside of any romantic entanglement and make sure I didn't just fall into another relationship because it was safe. I had imagined being single longer, but something Jayne said to me while she was here really hit home. I've always been myself, and my light, if you will, has only shone brighter since I've been here. Part of that was you, but the rest was because I've really been able to be me again. You did a really good job of making me think you just wanted to be friends because I have missed you so much in the last few weeks. And you wouldn't believe the number of times I pulled out that vibrator while you were in the shower!"

Blaine laughed. What started as a small chuckle grew until tears streamed down his face. Hattie looked at him like he had lost it. "Do you know how many times I fantasized about you while taking myself in hand in the shower?"

Hattie's cheeks reddened as she realized what he meant. "So all that time we were having sex alone when we could have been doing it together?"

"Yeah."

"Well, then maybe we should make up for lost time," she said, trailing her hand down his belly, past the dip where his thigh met his hip. Blaine was instantly hard again.

"Hmm, now there's a thought," he said as he rolled on top of her, capturing one of her nipples with his mouth, swirling his tongue around the bud in his mouth. "What do you think we should do about that?" he asked, kissing his way across and capturing her other nipple in his teeth, giving it the same treatment.

"I... um... ah..." she uttered.

"You seem to be having some trouble forming words. Maybe this will help," he said, sliding his fingers into her slick folds.

"Ayeyuh..."

"Tell me what you want, Hattie. I will give you anything you ask for." Hattie made another unintelligible sound as he swirled his fingers deftly around her sex.

"Mouth. Now."

"Uh, uh. You didn't say please," he teased. When Hattie groaned in frustration, he continued, "I'll let it slide this time." Blaine slid his long frame under the covers to the apex of her thighs and feasted on her beautiful cunt.

"Oh, Blaine," Hattie said, gripping his hair firmly while he devoured her sex with the enthusiasm of a puppy with a jar of peanut butter. "So good. So, so, so good," she moaned.

"Are you close, Hattie?" he asked, kissing her thigh.

Hattie was writhing, biting down on her lower lip. "Mmmhm," she mumbled out. Blaine pulled away, making Hattie cry out his name in frustration.

"Good things come to those who wait," he said cockily. "I need to be inside of you, Hattie, please."

"God, yes," she groaned out. Blaine grabbed another condom from the bedside table, slipping it on himself this time.

Blaine reached down, sliding his fingers in and out of Hattie's slick sex. Hattie moaned, gripping the sheets and turning her head side to side. "You look so beautiful, writhing beneath me like that, the sheets all twisted up around you."

"This is no time to be a poet, Blaine. Please, please fuck me now before I combust right here on the spot."

Blaine lined himself up with her entrance, sliding into the hilt. It was incredible how wet she was. Grabbing her hands in his, he raised them above her head as he began to rhythmically slide in and out of her. Hattie adjusted one of her legs so that it wrapped around his back. The change in position allowed Blaine to go even deeper, making him groan.

"I love the sounds you make," she whispered, making him release a feral sound as he picked up his pace.

"Hattie, I'm not sure how much longer I can hold on," he gritted out, the pleasure overwhelming his senses.

"Then don't," she said, "I'm right there with you. Come for me, Blaine." That command was all he needed. He slammed frenetically into her a few times, and then he felt his balls draw up and that tingling sensation at the base of his spine, and then he was coming. Reaching down, he gave Hattie's clit a few circles of his fingers before she was coming apart as well.

Afterward, they lay side by side, panting. Blaine pulled Hattie close, her head resting on his chest, while she played with the hair on his chest. When he could manage to speak again, he said, "Will you stay with me tonight, Hattie?"

"I'd love nothing better, Blaine."

Epilogue

Blaine

Almost 11 months later

Blaine finished buttoning his suit coat and checked his reflection in the mirror. He tugged down on his jacket, smoothing it out. He had to admit he looked good. The thought surprised him less than it used to. Blaine kept working with his therapist to overcome some of his body issues without going too far in the opposite direction. Now, more often than not, when he looked in the mirror, he saw the confident, attractive man he had become. Having Hattie in his life had helped him embrace that. She never made him feel less than and was there to support him in the moments of self-doubt that occasionally flared up, although less and less now. When she looked at him, she only saw the man who loved her and who had a part in helping her reclaim her life. Hopefully, after tonight, it would become their life.

Eli walked into the room and asked, "You nervous, man?"

"About tonight? No, I'm pretty sure she is going to say yes. What about you?"

Eli didn't answer, instead fighting with his pink tie. "I'll take that as a yes. Let me," Blaine said. After tying the knot, Blaine stepped back and said, "You look great, Eli. I'm really happy for you. Now come on," he said, "we can't have you be late to your own wedding."

As they entered the church to take their places, Blaine thought back to everything that had happened nearly a year ago. A few days after Eli's birthday, Blaine went to London's and found Marcus. It was early afternoon on a weekday, so the restaurant was relatively quiet, which was exactly what Blaine had hoped for. He called ahead to see if Marcus would be there. When Marcus saw him, he quickly looked around to check if Eli was there as well.

"He's not here," Blaine had told him. Marcus had looked both relieved and disappointed at the same time.

"Wait, you know?" Marcus asked, looking surprised.

"He told me everything that happened, including how heartbroken he is. Can you sit for a minute?" Marcus slid into the booth across from Blaine. "Look, Marcus, you seem like a good guy, and Eli sounded like he was really happy when the two of you were together. This is a conversation you two should be having, but I am just here to give you a little nudge. He doesn't want to hide you anymore. He wants to be open and honest about your relationship, but he is afraid to call you because he thinks you will reject him. If you don't want him or don't want to deal with the fact that he's new to the whole being bisexual thing and may still occasionally freak out, then don't call him. If you do, just know that he is miserable without you and would love to hear from you."

"Did he send you?" Marcus asked, keeping his eyes fixed on the table.

"Eli has no idea that I am here. I hate seeing him sad, so I decided to take a chance that you weren't an asshole and that maybe you missed him too. I don't blame you for not wanting to be hidden in the shadows while he figures his shit out, but you also need to understand that his whole life, he thought he was straight. That's quite a bit to process, plus worrying about how your friends and family might react, although it shouldn't matter who you love. I'm here because Eli told me I was making the same mistake he had, and once I pulled my head out of my ass, I realized he was right, and I was the only thing standing in the way between me and the woman of my dreams. So, to return the favor, I am here, telling you the things he is too afraid to say because I am not sure he would survive if you rejected him again."

Marcus called Eli that night. A few nights later, Eli introduced Marcus to his family. They stopped hiding and started loving each other openly. Except for Eli's uncle, who refused to accept that he and Marcus were together and referred to Marcus as 'Eli's friend', everyone else accepted them as a couple. After dating for a few months, Marcus asked Eli to move in with him. A few months later, Eli asked Marcus to spend the rest of their lives together.

Blaine wasn't quite ready to ask Hattie to marry him, but he was getting closer. He was, however, ready to ask her to move in. Since they were both working through things, they had been living separately, officially, but in reality, Hattie spent most of her nights in Blaine's bed. He knew her lease was ending soon, so he planned to ask her tonight. First, though, best man duties called.

As they walked up the aisle to their positions, Blaine spotted Hattie sitting in a seat along the aisle. Not giving a damn who saw, he pulled her into a passionate kiss, breaking apart only when someone wolf-whistled from the back of the church. She simply smiled and laughed as he gave her a quick kiss on the nose, then went to take his place next to Eli.

Eli tugged at his tie, shifting nervously on his feet. When Blaine stepped beside him, he turned and said, "Honestly, I thought you would be up here before me."

Blaine glanced back over at Hattie, smiling. "Guess you beat me to it," he teased. Eli laughed.

"Not by much. I bet we'll be back up here within the year," he said. The music started playing, and both men turned to watch as the love of Eli's life walked down the aisle.

The reception was held at London's. The owner closed the restaurant to the public for the night so Eli and Marcus could celebrate their union with their friends and family in the place where they first met. Blaine held tightly to Hattie's hand as they entered the space that had been transformed into a pink and Tiffany-blue wonderland.

"What?" she asked as Blaine looked over at her.

"Nothing," he said. "You just never fail to amaze me with how beautiful you are." He leaned over and added, "That dress is driving me almost as crazy as the one you wore on our first night together."

The dress in question was actually a skirt and top. The top was just short enough to reveal a strip of bare skin between the top of the floor-length skirt and the bottom of the blouse. The top was cut almost like a cropped blazer with a deep V and three-quarter-length sleeves. Hattie, of course, wasn't wearing anything underneath. It was sexy but tasteful enough to be worn to a wedding. She had chosen a light pink shade to match Blaine's best man attire. It didn't escape his notice that it was the exact same shade as her matching pink lace bra and panty set.

"Please tell me you're wearing my favorite pair of underwear under there," he whispered in her ear.

"You'll just have to wait and see, I suppose," she said, giving him a mischievous smile. Blaine was already ready to get her home and naked, and her comment had only made matters worse. But, being the good friend he was, he wasn't going to bail on his best friend just so he could go home and feast on his woman. Well, at least not on his best friend's wedding day. Any other day, he might not have felt so obligated to stay. Hattie really did have the most delicious pussy.

They ate, toasted, and danced the night away. Holding Hattie in his arms on the dance floor, Blaine was the happiest he could remember being. "Hattie?"

"Hmm?" she said as they swayed to the music, her head resting comfortably against his chest.

"I have a question I've been wanting to ask you."

"What is it?" she said, looking up at him.

"I was wondering what you thought about making it official."

"What do you mean, Blaine? Are you asking me to marry you?"

Blaine realized how what he said had sounded. If you had asked him earlier tonight if he was ready, he would have said no, but someday soon, maybe. But here, holding Hattie in his arms, surrounded by happiness, he realized he didn't need to wait. He was always going to want this woman. Today, tomorrow, or in two years, the answer would still be the same.

"I actually was just going to ask you to move in with me, but now that you mention it, Hattie Elizabeth Renaud, will you marry me?"

A huge grin spread across her face, tears threatening to spill from her eyes. "I would love to marry you, Blaine." With those words, she made him the happiest man alive. Blaine leaned down and kissed her softly and deeply.

"Let's wait on telling Eli or anyone else for now. I don't want to steal his thunder. Plus, I don't have a ring for you yet."

"That's okay," she said, pulling the gold chain she was wearing out of her top. "I have one for you." Blaine looked at the chain she was holding up, which was looped through a simple white-gold band with a single small diamond embedded in it. Blaine was speechless. Had Hattie intended to propose to him tonight?

"Is that for me?" he finally asked.

"Blaine, I love you, and I know this might seem a little bit spur of the moment, but I've been thinking about this for weeks. I've been happier this past year than I ever have been, and I want to spend the rest of my days with you. I thought tonight might be the perfect night to ask. I was planning on doing it later when I was naked, but this works too."

This woman was incredible. "When we get home, I am going to show you just how happy you just made me. You are such a good girl," he purred, lightly nipping the shell of her ear.

"I don't know about that," Hattie said softly. "I imagine good girls wear underwear to weddings." It took a moment for what Hattie said to slowly sink in.

"Are you telling me that you're bare under that full skirt of yours?" he whispered, slipping his finger into the waistband of her skirt. Hattie looked up at him and nodded.

"Bad girl," he growled.

"Am I in trouble, Daddy?" she asked, looking up at him through her lashes.

"Mmm, yes. The best kind. Now, how can we make this wedding go by faster so we can get the hell out of here and I can bury my face between your thighs?"

The End

Acknowledgements

This story would not have been possible without a whole team of people behind me offering me love and support. Guys—we did it!

My fantastic team of alpha and beta readers: Phara, Cathy, and Yasmine, who took their roles seriously and gave me feedback that helped shape the story so that it was one that readers would love, and Shari and Kim, who helped make sure there weren't any errors once everything was edited.

My best friend, Jess, who helped inspire this story. It was an awesome trip to Oceanside, and I would still move there in a heartbeat! Love you, Twinny!

Suzi, thank you for all your suggestions, guidance, support, connections, and overall enthusiasm for this project, despite everything life was throwing at you!

Megan and Catherine, for sharing your own journeys and helping guide me through being a new indie romance author.

Devan and Katherine from Grand Gesture Books for helping fine-tune the blurb and for just being wonderful, supportive humans.

OG Shaneiaks, I couldn't have done this without your love, support, and encouragement. If it hadn't been for our lovely little community that I stumbled into a few years ago, I don't know that I would be where I am today!

The "A-Team" of editors and designers: Amanda Brown, who was my copy/line editor and made sure my passive voice was kicked to the curb; Amy Parsons, who was my developmental editor and helped make Hattie and Blaine's story as beautiful as it could be; and Angela Haddon, who designed a stellar cover for me.

John York, narrator extraordinaire, whom I was lucky enough to meet, encouraged me to just do it and put it out there. Thanks for the reassurance that even big-name authors experience imposter syndrome and not to let it get in my way of doing something I love and that the world might benefit from.

Finally, my family, for only making a minimal amount of fun of me when I decided to pursue this wild idea. I love you all.

About the author

Harlow Scott didn't mean to become a writer. Like all great ideas, the inspiration for her first book came to her in the shower. She chooses to write about love because she believes in its power to comfort, heal, and offer a place to escape.

When she's not busy making people fall in love, you'll most likely find her in a museum or hanging out with her family and fur babies. Harlow is lucky enough to call the Pacific Northwest home.

Can You Hear Me Now?
Coming in 2026!

Did you love Hattie and Blaine's story? Sign up for my newsletter, get a bonus chapter, and get ready for more romance in Book 2 of the Pacific Hearts series, *Can You Hear Me Now?*

Thomas and Jessie have always been just friends — or so they thought. Beneath the surface, each is secretly falling for the other, but neither knows how to bridge the gap between friendship and something more. When Thomas lands an incredible opportunity to pursue his acting dreams, and Jessie's long-term relationship begins to unravel, their lives start to shift in unexpected ways. Through heartbreak, laughter, and late-night conversations, Jessie realizes Thomas is the one who's truly been there all along. Together, they discover a love that feels like home and a future neither saw coming.

Be the first to know all the details, see the cover, and more! Sign up for my newsletter at harlowscottbooks.com!